AN INDEPENDENT WOMAN

A Tabitha & Wolf Mystery Book 3

Sarah F. Noel

Copyright © 2023 Sarah F. Noel

All rights reserved

The characters and events portrayed in this book are fictitious. Any similarity to real persons, living or dead, is coincidental and not intended by the author.

No part of this book may be reproduced, or stored in a retrieval system, or transmitted in any form or by any means, electronic, mechanical, photocopying, recording, or otherwise, without express written permission of the publisher.

ISBN: 9798399957067

Cover design by: HelloBriie Creative
Printed in the United States of America

To my wonderful husband, Desmond.

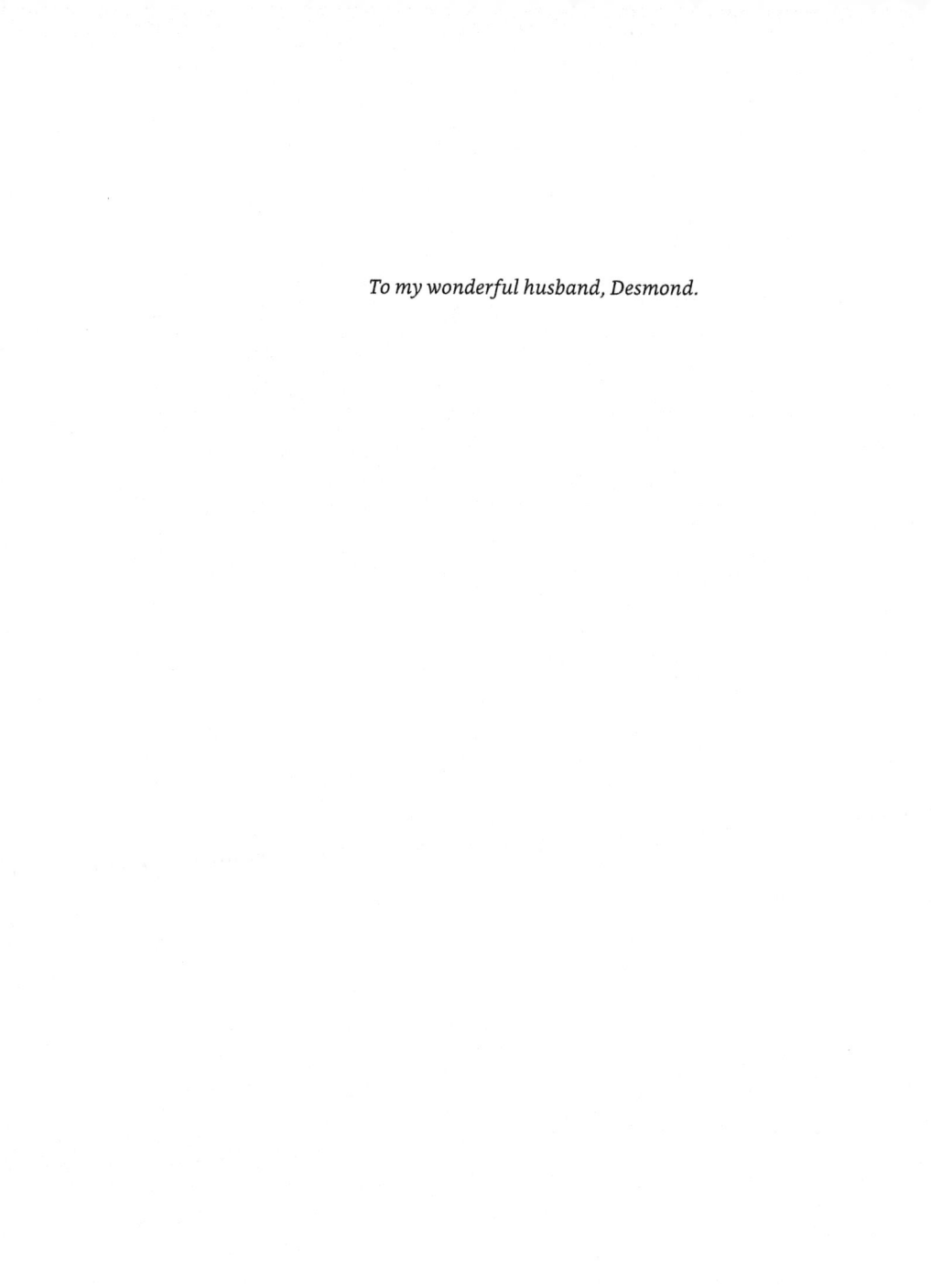

CONTENTS

Title Page
Copyright
Dedication
Foreword
Prologue   1
Chapter 1   2
Chapter 2   8
Chapter 3   12
Chapter 4   19
Chapter 5   27
Chapter 6   36
Chapter 7   43
Chapter 8   50
Chapter 9   59
Chapter 10   68
Chapter 11   76
Chapter 12   84
Chapter 13   94
Chapter 14   102
Chapter 15   116

Chapter 16	122
Chapter 17	130
Chapter 18	139
Chapter 19	156
Chapter 20	161
Chapter 21	170
Chapter 22	178
Chapter 23	183
Chapter 24	190
Chapter 25	197
Chapter 26	202
Chapter 27	208
Chapter 28	216
Chapter 29	223
Chapter 30	231
Chapter 31	237
Chapter 32	242
Chapter 33	247
Chapter 34	252
Epilogue	257
Afterword	263
Acknowledgement	265
About The Author	267
Books By This Author	269

FOREWORD

This book is written using British English spelling. e.g. dishonour instead of dishonor, realise instead of realize.

British spelling aside, while every effort has been made to proofread this thoroughly, typos do creep in. If you find any, I'd greatly appreciate a quick email to report them at sarahfnoelauthor@gmail.com

PROLOGUE

His breath became laboured as he gasped for air. Suddenly, his chest felt as if someone had piled a ton of bricks on it. The man felt dizzy and grasped at the table before him for support but to no avail. Within seconds, he had collapsed onto the cold, hard floor.

Behind him, a cold voice said, "Ye really left me nae choice."

CHAPTER 1

Wolf looked on, bemused, as their luggage was loaded onto the train. Previously, when he and Bear had travelled, before Wolf had inherited the earldom, they had each carried their light luggage in one hand. How many changes of clothes does a man need for a few days? It turned out the answer depended on whether that man was a thief-taker or an earl. At least according to his new valet, Thompson, he needed at least two changes of clothes each day. And so, now Wolf's luggage alone was enough to see a porter struggling, let alone Tabitha's. Wolf couldn't believe how much luggage a countess needed to travel with. The sheer number of hat boxes was beyond his comprehension.

Tabitha hadn't travelled by train since childhood when she would visit her grandparents. Ginny had never travelled by train, and even the ordinarily taciturn Bear seemed quite overawed by King's Cross station. The grand station was the main hub for travel on the East Coast Main Line. Built in 1852 and skilfully blending classical and Italianate styles, the station had been expanded multiple times over the last almost fifty years to accommodate the growing popularity of train travel. Now, the station was massive and awe-inspiring, and Tabitha had been happy to follow the porter as he weaved between the throngs of people who seemed to be walking in every direction.

Travelling to Edinburgh by train could typically take up to twelve hours. But Wolf, Tabitha, and their entourage were travelling in the Special Scotch Express, the miraculous train that could get them to their destination in a speedy eight hours, in luxury and comfort. When the porter had finally turned onto their platform, the ornately decorated train with its billowing plumes of steam had caused Tabitha to catch her breath at its magnificence. Over an early and quick breakfast, Wolf had explained to her what a marvel of engineering the train was. Tabitha had listened, but had been unable to match his enthusiasm for the sleek and powerful design of the train and the advancements in engineering that powered its great speeds. But seeing the train for herself, the grandeur of its gleaming, polished exterior and intricate detailing caused her heart to beat in excitement at the adventure ahead.

Wolf climbed onto the train and then put out his hand to help Tabitha. Walking through the train to find their carriage, Tabitha was as impressed by its interior as she had been by its exterior. They quickly arrived at their lavishly appointed carriage. Its plush upholstery, elegant wood panelling, and ornate decorations made it feel like they had entered a luxurious, if small, drawing room. Large windows would enable wonderful countryside views as they whisked through it at high speeds.

Finally, they were settled comfortably in their sumptuous carriage. Ginny and Thompson were in the second-class carriage, but Wolf had insisted Bear join him and Tabitha in first-class. With Thompson's introduction into the household, there was no need to pretend any longer that Bear fulfilled duties as Wolf's valet. While that did leave an open question about his role in the household, Wolf was happy enough to let that role be nothing more or less than a friend. And he wouldn't relegate his dearest friend to sitting in the servants' compartment. Of course, he would have been happy to have Ginny and Thompson sit in their carriage as well, but Tabitha, supported by Ginny, had persuaded him that would make everyone uncomfortable.

"Ginny seems quite nervous about traveling by train," Tabitha said. "I hope she will be alright."

"Thompson will take good care of her," Wolf assured her. "He's a very sensible sort of fellow and seems to be able to get any stain out of my clothes," he added, looking pointedly at Bear, who had fulfilled his valet tasks half-heartedly at best.

"Maybe you shouldn't get so many stains on your clothing, and then there'd be no need for other people to run around after you trying to remove them," Bear answered the implied tease jokingly. "The Wolf I used to know was more than willing to continue to wear a shirt with wine stains, even blood on it. I barely recognise this fop I see before me." This was all said and received good-naturedly.

By the standards of the typical aristocrat, Wolf was anything but a fop. It was a constant source of – albeit light-hearted – chivvying by Tabitha that he refused to dress formally in his own home and could barely be bothered when leaving the house. While Tabitha's deceased husband, Jonathan, had many sins that could be held against him, dressing to anything less than sartorial perfection was not one of them. Of course, when Tabitha reflected on the difference between the two men, she always concluded she would rather live with Wolf, even with his preference for slovenly dress habits, than her violent and abusive husband.

While Tabitha had inherited many of Jonathan's business assets, many more were part of the entail, and so inherited by Wolf on ascending to the earldom. As part of that portfolio of holdings, he was now a shareholder in the North British Railway. As he attempted to educate himself about the companies he had business interests in, he had been reading up on the history of train travel. He was particularly excited to see the company's flagship train in operation.

As the train pulled out of the station, Wolf told Tabitha and Bear what he had read about the changes that this technological miracle had brought about. The first public railway opened in 1825 with the introduction of the steam locomotive and the development of the early railway system. The Stockton and Darlington Railway's primary purpose had been to transport coal, but it also carried passengers. Over the ensuing seventy-five years, the railway system revolutionised travel throughout

Great Britain. And perhaps more importantly, had democratised it. Competition between railway companies and advancements in infrastructure ensured that train travel had become increasingly more affordable over the years, transforming how people lived and worked.

Even though she hadn't travelled by train since she was a child, Tabitha had always had a luxurious, well-sprung, comfortable horse-drawn carriage at her disposal. She had never considered the difficulties others might face trying to move around the country. Tabitha listened to Wolf enthuse about the miracle of train travel, and a little smile hovered around her mouth; his enthusiasm for the topic was clear.

Ever since Wolf had inherited and become the Earl of Pembroke, it had seemed to Tabitha as if the title were more a burden than a privilege much of the time. The son of a second son, his grandfather had made a minimal effort to ensure he was educated well enough, just in case. But at odds with his father, who was in turn at odds with his own, the late earl, Wolf had never seriously considered the likelihood of inheriting. Instead, he and Bear had built careers as thief-takers, often working in some of the less salubrious parts of London.

While Wolf's fortunes as a thief-taker had waxed and waned over the years, the career had given him a certain satisfaction; life as a thief-taker usually involved helping victims of crime. He and Bear helped people retrieve their stolen property and often helped ensure the acquittal of innocent people accused of crimes. Wolf was able to provide a very hands-on sort of help to people. Most of the time, it felt like an honourable way to make a living. Then one day, he found himself a peer of the realm with an enormous fortune at his disposal. Since then, he had spent the last few months trying to understand the power he now held as a member of the House of Lords and as a landowner and shareholder in multiple businesses.

As he had educated himself about his new business holdings, it had become clear to Wolf that Jonathan, the previous earl, had been miserly with his tenants and greedy in his business dealings. Wolf had already instructed his steward to rectify the situation on his estates. But Wolf was still trying to understand the businesses in which he was now an investor. Wolf was no Luddite, and he wasn't naive; he understood that progress usually left some people behind even as it improved the lives of others. But he felt strongly that he should try his best to ensure his fortune and investments did more good than harm. Sometimes, that was a very difficult line to walk, but he felt an unqualified pride in his involvement with train travel.

The chimney stacks and smog of London quickly gave way to the verdant English countryside with fields of green and yellow bordered by hedgerows. Flocks of sheep and sometimes herds of cows dotted the fields. Interspersed throughout the countryside were charming villages they passed so quickly that Tabitha missed them if she wasn't looking out of the window at the time. Tabitha was quite taken with the novelty of the experience, at least for the first hour or two. Watching her homeland pass before her eyes in almost a green blur, she was struck by Britain's beauty.

Their party had left the house quite early to make the train, and breakfast had been light. Within a couple of hours of travel, Tabitha felt her stomach rumble with hunger and said to her companions, "Perhaps it is time we investigate the dining car." Wolf was also beginning to feel hungry, and Bear never refused food, so they left their sumptuous carriage to seek sustenance.

Given the luxuriousness of their carriage, Tabitha would have expected nothing less in the dining car, and she was not disappointed. The dining car's decor was refined and tasteful throughout. Rich wood and elaborately detailed panelling throughout imbued the space with a warm opulence. Looking up as she entered, Tabitha noticed the ceiling's intricate mouldings and decorative elements.

The dining car's soft lighting fixtures created an intimate and inviting atmosphere. Large windows adorned with lace curtains let natural light filter in, offering passengers glimpses of the breathtaking scenery outside as they indulged in their meals. The tables in the dining car were elegantly set with crisp white linens, fine china, and polished silverware. Each table was adorned with fresh flowers, adding a touch of natural beauty to the surroundings. Comfortable upholstered chairs with plush cushions provided seating for passengers, ensuring they could relax and dine in the utmost comfort.

Attentive waitstaff, dressed in smart uniforms, moved gracefully through the dining car, catering to the needs of the passengers. They ensured the dining experience was seamless, providing impeccable service and attending to every detail. The head waiter immediately escorted them to a very well-appointed table. It was the man's job to know the rank and status of every guest aboard the train, and he immediately recognised some of that day's more illustrious passengers. When discussing the trip the evening before, Tabitha had insisted Wolf dress as befitted an earl. He had tentatively pushed back on the suggestion, unwilling to sit for many hours in the discomfort of such an outfit. But Tabitha had won out, and a slight raising of her eyebrows at Wolf as they were seated at the best table possible indicated her sense of vindication.

CHAPTER 2

Their meal ordered, Tabitha stared out the window, watching the countryside fly by. She was concerned about how Ginny was faring. She considered Wolf's statement that Thompson would care for her and tried not to worry. Thompson had only been a member of the Chesterton House staff for two weeks but seemed to have been quickly accepted into the household by the other servants. Tabitha knew it was often the case that upper staff, such as ladies' maids and valets, could hold themselves apart, creating distrust and resentment. Ginny assured her that Thompson, much like Ginny herself, was friendly and willing to pitch in to help the other servants.

Thompson was a comely man, not quite thirty, and Tabitha thought she'd detected Ginny blush when she mentioned his name. Perhaps her maid was not only prepared to sit separately from their group with the valet but was happy for the time alone with him. Tabitha smiled at the thought.

Catching her smiling, Wolf asked, "What's causing that smirk, Tabitha?"

"I am not smirking," she stated. "But I may have been thinking of something that made me smile." Not ready to share Ginny's possible interest in his valet, Tabitha changed the subject, "Why do you think the dowager has ordered us to drop everything and go to Edinburgh?"

"Honestly, it could be anything from a cat stuck up a tree to a body found floating in the bathtub," Wolf answered.

The Dowager Countess of Pembroke, Tabitha's mother-in-law,

was a formidable old woman. If she had been born a male, she could have been a great general, bestriding the battlefield, always four steps ahead of the enemy. As it was, she wielded her might and intellect in high society, ensuring her dominance by holding most of London's well-born in her thrall.

During Tabitha's short marriage to Jonathan, the dowager's disapproval had been directed at Tabitha's inability to deliver an heir for the earldom. Since Jonathan had died after drunkenly falling down the stairs during one of his many violent fights with Tabitha, the dowager had focused her disapproval on Tabitha's lack of stoicism when being used as a punching bag by her husband. As far as the dowager was concerned, if Tabitha had been the kind of wife she herself had been, she would have mutely, and obediently absorbed the punches, and then Jonathan wouldn't have fallen to his death. Of course, whenever the dowager stated this, Tabitha silently questioned whether the dowager was ever one to accept anything mutely and obediently.

Most recently, the dowager's disapproval had turned to Tabitha's unwillingness to stay in mourning clothes beyond six months. And then there was the outrageousness of Tabitha's continued residence at Chesterton House with Wolf, a single man only tenuously related to her. However, the dowager had taken quite a fancy to Wolf and now to Tabitha's four-year-old ward, Melody, and both had helped to thaw the relationship between the two women, at least somewhat.

Tabitha and Wolf acknowledged how helpful the dowager had been in their last two investigations. Her encyclopaedic knowledge of everyone in society and their histories had been invaluable, and her ability to draw all attention to herself and provide a distraction was indisputable.

Beyond whether Tabitha and Wolf had found the dowager a useful associate, the woman herself had made clear how much she had thoroughly enjoyed being, in her words, "a vital part of the investigative team." She had enjoyed it so much that she had installed telephones in her home and Chesterton House, without Wolf's permission, to facilitate team communications.

Usually reluctant to leave London for any reason, the dowager had agreed to travel north to stay with her married daughter, Jane, to help prepare her granddaughter for her coming out during the upcoming social season. The dowager had agreed to sponsor the girl, who, according to even her mother, needed some polish. The dowager would not have made the journey out of mere maternal devotion but rather agreed to undertake the trek out of fear of how some "country bumpkin" granddaughter would reflect on her when presented to London society.

So, despite grumbles about her Scottish heathen son-in-law, the dowager had hightailed it off to Edinburgh. Barely three days later, a telegram had arrived for Wolf, commanding, "Come at once. I am in great need of your expertise. Time is of the essence. I am depending on you."

Tabitha and Wolf had considered refusing. But that show of rebellion lasted for scarcely a minute. They had known insubordination would be paid for dearly for a long time to come.

"What do you know of your brother-in-law?" Wolf asked.

"Not a lot. Hamish and Jane attended my wedding to Jonathan, as did half of London. I'm not sure I said more than a passing greeting to them. And, of course, they were at Jonathan's funeral, where I talked with them briefly. From the gossip I've heard, Jonathan was newly elevated to the earldom after his father's death when Hamish began courting Jane. As the dowager tells it, Jane barely took when she came out. She's quite a plain-looking, shy woman, though I can only imagine what it was like growing up in the shadow of a mother like the dowager.

"While Hamish doesn't have a title, he has considerable landholdings, including collieries. Back then, his own father had recently died, and he had inherited a small fortune. The dowager will happily tell you what a poor match it was for an earl's daughter, but apparently, Jonathan believed it was the best offer, perhaps the only offer he was likely to get for a sister he was keen to have off his hands."

Tabitha paused, then added bitterly, "It goes without saying that no one mentions Jane's feelings on the matter." Tabitha could empathise all too well with a young woman whose guardian was enamoured of a wealthy suitor regardless of what might be in the woman's best interest.

"If memory serves me correctly, I believe Jane has four children, all girls. The daughter the dowager has been summoned to 'fix' is the eldest. I think her name is Lily or maybe Rose. It's definitely some flower. I think all the names are flowers. You can only imagine my mother-in-law's thoughts on this subject." Tabitha stopped and considered what she'd said, "Actually, now I think of it, maybe there are three girls and a boy. I distinctly remember the dowager saying something cutting about how it was a miracle he wasn't named Rhododendron."

"So, we have no idea what this emergency is," Wolf stated. "It may not even be an emergency. Just because she requires our so-called expertise doesn't mean anything."

"Well, she did say that time is of the essence," Tabitha pointed out. "That implies an emergency." Even as she said this, she wasn't sure why she attempted to defend the dowager. Yes, the telegram had said time was of the essence. But Tabitha knew as well as Wolf that this could be nothing more than hyperbole, something the dowager made frequent use of. "I promise if this turns out to be anything less than a genuine emergency, we will be on the first train back to London the next day," she added.

CHAPTER 3

After a delicious lunch, they returned to their carriage. They had been travelling for almost four hours but were only halfway to Edinburgh. Tabitha had brought books with her. An avid reader, one of her favourite novelists was Jane Austen. While she enjoyed the writer's entire canon, *Pride and Prejudice* was her favourite. She had read the book so many times that she could now start it at any point and immediately pick up the thread of the story.

When Tabitha first read the novel, she loved the heroine, Elizabeth Bennet. But she hadn't understood her statement, "Only the deepest love will persuade me into matrimony, which is why I will end up an old maid." Tabitha had been sixteen at the time and had been fairly indoctrinated by her mother over the years that, "One doesn't marry for love. One marries for status and security."

At the time, a family they were close to had suffered the indignity of having their eldest daughter, Nora, turn down a duke to marry a baron. "All in the name of love, supposedly," or at least that is what her mother, Lady Ashley, had said between bouts of wailing. Unfortunately for Nora's mother, the young woman had her own funds left to her by her a great aunt, so she could do as she pleased. According to Tabitha's mother, this was a cautionary tale about why girls should marry as young as possible; Nora was twenty-one when a match with the duke was proposed and old enough to refuse her parents' wishes.

Given her own mother's strong feelings on the subject, it was no wonder Tabitha was dangled in front of Jonathan Chesterton, the Earl of Pembroke, as soon as was socially acceptable. It never occurred to Tabitha to question the match, nor to examine her feelings towards the much older man. But now, not even five full years later, Tabitha was a chastened twenty-two-year-old who had realised she would never trust a man enough again to put herself in his power. But at times she second-guessed her own decision. She felt a strong attraction to Wolf, which she believed was reciprocated. But beyond that, he was a kind, generous, gentle man who had genuine respect for her intelligence.

As she read about Elizabeth Bennet's growing awareness of her love for Darcy, Tabitha wondered, was it possible to have this kind of deep love outside the pages of a novel? And more to the point, Tabitha, so mentally scarred from her abusive marriage to Jonathan, couldn't help but wonder if even the deepest love would truly protect her.

As Tabitha read her book and mused on the subject of love, Wolf was reading some business papers. But he couldn't help but sneak furtive looks at Tabitha. He loved to watch her in these unguarded moments. He could tell by the little frown mark on her forehead that her reading material troubled her thoughts. From what he could tell, she was reading *Pride and Prejudice*, not a book he would expect to cause discontent.

Just a few weeks before, Wolf had come perilously close to declaring his feelings to Tabitha. The declaration was unplanned, but he had found himself quite overwhelmed by his passions. Only Tabitha's clear indication that such a pronouncement was unwelcome had cooled his ardour. Despite some initial awkwardness in the moment, they both valued their friendship too much to let some hastily spoken words drive a wedge between them. Since then, it had been as if the moment had never happened. But even so, he had continued to think back to that evening. Was Tabitha's reaction indicative of nothing more than bad timing, or did it reflect a more deeply held desire on her part never to move their relationship beyond the platonic?

Just as Wolf was considering whether he was brave enough to

broach the subject of romance with Tabitha again at some point, Bear returned to the carriage. He had kindly offered to go and check on Ginny and make sure Thompson was taking good care of her. Retaking his seat, he said, "Well, by the way those two are looking at each other, I'd say a Michaelmas wedding is in the cards."

"What on earth are they up to back there?" Tabitha asked nervously. Her household was not one where staff were forbidden from courting and marrying. But Ginny was very dear to her, and the thought that the new valet might merely be trifling with the maid's feelings caused her great concern.

Realising his joke had been taken quite seriously, Bear quickly put Tabitha's mind at ease. He then took a sketchbook and charcoals from his valise and asked her, "Do you mind if I draw you?" Tabitha couldn't help but let her surprise show and immediately regretted it, apologised, and consented.

When Bear first joined the household, Tabitha, like many people, had made certain assumptions about him. He was enormous; tall, broad and muscled, with hair covering the back of his hands and creeping out of the neck of his shirt to meet a full beard that reached up his cheeks, nearly to his eyes. The overall effect was of some kind of mythical creature or a giant from a nursery rhyme come to life. In reality, Bear was one of the gentlest, kindest men Tabitha had ever known. While he often terrified many people on first meeting, he usually won them over quickly, at least when he chose to. However, the fear inspired by his bulk and visage had been extremely useful in Wolf and Bear's thief-taking days. Even during their recent investigations, Wolf found there was nothing like Bear's company to inspire cooperation.

Despite her immediate contrition at her surprise at Bear, the artist, she couldn't help but smile seeing the delicate charcoals gripped in his meaty paws. Tabitha continued reading but sat as still as she was able. No more than fifteen minutes later, Bear turned the sketch pad towards her and asked, "What do you think?" Tabitha was stunned; not only did the quick sketch perfectly capture her, but it had a vitality to it that made the observer believe the reader was about to raise her head out of her book and speak.

"Bear, it's wonderful," Tabitha said in awe. "I had no idea you had such talents. Do you only work in charcoals?"

"It depends on what's to hand and what I can afford," Bear admitted. "I love to paint, but our lives as thief-takers rarely gave me the luxury of space, time or money for supplies. Since being at Chesterton House, I've had more of all of those and started a couple of small canvases." He added shyly, "Including one of Miss Melody."

"You've been painting Melly!" Tabitha exclaimed gleefully. "May I see it when we return?"

"Certainly, but don't get your hopes up too high. I'm no John Singer Sargent," he said, referring to the renowned portrait painter.

"Sorry to interrupt," Wolf said to Bear, "But take a look at some of these papers. I think it'll help you understand better the issue I was talking about yesterday." Seeing Tabitha's cocked eyebrow, Wolf said, "Bear and I have been discussing how he might help me manage the estate and associated businesses. I've been going over some of the accounts with him."

"What a wonderful idea," Tabitha said with genuine enthusiasm. She knew how much it meant to Wolf that his old friend stay by his side. She also knew enough of Bear to realise he would not feel comfortable living at Chesterton House as nothing more than a long-term houseguest. He would have to believe he made a genuine contribution to the household.

Tabitha had been anxious about leaving Melody behind. Some soothing words from Wolf had calmed her somewhat, but the anxiety returned after talking about the child. When she had taken on responsibility for Melody, she had also brought the girl's brother, Matt, known as Rat, into her household. Unlike Melody, Rat was a part of the household staff. Nevertheless, Tabitha had grown very fond and protective of the boy.

Once Tabitha and Wolf had decided they had no choice but

to obey the dowager's dictate that they follow her to Scotland, Tabitha was unsure what to do about Melody and her brother. During their previous investigation, Melody had been abducted by Maxwell Sandworth, the Earl of Langley. Unbeknownst to Tabitha and Wolf at the time, Langley worked for British Intelligence and had taken the child in a misguided attempt to force Tabitha and Wolf to stop their investigation. Melody was a delightful, intelligent child, and Langley had become as charmed by her as everyone else. He was so charmed that when confronted about the kidnapping, he'd had the audacity to request that Melody continue to visit regularly. And to Tabitha's amazement, she'd agreed. It seemed Langley had been acting as more of a doting godfather than a malevolent kidnapper and that Melody was as taken with "Uncle Maxi" as he was with her.

Tabitha's first inclination had been to take Melody to Scotland with them. But they had no idea how hospitable the dowager's daughter would be to the little girl's appearance in her nursery, and they had even less idea of the nature of the investigation they were being dragged into. It seemed the more prudent, if heart-wrenching, decision was to leave Melody behind in London. Wolf suggested they leave the little girl at Chesterton House in the care of her nursemaid, Mary. But to his surprise, Tabitha had suggested the child stay with Uncle Maxi. In the short time Melody had spent with Langley during the "abduction", he had taught her to read, and had even started her on basic multiplication. As much as Tabitha was loath to admit it, Langley was a good influence in the little girl's life.

Tabitha had also pointed out, "And he can take Dodo as well!" Dodo was the Cavalier King Charles Spaniel Langley had given Melody to keep her company during her stay in his home. Tabitha was not a dog lover, but even she had grown, if not fond, then tolerant of the puppy. But Tabitha had been unaware of how troublesome a puppy could be, and thought it only fair that the man who had imposed this destructive pet on their household staff would relieve them while she was away. The only question left by this whole arrangement was where Rat should reside during their trip.

When Tabitha had insisted on taking Melody and Rat into their household at Chesterton House, Wolf had expressed his reservations about the living arrangements; Melody was to live as Tabitha's ward in the nursery, but Rat would live in the carriage house and work as a member of the staff. This arrangement had been Rat's preference, but Wolf had anticipated such an unusual arrangement would lead to awkward situations for all of them. Leaving Melody with Langley had become one of those situations.

Did they send Rat with Melody to live with Lord Langley? The boy had been very protective of his sister since her abduction. Tabitha and Wolf had agreed that it was for the best if Rat did not know the details of how and why Melody had ended up spending so many days at Langley House. Luckily, Rat had been so relieved to have Melody home safely that he hadn't poked too many holes in their elaborate and rather absurd explanation. But could they send him to stay with Lord Langley?

Rat was a sharp and hardworking lad, and had been accepted by the rest of the staff, despite his unusual standing with the master of the house. But now that he was established in a routine, asking the other servants to accommodate his absence for who knew how long would be unfair. In the end, they had asked Rat what he wanted to do, and the boy had suggested he continue to take his evening meal with Melody in the nursery at Chesterton House as he often did when Melody was at home. Rat seemed comfortable with this arrangement, and even though Langley raised his eyebrows when told, he made no objections. Tabitha hoped she wouldn't regret leaving Melody at Langley House. She hoped to send a telegram as soon as possible after their arrival. Langley had promised to correspond regularly with her during Melody's stay. But even so, she would not rest easy until she heard how the arrangement was working.

The rest of the trip passed companionably. Wolf continued to read through papers and then pass them to Bear, pointing out aspects of the accounts he felt his friend should pay attention to. Tabitha continued to read her book and sometimes stare out the window as the glories of the British countryside flew past. Around 3pm, they agreed that some tea and cake would be welcome and returned to the dining room.

As they travelled further north, the countryside became more rugged and spectacular. Not long before they crossed the Scottish border, Tabitha caught sight of the brilliant blue of the North Sea and long stretches of white sand. The landscape's green began to be coloured by the purple of large swaths of heather.

Finally, the train slowed to a stop. They had arrived at Waverley Station, Edinburgh.

CHAPTER 4

The MacAlister carriage awaited them as they ascended from the station. The drive to Charlotte Square, the Edinburgh residence of Laird MacAlister, as his coachman referred to him, was barely fifteen minutes' drive. Settled into the comfortable carriage, Wolf asked Tabitha jokingly, "So, how does a laird rate next to an earl?"

"Actually, laird is not a noble title, at least in the legal sense that earl is. I believe it is an honorific title denoting that a man owns a substantial estate," she answered. "From what I've heard, the dowager was never happy that Jonathan allowed Jane to marry an untitled man. And a Scot at that. At some point, someone referred to him as Laird MacAlister, and she seized on it and refused to have him addressed any other way, even though he politely told her the first time she said it there was no need and that the title was not the same as earl or duke. The very last gossip she wanted spread around London was that her daughter had dropped in rank. So heaven help anyone who refers to Jane as anything other than Lady MacAlister."

"Should I be referring to her as Lady MacAlister then?" Wolf asked.

"If you know what's good for you," Tabitha said. "At least in front of her mother."

"And how should I address the laird?" he asked, amused as ever by the dowager's insistence on imposing her sense of reality on everyone around her.

Tabitha thought momentarily, then replied, "I don't remember enough about the man. But it goes without saying that the dowager's caricature of an uncivilised, heathen Scot should probably be ignored. But as for his own preferences, let's wait and see how he presents himself."

The house was in Edinburgh's New Town where the wealthy and powerful of Edinburgh could delight in the charm of viewing Edinburgh Castle and its environs from a genteel distance, leaving the poor to the filth and misery of their rotting tenements and the ensuant cholera, typhus and other deathly infectious diseases. Tabitha knew little about New Town's history but could appreciate its neo-classical and Georgian-architecture-lined wide roads.

The MacAlister home was a palatial Georgian building, quite as stately as many of the best London residences. Entering the house, Tabitha noted the vestibule's elegance, with marble tiles on the floor and a soaring ceiling complete with a crystal chandelier that wouldn't have looked out of place gracing any grand London home. It was clear that, despite the dowager's complaints at having to travel to the wilds of the North as if she were voyaging beyond the reach of civilisation, this was a house she would be happy to visit if it were in London.

The family, including the dowager, were assembled to greet them. A large, friendly-looking man, clearly the laird himself, immediately stepped forward to be the first to welcome their guests. He was tall and broad, though not in any way close to Bear's size. Hamish MacAlister had red hair, heavily laced through with grey. He sported a rather impressive set of mutton chops, and Tabitha could only imagine what the dowager thought of those. Her mother-in-law had said many times that she never trusted a man who wasn't clean-shaven, and that any kind of facial hair seemed something a man would only adopt if he were on the run from the law. The dowager had never commented on Bear's beard, but Tabitha believed the dictate only applied to the ruling classes.

Laird MacAlister had bright blue, twinkly eyes and a large, white-toothed smile. Everything about the man radiated genuine pleasure at their arrival. He grasped Wolf's hand in a firm grip and said, "Welcome, cousin. It's a pleasure to meet you."

Wolf looked taken aback for a moment. Somehow, it hadn't dawned on him that he was actually meeting family. He had viewed Jane as one of Tabitha's in-laws. But in truth, she was his cousin, and that seemed to have escaped his awareness until Hamish addressed him. He wasn't sure how he hadn't realised before that the dowager was then his aunt, at least by marriage. Had he been committing a social faux pas by not referring to her as such all this time? But on second thoughts, if she'd wanted to be referred to as such, there was no doubt she would have demanded it.

After greeting Wolf, Hamish moved on to Tabitha, enveloping her in a bear hug. While she might have felt this greeting inappropriately familiar under normal circumstances, the man seemed so guileless and enthusiastic that it was impossible to be offended, though Tabitha could only imagine the dowager's reaction to such a welcome. "Ye're looking well, lass," Hamish said in a booming, jolly voice. Everything about Jane's husband was larger than life.

When describing her son-in-law previously, the dowager had made their host sound like a barely literate, uncouth lout of a man. But in truth, while he lacked the reserve and polish expected in the best circles of London society, he was clearly a gentleman. Even his accent was a pleasant burr, with quite a melodic quality rather than the incomprehensible guttural growls the dowager had once described. "It is a pleasure to see you again, Laird MacAlister," Tabitha said.

"We dinnae bother wi' formalities in this hoose, lass," the man answered. "Particularly wi' family. Hamish will do for me."

Tabitha could see the dowager's reaction to this statement. She was not someone to let standards slide, even within the bosom of her family. Nevertheless, Tabitha inclined her head and said, "Then Hamish it shall be. And I hope you will call me Tabitha. And," she paused, glanced at Wolf, then said, "And Lord Pembroke prefers to be called Wolf, instead of his given name,

Jeremy."

"Wolf, is it?" Hamish laughed. "Weel, ye're baith very welcome."

Tabitha had hoped to keep Wolf's nickname from the dowager. But it had been revealed inadvertently during their last investigation, and it seemed churlish to refuse to introduce him as he wished now that the cat was out of the bag.

The greetings of the head of the household dispensed with, Wolf and Tabitha approached Jane, Lady MacAlister, who was flanked by her eldest daughter and mother. Jane was much as Tabitha remembered her: a plain, mousey-looking woman dressed in a well-made but unflattering dress. While not as short as her mother, Jane lacked the older woman's presence and seemed to shrink in on herself as she received her guests' attention. Tabitha held out her hand to her sister-in-law, feeling that, as virtual strangers, a kiss on the cheek would neither be appropriate nor welcome.

"Welcome, sister," Jane said timidly, her voice matching her wan complexion. "We appreciate that you are visiting on such short notice and with so little explanation as to the circumstances we find ourselves in."

Before Tabitha could answer with matching polite formality, the dowager said dismissively, "Pish posh, Jane. Why wouldn't they come? You are a family in crisis, and more to the point, I requested their presence." The dowager paused and amended her statement, "Well, I requested dear Jeremy's presence. Clearly, it was too much to expect he might be allowed to attend me unaccompanied."

The dowager could always be counted on to use as few words as necessary to offend as many people as possible. In two sentences, she managed to imply that Wolf was henpecked by Tabitha, who, in turn, the implication was, exhibited a pathetic need to be involved where she wasn't wanted.

"Lady Pembroke, I assumed you realised by now that Tabitha has been an invaluable part of recent investigations and that any request of me was an implicit request of us both," Wolf said pleasantly but firmly. The dowager's only answer was a harrumph which usually indicated she had no good answer but refused to concede defeat.

Once Wolf greeted his cousin Jane, she said nervously, "And this is my eldest daughter, Lily." Despite the dowager describing her granddaughters as mousey, insipid copies of Jane, the young woman standing before Tabitha could not have seemed less like her mother's child. Lily was as tall as Tabitha, that is to say, almost unfashionably tall for a woman. She had the graceful, swan-like neck so admired in young, marriageable women. Her skin was a perfect alabaster with a hint of pink on her cheeks that no makeup could replicate in its natural beauty. Lily had inherited her father's bright blue eyes, but on the daughter, they were framed by dark, thick, long lashes. To top off the look of unstudied beauty, the young woman had thick, curly, dark auburn hair that tumbled over her shoulders.

While Lily was undoubtedly a true beauty, unflattering, overly large glasses framed her sparkling eyes, and a hideous brown dress draped the tall, slender frame. As if determined to be the icing on the ruined cake of the girl's outfit, there seemed to be multiple twigs stuck in her hair.

Noticing Tabitha's eyes drawn to her granddaughter's head, the dowager walked over to Lily, "Child, you have what seems to be a bird's nest as part of your coiffure. Jane, does the girl not have a lady's maid to see to her?"

Flustered by her mother's criticism, Jane blushed deeply and muttered, "Lily, could you not have stayed in the house just for one morning? You knew we were to have guests."

Lily, who seemed unperturbed by her grandmother's comments and her mother's embarrassment, merely approached Tabitha with an outstretched hand and said, "Aunt Tabitha, it is so lovely to meet you after hearing so much about you from Grandmama." Seeing Tabitha's look of scepticism at the thought that her mother-in-law had said anything about her that might merit such a statement, Lily added, "The more she made you sound like the worst kind of termagant, flouting society's strictures and immune to its censure, the more I couldn't wait to make your acquaintance."

Even the dowager had the good grace to look a little shamefaced at this, albeit almost certainly accurate, repetition of her words, "Child, what nonsense are you speaking? I said no such things." Neither Lily nor Tabitha bothered to address this blatant lie.

Tabitha regarded her niece with real interest; this was no demure, milksop young girl. It was not merely in looks that the girl bore no resemblance to her mother. "Lily, I am delighted to make your acquaintance. Let me introduce you to Jeremy Chesterton, the Earl of Pembroke and your first cousin once removed."

Wolf moved forward to take the young woman's hand, and she gave him a firm, no-nonsense handshake so very like her father's. The young woman did not lower her face, demurely glancing through her lashes at her handsome cousin as so many girls her age might have, but instead looked him in the eye, "Welcome to Scotland, cousin. You cut a finer figure as earl than my Uncle Jonathan ever did, for all his fancy clothes and airs."

At this, the dowager looked as if she were going to explode, and Jane looked as if she wished the earth would open up and swallow her. Hamish merely chuckled and said, "I supposed I should apologise for Lily; the lass got her blunt speaking from me, I'm afraid. My mam used to say I was born with my foot in my mouth."

Tabitha noticed that, unlike her father, Lily had barely any Scottish accent and could have easily passed in the best London drawing rooms. She assumed imported English nannies and governesses were responsible for this. "Laird MacAlister, your daughter's candour is refreshing and charming," Tabitha assured him.

"Is that what we're calling it?" the dowager interjected, "Refreshing and charming? I can think of some other words. Certainly, more than a little work is needed. Definitely more than the mere final polish I was led to believe I was to aid with."

At this, the dowager looked accusingly at her daughter, who visibly shrank back at her mother's disapproval.

However, Hamish, seemingly unaware or uncaring of the dangerous waters he was wading into, replied, "Aye, the lass is a breath of fresh air. I'm unsure how I'll part with her when she marries."

At this, Lily went over to her father and took his arm affectionately and said in what was now a decidedly different accent, "Dinnae fash yersel', ma bonnie faither. Ah winnae be marryin'."

Hamish patted her hand, shook his head, and replied in a similar stronger accent than he had been using, "Lass, ye ken ye hae tae."

"I will not stay one moment more in this house if English is not spoken," the dowager said imperiously, adding, "by every member of this family at all times."

Desperate to defuse the situation, Jane said, "Mama, our guests must be eager for their rooms and to change out of their travelling clothes." Then addressing Tabitha and Wolf, she said, "Whenever you're ready, we thought we would have some sherry in the drawing room before an early dinner. You must all be exhausted." Just as she finished speaking, Bear appeared, filling the doorway. He had been helping Thompson and Ginny indicate to the MacAlister servants each guest's luggage.

Seeing the hairy giant of a man dramatically framed by the doorway, almost blocking out the light, Jane gasped, and instinctively put her hand to her throat. Even the seemingly unperturbable Lily looked concerned.

Wolf had decided this trip was the perfect time to reintroduce Bear in his new elevated role in the Pembroke household. Given this, he didn't want the dowager to leap in and treat the man as a servant, "Hamish, I would like to introduce Mr Caruthers, my private secretary." The dowager's eyebrows shot up at Bear's unexpected promotion, but she kept her own counsel.

Bear walked further into the vestibule, and Hamish grasped the other man's large paw, "Ye're verra welcome, Mr Caruthers."

This final introduction made, the guests were shown to their rooms.

CHAPTER 5

Tabitha entered her assigned bedroom and was happy to find Ginny unpacking. Thanks to Ginny's foresight, there was an easily accessible bag with a suitable evening gown, shoes, and accessories for dinner that night. "M'lady, I've started running you a bath. I'm sure you wish to wash the grime of the trip off."

"Ginny, you're an angel. But once I'm dressed, leave the rest of my unpacking and get yourself settled and something to eat. The rest of my stuff can even wait until morning," Tabitha added.

"That's very kind of you, m'lady, and I will go and get a little something to eat. But I'll return and finish the unpacking after. I don't like to go to bed with chores left undone. Never have." Tabitha smiled at her highly efficient and conscientious maid.

A quick bath and fresh clothes did wonders to reinvigorate Tabitha. They still had no idea why they had been summoned to Scotland, and she assumed this reveal would happen over dinner and wanted to ensure she had the stamina for whatever drama awaited them.

On entering the drawing room, Tabitha saw that Wolf was already standing near the elegant marble fireplace, a cut glass tumbler of what she assumed was whisky in his hand. She took a moment to admire how well he looked in evening wear, and to note the added touches of elegance the new valet, Thompson, had subtly introduced into Wolf's attire. Their butler, Talbot, had done his best to help dress his master while Bear was the putative but wholly inept valet. But, as with many butlers, Talbot had risen through the ranks of footmen and had never officially performed valet services. However, Thompson had come highly recommended by the household of the Marquis of Winchester after his employer died suddenly in a boating accident. Thompson knew all the tricks to turning out an appropriately dapper peer of the realm.

Tabitha had thought long and hard about the clothes she had brought. Before marrying Jonathan, she had been expected to dress appropriately for a demure debutante. After her marriage, Jonathan demanded an almost puritanical austerity of dress. Then, after six months of mourning, Tabitha had decided, despite the dowager's disapproval, to throw off even the lilacs and greys of half-mourning. But she had been unsure of her chosen style as a young, wealthy widow.

After a few experiments, including a few rather brazen costumes during their investigations, she was beginning to find her personal sartorial voice. Her new clothes were far less demure than anything her mother or deceased husband would have approved of. However, they were still well within the boundaries of acceptable style within aristocratic circles. Acceptable by the standards of anyone except her mother-in-law, that was. The Dowager Countess of Pembroke never missed an opportunity to denounce Tabitha's outfits as almost befitting a scarlet woman, which she also never failed to point out was appropriate given the scandal of Tabitha living with Wolf, an unmarried man.

And so, the question Tabitha always faced when dressing for the dowager's company was: how much of a red flag to a bull did she wish to be? More importantly, Jane was Jonathan's sister, and she did not wish to offend her hostess. Although it hadn't been lost on her that, like her mother, Jane had also thrown off mourning attire. It appeared Jonathan was no more missed as a brother than a husband. Finally, in consultation with Ginny, Tabitha had left her more revealing and potentially scandalous outfits behind in London. But she wouldn't let her wardrobe be dictated by a judgemental old woman who would likely disapprove regardless.

That evening, Ginny had chosen a simple but beautifully tailored pale, mint green silk dress for her. It showed a hint of decolletage but was still suitably demure, or at least that was Tabitha's hope. Tabitha paired the dress with a triple strand of pearls given to her by the dowager on her marriage to Jonathan. Ginny dressed Tabitha's hair in a modern yet sophisticated style, and the overall effect was of fashionable refinement. Of course, this was no guarantee that the dowager wouldn't disapprove, and Tabitha entered the drawing room with trepidation. She usually paid little attention to the dowager's inevitable sniping, but she cared about how it might poison her reception by Laird and Lady MacAlister.

Tabitha needn't have worried; while the dowager did purse her lips and narrow her eyes on Tabitha's entrance, she kept her thoughts to herself. Tabitha reflected, for not the first time, that there was something to be said for having the dowager in her debt. Or at least in need of her help. Of course, the older woman would never allow that truth, at least explicitly. But her acknowledgement of her hitherto social pariah of a daughter-in-law very publicly at a recent ball was at least a nod to Tabitha's recent assistance.

Hamish welcomed Tabitha warmly into the room, and Jane acknowledged her politely. Tabitha realised Lily was not yet down, but no sooner was Tabitha seated with a glass of sherry in her hand than the young woman made her entrance. While she had changed for dinner, her evening dress was no more flattering than her day dress had been. However, at first glance, it seemed the tree parts were no longer part of her hairdo. Tabitha didn't often agree with the dowager's pronouncements, but she had to admit that the young woman needed a bit more than just some polish if she was to make her debut that season.

Lily sat beside Tabitha, her eyes blinking nervously behind the unflattering glasses. Looking around her to ensure they had some privacy, she asked in a low voice, "Did Grandmama tell you why I need your help?"

Tabitha couldn't help the surprise in her voice when she

replied, "Neither Lord Pembroke nor I were aware it was you we had been summoned to help. How can we assist?"

"I need you to find my friend, Peter."

Tabitha wasn't sure what she had expected, but it wasn't that the demand they drop everything and make all haste hundreds of miles to the North was merely to find a missing young man who was likely doing nothing more than sowing some wild oats. Tabitha's thoughts must have been clear on her face because Lily continued, "I assure you, I would not have asked if I believed this was nothing more than a young man blowing off steam. Peter isn't like that. He isn't one of us," she said knowingly.

Before Tabitha could ask who he was, if not "one of us", Lily answered the unspoken question, "He's not of noble birth or wealthy. In fact, he's very poor. He grew up in an orphanage. He managed to get a scholarship to a fine school and then to attend Edinburgh University, where he studies medicine."

"So, he's a student," Tabitha said, scepticism that this anything more than student high jinks still evident in her voice.

"Peter is a very serious young man and an ardent supporter of the cause," the young woman said, eyes blazing. Tabitha knew that look, and it didn't bode well for persuading Lily to accept a society marriage to a man deemed appropriate by her grandmother. Lily clearly had very passionate feelings towards this missing young man.

"Lily," Tabitha began gently, unsure how best to broach her suspicions, "it is evident Peter means a lot to you–"

But before she could continue that thought, the young woman interrupted her impatiently, "I'm not in love with him. Why does everyone immediately think that? Isn't it possible for a man and a woman to think highly of each other and yet be nothing more than friends?"

Tabitha considered the question. It was not far from her recent ponderings regarding her relationship with Wolf. Was it possible? Did this young woman, barely out of the schoolroom, somehow have the maturity to manage something Tabitha had struggled with every day recently? But then Tabitha considered

Anthony, the Duke of Somerset. She thought highly of him and considered him a dear friend, but there was nothing more to it than friendship. Perhaps it was possible to be merely friends with someone of the opposite gender. However, was it possible for her to be merely friends with Wolf? Realising her thoughts had drifted in an unhelpful direction, Tabitha pulled her focus back to the interesting young woman before her.

"I believe it is possible. Perhaps not common, but yes, possible," Tabitha acknowledged.

Before they could talk anymore, dinner was called. Tabitha was seated next to the right of their host, Hamish, with the dowager to his left. With uneven numbers, Tabitha found herself with Jane on her right as the dowager commandeered Wolf for her other side.

Tabitha noted that Bear had not joined them for dinner. She didn't blame the man. At best, a private secretary hovered in an uneasy netherworld, not upper servant, but not a friend under normal circumstances. Of course, he was Wolf's dear friend, but he hadn't benefited from the new earl's education or upbringing. Tabitha was sure Bear was far more comfortable eating in the kitchen than with the dowager, who had only ever known him as Wolf's valet. Lily was seated between her mother and Wolf, so any further confidences would have to be postponed.

Conversation through the soup and fish courses was banal enough. Tabitha realised that Hamish, likely an amusing dinner companion under normal circumstances, was holding himself in restraint with his mother-in-law sitting at his elbow, ready to cast judgement at any moment. At least there was nothing to criticise in the food, and Tabitha was happy to be able to offer Jane her genuine compliments on her cook. The compliments given and received graciously enough, Tabitha then cast about for a suitable topic for discussion with her less-than-chatty sister-in-law. Luckily, the dowager was keen to make the most of having dear Jeremy as a captive audience, and so Hamish was freed up for conversation, even if restrained.

Tabitha was eager to learn about Edinburgh's history,

and Hamish was an enthusiastic and knowledgeable conversationalist on the topic. He told her how the population had outgrown the Old Town, which had initially coped with the demand for housing by building upwards, creating tenements of sometimes as many as twelve storeys high. Eventually, in the middle of the prior century, building began across the river of what was now known as New Town. There was a quick exodus of the wealthy inhabitants of Edinburgh to the new, expensive part of the city.

"I would be interested in visiting the Old Town and seeing the Castle," Tabitha told Hamish.

Overhearing this comment, the dowager interrupted any reply Hamish might have made, saying, "What a ridiculous idea, Tabitha, even for someone as prone to courting trouble as you are. It's like saying you are curious about visiting Whitechapel. For heaven's sake!"

Unbeknownst to the dowager, Tabitha had visited the notorious London neighbourhood during their first investigation. Of course, she had been disguised as a young man then, but even so, she had felt the desperation and danger alive in the air. If she was honest, it had scared her.

"Lady Pembroke has a point, Tabitha. It's nae a place for a fine lady tae visit," Hamish agreed.

Tabitha didn't press the point; she had other things on her mind. When would they be told why they had been summoned to Scotland? While it was true Lily had begun to explain, Tabitha was certain the dowager hadn't felt the disappearance of a poor, unconnected young friend of her granddaughter's a sufficient reason to rouse herself to action. It had been clear from Jane's vague allusions about 'circumstances' when welcoming them that there was a reason for asking for help. But whatever it was, the family felt no great urgency to communicate that reason.

Finally, with dinner at an end, it was the juncture when, under normal circumstances, the women would withdraw, leaving the men to their port and cigars. "Laird MacAlister," the dowager said, addressing her son-in-law formally, "I believe it is time to explain our dilemma to Jeremy and Tabitha. I suggest you men foreswear your cigars and that we all repair to the drawing room."

The dowager never intended for her suggestions to be disputed or debated, and with a collective recognition of this fact, the entire party stood and made their way back to the drawing room.

Hamish offered Wolf some single malt whisky, "I have a fine Glenlivet, or if you prefer something peatier, I have some of the Talisker you drank earlier."

"I enjoyed the Talisker, but it was a little peaty for my tastes, so I'll have a Glenlivet," Wolf replied.

Hamish chuckled, "Ye English are ower delicate for oor finest whiskies. If ye foond that tae peaty, I should let ye try a Laphroaig."

As it happened, Laphroaig whisky had been a pivotal clue in their last investigation, and Wolf had learned enough to know it was an acquired taste. Instead, he gladly accepted the Glenlivet. In truth, he preferred a fine French brandy to Scottish single malt, but knew better than to ask for anything other than a whisky while he was this side of the border.

The butler, Dawglish, brought in tea for the women, and finally everyone settled with a drink of some sort in hand. The dowager then cleared her throat to indicate she expected everyone's attention, put down her teacup and stood. It seemed she intended to milk this moment for maximum dramatic effect.

"Dear Jeremy, and Tabitha, of course, I'm sure you've been waiting expectantly to hear why your help is so needed." She then paused, looked around the room to ensure she had a suitably rapt audience and continued, "As you know, my granddaughter Lily will be having her season shortly, and I will sponsor her. It is shockingly self-evident that there is much work needed to ensure she is a good reflection on me." Anyone else might have phrased this criticism in such a way as to avoid offence.

The dowager continued, oblivious or unconcerned about any affront her words might have caused, "However, an unfortunate stumbling block has been placed in the way of the commencement of the necessary campaign of action." Tabitha reflected that most grandmothers would hardly refer to the process of readying a debutante in such military terms. However, the dowager was not most grandmothers and continued, "Lily has informed us she will not participate in any of the much-needed visits to the modiste or the shockingly necessary deportment lessons, at least for now. Apparently, there is a young woman she has been allowed to become acquainted with." At this, the dowager threw a look in her daughter's direction that might have withered even a more indomitable woman.

Tabitha noted that the dowager seemed to be under the impression that the missing friend was a young woman rather than a young man. That was interesting.

"This wholly unsuitable young woman is unwilling or unable to make her whereabouts known, and Lily thinks this is somehow her responsibility to rectify. And in taking on this responsibility, she has now transferred it to me via blackmail."

At this accusation, Lily put down her teacup, stood up to face her grandmother, and said in a tone quite as imperious as her forebear's, "Grandmama, that is an outrageous lie. I never blackmailed you."

Unused to interruptions and rebuttal, the dowager was momentarily flummoxed, but she quickly regrouped and came back with her counteroffensive, "You said very clearly that you would not participate in any activities until this young person is found or reappears somehow. Given the vital importance you know your parents and I attach to your debut, I am at a loss to see your statement as anything other than a Sword of Damocles held over my head."

Tabitha could see this particular argument wasn't getting them any closer to understanding what Lily believed might have happened to Peter, so she held up her hand and said, "Regardless of how and why the request for assistance was made, Lord Pembroke and I are now here. Lily, why don't you tell us what you know and why you believe your friend has done anything other than leave Edinburgh without informing you." Seeing the dowager about to weigh in again, Tabitha made a decision, "Actually, I am quite exhausted from our trip and would prefer to listen to Lily's story with a clear head. Lily, I suggest you meet with Lord Pembroke and me after breakfast. And only Lord Pembroke and me," she said pointedly.

CHAPTER 6

The following morning at breakfast, Tabitha asked Lily where they might talk uninterrupted. This less-than-subtle reference to the dowager was answered with a loud harrumph from across the table, but the old woman did not comment otherwise. Lily suggested they walk in the garden, and she could show them some of her prized plantings. Tabitha was genuinely curious to learn more about the young woman and felt being out of the range of possible eavesdropping was not a bad idea.

London had begun to cool down noticeably as autumn took hold, and Scotland was significantly colder. Tabitha, Wolf and Lily went to retrieve their coats, agreeing to meet in the summer room, enabling them to exit through the French doors to the garden.

Tabitha knew very little about horticulture, but she did appreciate beauty. Whatever scientific purposes this garden had been cultivated for, it seemed it had also been created for the sheer pleasure of viewing nature's beauty. Tabitha could see some crocuses, which she didn't realise could grow in the autumn. They were in a variety of colours from purple, to lilac, and white. There were also some beautiful, elegant pink blooms that Tabitha didn't recognise. She asked and Lily told her they were Japanese Anemones which had been recently introduced to Britain.

As Lily led the way further into the garden, she explained, "Of course, this garden is small compared to MacAlister Castle. Nevertheless, I've worked with Mr McManus, the gardener, to replicate some of the more experimental plantings I've had success with there."

Tabitha was intrigued to hear more. Certainly, the twigs in the girl's hair the day before made a lot more sense now. "I'd love to hear more about your botanical studies," she said sincerely.

The younger woman blushed prettily, "I would hardly call them studies. I wish I could study botany. I find everything about plants to be fascinating. My hero is Mr Joseph Dalton Hooker." Seeing Tabitha and Wolf's blank look at the mention of this name, she continued, "He has travelled the world collecting and documenting numerous plant species. Until recently, he was the director of the Royal Botanic Gardens at Kew. I would give anything to be able to have half the career he has. But of course, I'm a woman, so I don't get the chance to have a career of any sort. It seems all I am fit for is to be a broodmare."

Tabitha couldn't dispute the young girl's grievance. Some women managed to penetrate the male spheres of academia, however slow and painful the effort. However, for women of their class, there was only one acceptable path in life: a good marriage leading to enough children to ensure the continuation of the line. But while there was no doubt Lily's grandmother saw no other path for Lily, Tabitha sensed Hamish was not the kind of father to impose his will on his daughter. "It is almost 1900, Lily. The world is changing. Even our world," she added, seeing the young woman's scepticism. "Have you talked with your parents about your interests and ambitions?"

Tabitha could have sworn Lily rolled her eyes at this statement and suddenly felt far older than the four years that separated them. "Mama believes my 'playing in the dirt' is merely a tomboy phase and will pass. Papa is a dear man and would never force me to do anything. However, he defers to Mama, and she is far too terrified of Grandmama to allow anything but the traditional path of wedlock and raising a brood of entitled brats."

It was hard for Tabitha to envision Jane as the domineering wife Lily was portraying. However, she could far more easily imagine her as the petrified and cowering daughter, pandering to her mother's shrewish demands. The dowager might portray her daughters and their families as out of sight and out of mind. Still, they were now her only progeny, and it made sense to think she continued to manipulate them, even from as far away as London was from Edinburgh. The continuation of the bloodline was everything to the Dowager Countess of Pembroke. With Tabitha's failure to produce even a female child, the family matriarch had been forced to resort to her disappointing daughters.

Wolf cleared his throat and glanced at Tabitha, reminding her they had strayed off the topic at hand. He took over the conversation, "Lily, I believe you began to tell Tabitha something of your friend Peter last night, but why don't you start at the beginning for my benefit."

The garden was not large, so they made a couple of circuits before finally sitting on a bench under a broad yew tree while Lily told her story. She confessed that she harboured a passionate belief in women's suffrage along with her interest in botany. Of course, this interest was one she kept secret from her parents.

The previous year, while the family was visiting Edinburgh, Lily had attended a rally on the pretence of visiting the library accompanied by her maid. The rally by the Scottish Labour Party promoted workers' rights, nationalism of land, Scottish Home Rule and universal suffrage. Lily had been caught up in the convergence of activism for workers' rights with the cause of suffrage, both for women and the almost thirty percent of men in Edinburgh still denied the right to vote.

A fiery young speaker at the rally had passionately espoused social justice and equality. Lily's eyes had been opened to the unfairness of the system of inherited wealth and status she benefited from so greatly. That fiery speaker had been Peter Kincaid.

Lily had approached the electrifying Mr Kincaid and immediately pledged herself as a disciple. When her family had left Edinburgh and returned to MacAlister Castle, Lily and Peter had begun a clandestine correspondence facilitated by her maid. Over the past year, through his letters, Peter had educated and inspired Lily with his hopes and dreams towards making Scotland a fairer, more egalitarian society.

Peter's letters had been a revelation to Lily, who, like all girls of her class, had been raised to be nothing more than an appendage to the aspirations and ambitions of the men in her life. The young man's words opened up whole new vistas of thought. He helped Lily understand that women's suffrage was not merely a fringe cause but rather a critical component to advancing the rights of all Scots, including working-class men and women.

"His letters made clear there was an exciting world waiting outside of the luxurious prison that had been my life so far. A life that, if my mother and grandmother have their way, will one day merely substitute one jailor for another on my marriage," Lily exclaimed, her beautiful eyes shining with excitement as she recalled the Eden the young man had conjured for her with his words.

Watching Lily's face and hearing how she spoke about Peter, Tabitha was even more sceptical that Lily's only infatuation was with the man's politics. However, she kept her own counsel and encouraged the girl to continue.

With the family's imminent return to Edinburgh a week before, Lily and Peter had made plans to meet. Lily explained, "A large rally was being arranged, and Peter was to be one of the speakers. We had planned that I would find a reason to leave the house, accompanied by my maid Grace, and would attend the rally. After, Peter and I would find a coffee house and talk." Lily's eyes filled with tears as she came to the pivotal part of her story, "He never showed up. Not even for the rally. He would never have let the party down, Aunt Tabitha. Something must have happened."

"And you never heard anything from him after that?" Wolf asked, unsure what to make of this story. Was it nothing more than a young, naive, and sheltered girl caught up in the poetry and passion of an intense and idealistic young man who then disappointed her?

"Not a word. I might have believed something even more important had prevented him from attending the rally, however unlikely that might be. But I sent a note with Grace to his rooming house the next day and received no reply. The woman who runs the house told Grace that Peter hadn't been home since early the day before. I know something terrible must have happened to him," Lily cried, tears rolling down her beautiful cheeks.

Wolf exchanged a look with Tabitha. That a young man might spend the night in a bed other than his own was not a radical notion but also not one Wolf wished to share with his young cousin. But there was a question he still needed answered, "How did your Aunt Tabitha and I come to be involved in the search for this young man?"

At this question, Lily looked a little shamefaced, "I have been at a loss as to how I might go about finding Peter. A young woman, even accompanied by her maid, cannot wander the streets of Edinburgh asking questions. But then, Grandmama showed up a few days ago and started making plans to prepare me for the season. At dinner the second night, she told us how she helped you investigate two recent murders." Tabitha's eyebrows shot up at this, but again, she kept her thoughts to herself.

Lily continued, "She mentioned that during the last investigation, your ward was abducted and that you, Aunt Tabitha, helped her track the kidnapper to the house where he was holding the child. And that made me think that perhaps you and Cousin Jeremy could help me find Peter."

"So, you told your grandmother the story, and she offered to send us a telegram asking for our help?" Tabitha asked, quite sure that wasn't what had happened.

"Not exactly," the girl admitted. "As you may have noticed, I said that a female friend of mine had gone missing, and I needed your help and that I wouldn't participate in the season nor any admit.

admit.

preparation for it until she was found. Of course, Grandmama appealed to Mama and Papa. Mama would have gladly allowed Grandmama to lock me in my room and force me to dress fittings, but Papa has always been the soft-hearted one. I gave them an edited version of how I had come to meet Peter and of his activities, and Papa saw how genuinely concerned I was. He then asked Grandmama to send the telegram. Realising it was the only way to gain my cooperation and achieve her ends, she agreed."

Well, this made more sense, Tabitha thought. It had always been clear to her that the dowager had not called them to Scotland out of the goodness of her heart. That she had done so to win her granddaughter's compliance with her schemes was very believable. She asked, "How much do your parents and grandmother know about this friend?"

Lily lowered her eyes, bit her lip and then admitted, "Well, given that they believe my friend is a young woman, they know her as Petra. I told them I met her at the library this trip. I said she is of a lower class and that we became friendly."

Seeing the looks on their faces, Lily said hastily, "Trust me when I say that story was quite shocking enough, particularly for Mama and Grandmama. We thought we might have to bring Mama's smelling salts for a few moments, but Grandmama told her it wasn't the time for her histrionics. If I had said Petra was, in truth, Peter and I had known him for a year, even Papa might have agreed to lock me in my room." The young woman paused, then added hesitantly, "I realise that by telling you this, I'm making you a party to my deception. Aunt Tabitha, I believe you may know something of what it is to be a young woman dealing with the expectations of your family. I believe I can trust you to keep the most alarming parts of my story to yourself." Tabitha and Wolf didn't disagree. Lily ended her story, "I told my family enough of the truth to explain why I was upset and to impress upon them the need to help."

Tabitha tried to suppress a smile; Lily was far more like her grandmother than perhaps either one of them might like to

CHAPTER 7

After gathering the few details about Peter that Lily knew, including the address of his rooming house in the Old Town, Tabitha and Wolf agreed to collect Bear after lunch and begin the investigation. They both had serious doubts that there was any real mystery to solve. But they had come all the way to Scotland, and Lily refused to engage in any kind of preparation for her debut until they promised to do their best to find the young man.

Over a delicious lunch of Scottish salmon served cold with a green bean salad, the dowager leaned over to Wolf, who was on her left, and said in an overly loud whisper, "Did you get all the information you needed from the child? I'm sure this is nothing but a storm in a teacup. However, she wilfully refused to participate in any preparations for her debut or even contemplate her visit to London until you were here investigating."

Wolf assured the dowager they had spoken to Lily and had enough information on "Petra" to begin. The old woman shook her head sadly and said, "I cannot imagine where Lily gets such wilfulness from. Certainly not her mother, who has always been the biggest wet rag. It must be from Hamish's side of the family. All that red hair, you know!"

Unsure of what he was supposed to say, Wolf kept silent any thoughts about from whom Lily had inherited her resolute personality.

Sitting next to Hamish again was no chore, as far as Tabitha was concerned. He was a delightful dining companion, amusing without being lewd, informative without being pompous. He told her they planned to hold a small soiree to welcome their guests the following evening. With some trepidation in his voice, he told her that in Edinburgh, the upper class comprised those with titles and those with mere wealth in equal measure. This was not London, where the ability to earn money instead of inheriting it was considered a character flaw. Of course, Hamish did not put it quite like that but instead seemed anxious that his titled guests not feel slighted at the idea of fellow dinner companions who were not similarly illustrious. Tabitha assured him this would not bother either Wolf or her but paused momentarily, and her gaze went involuntarily to the dowager.

Seeing the direction in which Tabitha's eyes flickered, Hamish smiled, leaned towards her, and said quietly, "Aye, I ken the same can't be said of everyone around this table."

Hamish had offered his comfortable carriage to Tabitha and Wolf as they conducted their investigation. Tabitha had been concerned that the dowager's new enthusiasm for being part of the investigative team might drive her to insist on joining them. But with Tabitha and Wolf summoned to Scotland and searching for Peter, the dowager reminded Lily she was now honour-bound to participate fully in all preparations deemed necessary for her debut.

Tabitha wasn't sure the young woman fully understood the Faustian bargain she had struck with her grandmother. As far as the dowager was concerned, in fulfilling her side of the agreement, she had assured herself of Lily's full cooperation no matter what. Tabitha only hoped they could locate Lily's friend and ensure the bargain was worth the price.

Lily knew two definitive things about Peter: where he lived and what he was studying. Given this, the plan was for Tabitha and Wolf to visit his room first and then the university. Perhaps if they talked to his professors and perhaps some of his fellow students, they could piece together a preliminary picture of the man.

Remembering what Hamish had told her about the

overcrowding in the Old Town, Tabitha had thought she was prepared. But it was very different hearing about the results of squeezing far too many poor and sick people into too small an area and experiencing it for herself. Bringing Bear with them seemed an increasingly wise move. The coachman and footman should be able to ensure the safety of the carriage, but even in the plainest walking dress, Tabitha could see what an immediate target she and Wolf were.

For his part, Wolf was sorry he hadn't been able to change into his thief-taking outfit. He had brought the old, worn clothes from his previous life to Scotland, but there seemed little point in wearing them when he was with Tabitha. There was no hiding that she was a well-born lady. And during their last two investigations, Wolf had come to appreciate that there were times when his rank and title could be advantageous. Doors opened for the Earl of Pembroke, and people were eager to ingratiate themselves. Wolf just hoped that trick worked as well in the slums of Edinburgh as similar ones had in London.

Wolf and Bear could easily make their way around London. But they were at a total loss in Edinburgh, particularly once they crossed over the divide from the wide, elegant thoroughfares of the New Town to the steep, winding, cobblestoned streets of the Old Town. Wolf hoped the coachman had a sense of where to go. The Old Town was not a very large area, constricted as it was by its mediaeval boundaries, and in no time at all, they pulled up outside a dilapidated building in an equally dilapidated street.

Wolf had learned some lessons over the last few months about how to bring to bear the full force of the earldom when needed. He nodded to the footman, indicating he should knock on the front door and ask for the landlady.

The door opened just a sliver, and a thin woman of indeterminate age peered out suspiciously. Her face had a greyness that washed out whatever prettiness the woman might have once had. Her entire body stooped with world-weariness. Mrs Farley was a woman who had seen it all. Even so, the grand carriage and the liveried footman outside her front door were enough to surprise even her. Informed that the Earl and Countess of Pembroke wished to enter her house and speak with her struck the woman dumb, and she could do no more than nod her head and open the door wider for her illustrious guests to enter.

The sight of the MacAlister carriage on Bakehouse Close, Canongate, had caught the attention of the entire street. As Tabitha, Wolf and Bear stepped out of the carriage onto the street, it felt like a hundred pairs of eyes were upon them. Ragamuffin children ran up to the carriage begging for a few coins. The sight of Bear kept them at a distance, but even so, the footman quickly shooed them away.

Bear remained outside the house, helping to keep an eye on the carriage and deterring any local criminals who might be tempted by the unusual sight presented by their little party. Tabitha and Wolf followed the still mute Mrs Farley into the house and then into a shabby but at least clean parlour. Mrs Farley finally found her voice and apologised for being unable to offer any tea, "Ah'm sorry, but I cannae offer ye any tea. Ah hate the stuff, masel'. But Ah can offer ye a wee dram o' whisky."

Torn between risking offence by refusing and being concerned about drinking whisky in the early afternoon, Tabitha politely turned down the "wee dram." She needed her wits about her. Wolf, who knew the value of prefacing witness questioning with the niceties of socialising, accepted. The wee dram was anything but small, and the whisky had none of the smoothness of Hamish's offerings, but Wolf had drunk worse. A lot worse in his time. Mrs Farley poured herself a glass and sat in a worn old armchair opposite the equally worn sofa Tabitha and Wolf perched on.

They had agreed in the carriage that Wolf would take the lead in questioning the landlady. His years as a thief-taker working in some of the roughest neighbourhoods in London meant he knew how to talk to the Mrs Farleys of this world. He quickly told a reasonably matter-of-fact, if pared down, version of the story Lily had told them. At this point, he was still deeply sceptical that there was anything nefarious about Peter's nonappearance at the rally, and he had no reason to prevaricate.

The landlady seemed unconcerned about her lodger's absence from his bed for a few nights, "He's a young lad, and young lads will dae whit they'll dae, eh? No that Ah've kent him tae be like that. He's ower keen on his politics, ye ken." She then added with pride at her modern sensibilities, "As lang as they dinnae bring ony weemin here, Ah dinnae care whit my boys get up tae."

Tabitha found her accent rather hard to understand, but from what she could tell, Peter wasn't the kind of young man to normally spend the night out, but as long as women weren't brought back to the house, Mrs Farley kept her opinions to herself.

Seemingly over her awe at the magnificence of her guests, Mrs Farley then spent quite a few minutes describing some of the less serious-minded lodgers she'd had over the years and how she'd dealt with their shenanigans. Politeness prevented Wolf from interrupting her while she was in flow, so he sipped his whisky and waited for a lull in her stories. Eventually, she stopped long enough that he was able to ask, "Do you know anything of friends Peter might have?"

Visibly regretting she didn't have more to report, Mrs Farley nevertheless attempted to make the most of what she did know. Peter had one friend who would sometimes come and call. From what she could remember, his name was Mr Trent. Or at least she thought it was. A fine-looking young man, if ever she saw one with dark, curly hair and long eyelashes, pretty enough for a girl.

It soon became clear that, while Mrs Farley had nothing more to tell that would be useful, she'd be happy to tell them much useless information if they weren't careful. After letting her prattle on for a short while, Wolf asked if they could see Peter's room.

"Ah dinnae ken," the woman protested weakly, claiming concern for her lodger's privacy. And if he were to find out, he might even find other lodgings. Then she'd be out of pocket, the wily woman said suggestively.

Picking up quickly on the suggestion, Wolf pulled some coins out of his purse. The pure avarice gleaming in her eyes gave all the consent they needed. With the coins deposited safely in her apron pocket, Mrs Farley led them upstairs and opened the door to a room on the first floor.

It was a tiny room, barely big enough for a narrow bed, a desk, a chair, and a small wardrobe. The room was tidy, and the bed was made. Realising she had milked this visit for all the entertainment value and coin possible, Mrs Farley left them to it.

"You take a look through the desk drawers, and I'll check the wardrobe," Wolf said.

The desk drawers were as tidy as the rest of the room. Tabitha found a few papers neatly stacked and tied together in one drawer. Reading someone's private correspondence felt deeply invasive, particularly given that they weren't even sure Peter was missing. However, they had made a promise to Lily and needed as much information about the young man as possible.

On closer inspection, the letters turned out to be from Lily. Now Tabitha felt even more uncomfortable reading them. However, a quick perusal confirmed Lily's claim that their friendship was purely platonic. That at least made Tabitha feel a little less guilty. Sitting on the bed, she started skimming the letters looking for clues.

Tabitha only had one side of the correspondence, but from what she could tell, Lily and Peter primarily talked about the cause of universal suffrage. It seemed Peter's letters were instructive in the history and the rationale for suffrage, with Lily's full of questions and references to things he must have taught her. He must have branched out in the later letters and started telling her about workers' rights and unionisation efforts. And in the most recent letters, Lily quoted some quite radical ideas it seemed she had learned through their correspondence.

The letters revealed few personal details about Peter. Occasionally, Lily referred to a person called Louis Trent, and

Tabitha assumed this was the young man Mrs Farley had referred to. In the last letter, Tabitha found an intriguing line: "Your benefactor, Mr Sinclair, will attend a dinner at our home next week. The dinner is being thrown in honour of Grandmama's visit. Would you like me to speak to him about you?"

Tabitha showed Wolf that letter, then tied them up as neatly as she had found them and returned them to the drawer. Wolf had found nothing of interest in the wardrobe, and an inspection of the bed didn't turn up anything hidden under the mattress. Realising there was nothing more to find, they let themselves out of the room and exited the house as quickly as possible.

CHAPTER 8

Back in the carriage, Tabitha and Wolf told Bear the little they had discovered. "I think the next step is to go to the university and see what we can find out," Wolf said. "I think you should stay in the carriage for this one, Bear," Wolf added. Bear's ability to intimidate people could sometimes be as much a curse as a blessing.

Wolf called to the coachman to take them to the medical school. It wasn't a long drive, and within a few minutes, they arrived at the ornate, Italianate-designed Faculty of Medicine building. A plaque on the wall told that the school had been founded in 1726, and this building opened in 1884.

They left the carriage at the elaborate wrought-iron gates and made their way through the impressive arched walkway lined with brick-red columns. Tabitha had never visited a university, and wondered if they were all as breathtaking as this, and whether the students were inspired to greater academic heights every time they walked through the gates.

During their previous investigation, Wolf had visited St Thomas' Hospital and a prison. In both instances, his success in gaining information had helped him realise the full power of the earldom. Given the useful fawning his earl posturing had engendered in everyone from porters and doctors to the prison warden, Wolf saw no reason not to repeat the performance. An older man seemed to be standing guard at the end of the walkway, inspecting and questioning visitors. Wolf assumed he was the porter.

Despite his disinclination to dress formally at home, Wolf

had no wish to embarrass Tabitha by being anything less than a credit to his title while they stayed with the laird and his family. And, of course, that the dowager was in residence made an even more compelling argument for keeping up standards. Today, Wolf was glad he was dressed in his best peer of the realm finery. Approaching the porter, Wolf threw his shoulders back slightly, straightened his back, and raised his chin just enough that, when he spoke, he was looking slightly down his nose at the man.

Tom McDonald, the porter, took one look at the couple walking towards him and immediately knew they were quality. And likely English quality, if he had to guess. There was something just a bit more fashionable about their outfits than the average Scottish noble would likely wear. Tom was immediately on his guard; he had no time for the English. He wouldn't have referred to himself as a Scottish Nationalist, but he certainly agreed with much of what they said.

Tom's family had been Highlanders; family lore had it they were Jacobites and that a distant ancestor had found his way to Edinburgh when he lost his lands after the battle of Culloden. So, Tom McDonald had no reason to pander to the English. But he was no fool; these were not the kind of people a man such as he should be slighting. And so, he doffed his cap as they approached. "G'day, sir and madam. How can I help ye?" he asked.

Tabitha hadn't witnessed Wolf's impersonation of his late grandfather and stifled a giggle as he launched into it. His speech became a little smoother, his vowels more rounded, "Good morning to you, my man. I am the Earl of Pembroke," Wolf said in a sonorous voice that seemed to echo with all the superiority and privilege of five hundred years of family power and influence. Tabitha wasn't sure if she was impressed or worried he could become this person so easily. More than anything, he sounded just like Jonathan. The two men had never met, even as children, and yet if she had closed her eyes, Tabitha would have sworn she was on her dead husband's arm. And that scared her.

Wolf continued in the same tone, "I need to make inquiries about a student here, Peter Kincaid."

Even though Tom had guessed the couple was quality, he hadn't expected to be talking to an earl. Wait until he told Mrs McDonald. "Ah, Mr Kincaid, I know him well, m'lord," the porter said with appropriate deference. He knew all too well how the Master would take it if word got back that he'd been anything less than respectful to a member of the English nobility. "He's a fine young lad, not like some of them. Very serious, he is. None of the japing some of them get up to."

Wolf knew all too well from his university days the kind of antics students often got up to. "Exactly what I had heard about Kincaid. In fact, that is precisely why I am hoping to find him. My cousin's daughter has become rather a champion of the young man and has asked me to meet with him and consider mentoring him, so to speak." Wolf had no idea what kind of mentoring a medical student might need from a peer of the realm. However, he had learned quickly that people normally accepted unquestioningly whatever an earl said, no matter how ludicrous.

"Aye, I wish I could be o' some assistance, m'lord. But I've no laid eyes on Mr Kincaid the day. Truth be told, I havenae seen him for a few days now. What day is it? Thursday, ye say? Aye, the last time I clapped eyes on him was last Thursday afternoon. I mind it well 'cause ma Mabel aye packs me some haggis on Thursday, since she cooks it on Wednesdays. And just as I finished gobblin' it up, young Mr Kincaid happened to pass by and remarked on the broad smile plastered across ma face. Mabel's haggis aye brings a smile tae me mug, ken." Tom McDonald finished his story with a smile that made Wolf believe the man was thinking fondly of the aforementioned haggis.

Tabitha asked, "Would you normally see Mr Kincaid most days? Mr... sorry, we never caught your name."

"McDonald, Thomas McDonald, Tom tae ma pals, at yer service, m'lady," the man said, tipping his cap again. "Tae answer yer query, Mr Kincaid isnae one o' those students who skip classes for drinkin', or worse. He's here every day, mark ma words. He's bound tae be a bonnie doctor one o' these days. No' that I put much trust in doctors, mind ye; I'd rather stick wi' ma Mabel's poultices and potions any day, and I'll no' pay a penny for the privilege. But if I were tae seek out a doctor, I'd surely seek out Mr Kincaid."

Wolf was keen to get confirmation from the loquacious porter, "So, Mr McDonald, you would expect to see Mr Kincaid every day but haven't seen him for over a week. Is that correct?"

"Aye, that's right, ye've got it."

"Just one more question, Mr McDonald. We had heard mention of a friend of Mr Kincaid's. A fine-looking young man with dark curly hair. Would you have any idea who that friend might be?" Wolf asked.

"Aye, that's young Louis Trent, indeed. A rotten apple, that lad. I've never fathomed why a fine young man like Mr Kincaid would associate with him. Louis Trent is one o' those fellows who wastes his days and nights in drink. He's been cautioned before, mind ye. If he disnae straighten up his act, he'll be kicked out o' here. The only reason he's lasted this lang is 'cause his father happens tae be a highfalutin' doctor in the New Town and teaches here."

Wolf found this last part interesting. He wasn't sure how large the upper echelons of Edinburgh society were, but perhaps their hosts knew who Louis' father was. Of course, he and Tabitha would have to find a way to ask the question without revealing that 'Petra' was, in reality, Peter. The more he thought about it, the more he realised that if they were to have any chance of finding this young man, they would likely need some help from the MacAlisters or at least people of their acquaintance. To do that, they would have to reveal the truth, or at least the gender, of Lily's friend. They needed to persuade the young woman to confess to her family.

Putting this thorny issue aside, Wolf asked one final question, "Have you seen Louis Trent recently?"

Tom McDonald laughed ruefully, "Aye, I've laid eyes on him

as well. He stumbled in here this mornin', well past the start o' classes, lookin' like a proper mess after a night o' heavy drinkin'. I caught a glimpse o' him foolin' about in the courtyard afore he took off. He didna spend more than a couple o' hours, at the most, in these halls. If ye ask me, I reckon he's actually hopin' they kick him out o' here."

Wolf handed the man some coins, which were quickly pocketed. "If Mr Kincaid happens to turn up, please tell him his friend Lily is very worried about him."

In the carriage, Wolf expressed his belief that Lily needed to tell the truth about Peter. "I was thinking much the same thing myself," Tabitha admitted. "It seems as if the man may have gone missing. It's still unclear whether his disappearance is voluntary or whether there is something more worrying at play, but I'm not sure how we start to investigate without Hamish's help."

"Indeed," Wolf concurred. "This isn't London. I don't have my usual Whitechapel sources. We don't even benefit from the dowager's encyclopaedic knowledge of everyone in society's darkest secrets and peccadillos. We know no one. We don't even know how to navigate the city. Sometimes, I can barely even understand what is being said. We are going to need help."

Back at the MacAlister home, Tabitha and Wolf were told by Dawglish that the family was taking tea in the drawing room and were eager for them to join and report back. Wolf exchanged looks with Tabitha. "Is Miss Lily also in the drawing room?" Tabitha asked. The butler indicated she was.

The gathered family looked up as Tabitha and Wolf entered the drawing room. "Well, about time," the dowager stated impatiently. "Do you have any idea how much of Jane's tedious sewing circle gossip I've had to endure?"

Her daughter looked pained at this slight and said timidly, "Mama. It is hardly gossip. I merely told you the names of the women in our circle, whether they are married and to whom."

"Exactly my point! The most tedious excuse for gossip ever. How are you a child of mine?" She mused to herself. "But thankfully, now dear Jeremy and Tabitha have returned, I can stop pretending to be even somewhat interested. Honestly, Jane, I thought you were boring as a child, but I believe you have become even more so with age."

Tabitha and Wolf were seated and supplied with tea and cake. Lily looked even more eager to hear their report than the dowager. Tabitha was quite hungry and thirsty and was keen to drink some tea and have at least one of the delicious-looking shortbread biscuits. But it was clear their audience was too impatient to allow them even five minutes. Taking at least a sip of tea and a bite of a biscuit - as delicious as she'd anticipated - Tabitha said, "Before we tell you all we have discovered, I need to speak privately with Lily."

Lily looked panicked at this statement, and the dowager irritated. "Oh, for heaven's sake, Tabitha. Just spit it out, whatever it is. Do we really need to indulge in such skulduggery? Just tell us what you've found out."

"I must insist, Mama," Tabitha insisted.

Looking very nervous, Lily stood and said, "Perhaps we can speak in the summer room, Aunt Tabitha." Wolf looked at Tabitha, and she gave a little shake of her head. She thought it was best if she had this conversation with Lily alone. With the dowager still huffing and puffing about how unnecessary it was and how she refused to revisit the unimaginably bland lives of the sewing circle ladies, Lily led Tabitha out of the drawing room.

Looking over her shoulder to confirm a nosey old woman wasn't behind them, Tabitha followed Lily into the room and closed the door. She indicated to the nervous girl that they should sit. Taking a deep breath, Tabitha began, "Lily, we believe your friend Peter is missing. We're still unsure whether he has disappeared of his own volition, but we have had confirmation from his landlady and a porter at the medical school that he hasn't been seen since last Thursday sometime."

Lily's expression changed from vindication to worry, "I knew he was in trouble!" she exclaimed.

Tabitha corrected her, "We don't know he is in trouble. There are a myriad of reasons a young man might choose to make himself less available. You are an innocent, Lily, but…"

Lily cut her off, "Please don't condescend to me, Aunt Tabitha. I may be a young woman, but I understand more of the ways of the world than you might think." Tabitha didn't want to consider how she might have acquired this knowledge. Lily continued, "As I've told you and Cousin Jeremy, Peter is a serious young man. There is nothing more important to him than the cause and his studies. He wishes to become a doctor so he might care for the poor and indigent of Edinburgh. He sees so many people dying from preventable diseases. At least preventable if people had adequate housing, nutrition and basic care."

The girl's eyes lit up with the fervour of a true disciple, "Peter believes equality must be more than a political statement. Becoming a doctor is a practical way for him to do his part. I do know what young men can be, but please believe me when I say that Peter cares nothing for women, or drink, or cards. He is single-minded in his vision, and if he has disappeared, it's not because he is carousing around town."

Tabitha was still not wholly convinced, but it was obvious Lily would not be dissuaded from her belief. Instead, treading carefully, Tabitha said, "If you are right, Lily, then what I am about to say is even more true. Cousin Jeremy and I both feel we cannot solve this mystery alone."

"Why not?" Lily demanded. "Grandmama told me you have solved two murders in just a few weeks."

Not wanting to know any more about the dowager's likely melodramatic exaggerations of their recent investigations, Tabitha said gently, "In London. We solved those mysteries in London, where we know people and Wolf, I mean Cousin Jeremy, has connections. We know no one here. We have no connections. We don't know the city. Even your grandmother doesn't have social connections here we can take advantage of."

"But I do!" the girl stated boldly. "My family does!"

Tabitha pounced on that comment, "Exactly! Your family

does. Your father is well-connected. He knows people throughout the highest echelons of Edinburgh society. But we cannot ask him for help without revealing more of the case than you have currently admitted."

It was clear from the look of horror crossing Lily's face that she suddenly realised what she would be asked to do. "No! I can't tell them the truth. You said you wouldn't make me."

"I'm not sure we promised that," Tabitha told the distraught young woman. "And even if we had believed we could keep the truth about 'Petra' a secret, it's become clear to us we cannot. Or at least, we cannot both keep it a secret and effectively investigate what may have happened to Peter. I will not force you to reveal anything. But if you don't, then I also make no claims as to the likelihood of us making much headway in finding your friend."

It looked as if Lily was about to burst into tears. Tabitha put her hand on the young woman's arm and said kindly, "Lily, I am not trying to blackmail you. We will still do our best. But I want you to understand how hamstrung we will be. Cousin Jeremy and I want to treat you like the capable, intelligent young woman you are and ensure you are fully aware of the low probability of success we believe we will have under the current circumstances. But, if you choose to say nothing more to your parents, we will support that decision and think no less of you for making it."

Lily didn't speak right away, but finally, taking a deep breath, she said resolutely, "If I truly believe in the cause, then this is the sacrifice I must make for it. And it is so much less than most have to suffer. But, please, can I tell just Da? It will be so much easier telling him without Mama wailing and Grandmama doing, well, doing what she does."

Tabitha thought this was a very wise idea. "Would you like me to be in the room when you tell him?"

Lily nodded, "Yes, if you don't mind. Cousin Jeremy as well."

"Let me go and fetch them both, then," Tabitha offered. She could only imagine how the dowager would receive this request.

But if Lily could be brave and tell her father the truth, Tabitha could face the likely wrath of her mother-in-law.

CHAPTER 9

When Tabitha walked back into the drawing room, she could tell from the look on Wolf's face the grilling he had been receiving during her absence. She could only imagine how unwilling the dowager had been to wait to receive their news. This latest request would not help that situation but needed to be made.

"What has kept you, Tabitha?" the dowager demanded. "I hope you can now fill me in on what you have discovered. This cloak-and-dagger nonsense is worthy of a penny dreadful."

Tabitha sighed; this was not going to be easy. "Mama, my apologies, but I must keep you waiting a short time longer. Wolf and I need to speak with Hamish in private."

It looked as if the dowager was going to explode. She stood up and waved the cane that she didn't need to use for walking but sometimes used because she enjoyed brandishing it threateningly, saying, "Enough of this nonsense! I have no idea what is going on in this house. But it stops immediately! Do you hear me? Tabitha, let me remind you that you are only involved in this investigation at my invitation. By all rights, this is my case, and I should be leading all questioning. I certainly shouldn't be excluded."

Tabitha could see that this situation was quickly getting out of hand. She did not doubt that allowing the dowager to be included in Lily's confession would be unhelpful. And it was hard to imagine that even mousey Jane would agree to be the only person excluded. She looked to Wolf for help; if anyone could placate the Dowager Countess of Pembroke, it was dear

Jeremy.

"My dear Lady Pembroke," he said, "You are entirely correct, of course. We are only here at your kind invitation and investigating at your instigation." Tabitha wasn't sure how he said all this with a straight face. But it was clear as the dowager sat back down and lowered her cane that his words, however disingenuous, were having their desired effect.

"Well, I'm glad to hear that someone at least recognises my pivotal role," the dowager grumbled.

"How could I not?" Wolf conceded. As he said this, he crossed the room from where he was seated and knelt beside the old woman's chair. He took one of her aged, blue-veined-lined hands in his. It almost looked as if he were about to ask for her hand in marriage, and despite the gravity of the situation, Tabitha had to try hard not to giggle.

"Lady Pembroke, I would not ask this of you if I wasn't sure it was of the utmost importance to the investigation; please allow us a brief, private audience with Laird MacAlister. I can assure you that, as soon as I can, you will be fully apprised of the current status of the investigation." As he said this, Wolf had lowered his voice somewhat and injected it with the tones of a pleading lover. Tabitha wasn't sure whether to be appalled or impressed. Either way, it seemed to work.

"Dear Jeremy, I will allow this, for your sake. But I am not happy. I assume that goes without saying. However, I will be reconciled for the moment. But do not seek to play on my magnanimity. I expect to be fully informed long before I go to dress for dinner!" Wolf nodded in acknowledgement of this unmoveable deadline. In truth, he didn't know what Lily had agreed to and was unsure how much they could reveal to the dowager. But that was a battle he was prepared to postpone until he had a stiff drink in his hand later.

Wolf rose from his knees, glanced at Tabitha, noting the twitching of her lips as she attempted to stifle her amusement at his performance, and said to the laird, "Now that we have resolved this issue, Hamish would you mind joining Tabitha and myself in the summer room?"

The laird nodded his acceptance, clearly aware that any more discussion was unwise until they had left the drawing room. The three of them entered the summer room, where a visibly upset Lily stood by the windows, wringing her hands and chewing her lip with anxiety.

Hamish was a doting father, and his daughter's obvious distress was enough to have him cross the room and take her in his arms, saying in the broad Scots accent he tried to soften when the dowager was around, "Dinna fash yersel', ma bonnie lass. Whatever it is, it cannae be as dire as ye reckon. What can I dae tae mend things?" the man said lovingly.

"Oh, Da!" Lily exclaimed, crying on his shoulder. "I'm so sorry. I didn't mean to lie to you. I just didn't know what else to do. You're the last person in the world I'd want to deceive."

Tabitha's father had been loving and indulgent, and she had known exactly how to wind him around her little finger. So, she could appreciate Lily's manipulation of her parent. While there was no doubt the girl was genuinely upset and anxious, she had injected just enough wheedling into her tone to ensure a loving father's indulgence.

"Why don't we all take a seat," Tabitha suggested. "And then you can tell your father everything." She said this last word pointedly. There was little doubt the girl would tell yet another limited version of the truth if left to her own devices. But, while it would likely be necessary to modify the story for the dowager and Jane's ears, Tabitha felt that Hamish needed to know the unvarnished truth. He was their best resource and most likely ally. Tabitha knew all too well from past investigations with Wolf how frustrating it was to work with only a partial knowledge of a situation.

It seemed Lily had correctly interpreted the tone in Tabitha's voice, and she quickly told her father the whole truth about how she had come to know Peter and her continued correspondence with him. Hamish didn't interrupt her, and after she was finished, he continued to sit with a look of shock on his face.

Tabitha could imagine how he felt; he was a devoted father, and it must be devastating to hear that his adored daughter had been so deceitful. To say nothing of what she had been lying about. No well-born man wanted to hear that his genteelly-raised daughter had been sneaking around to consort with a rabble-rousing man of no consequence.

The silence dragged on while Hamish just sat there with a devastating look of disappointment on his face. Finally, when even Tabitha could take it no more, Lily ran to her father and fell to her knees, hugging his legs. "Please, Da, dinna be angry. I ken I've let ye doon. But I got sae caught up in Peter's words."

Tabitha wasn't sure if Lily's reversion into Scots was a further attempt at manipulation or a genuine lapse due to shame, but whichever it was, it had the desired effect. Hamish raised the girl from the floor onto his lap as if she were still a child of five. He pulled her into his chest, where she began to sob as he stroked her hair. Watching the scene unfold convinced Tabitha that the girl, whether wittingly or unwittingly, had ensured her father would support her, however reluctantly.

"I'm no' pleased aboot this. And I'm certainly no' pleased that ye lied and were skulkin' aboot. But ye ken I cannae stay angry at ye," Hamish said soothingly. The words had no bite to them, and it was clear any danger was over.

"Hamish, now that you know the full story, you will appreciate that we may need to tell a modified version to the dowager countess," Tabitha said, adding," and perhaps even to Jane."

Hamish laughed, "I hae nae doot aboot the truth o' that statement. I love ma Janey dearly, but she lacks her own will when it comes tae her mither. If we cannae reveal the entire story tae the dowager, which we certainly cannae, then we cannae disclose it tae Jane either."

Tabitha hadn't had much time to consider what an acceptable but credible modified version of the truth might be. Whatever else she was, the dowager was no fool. If the story was anything but watertight, the woman be immediately suspicious.

Considering this danger, Tabitha said hesitantly, "Lily, I'm assuming your grandmother knows about your botanical interests?"

Lily snorted and said sardonically, "Knowing and accepting them are two very different things. But yes, Grandmama is aware that I, as she likes to say, 'Enjoy playing around in the dirt.'"

Tabitha continued, "Does your mother know of your desire to study at university?"

Lily snorted again, "As with Grandmama, this is not something she takes seriously. But she has heard me say as much many times."

Hamish defended his wife, "Yer mither only wants whit she thinks is best for ye, lass."

All tears forgotten, Lily got off her father's lap and replied with eyes blazing, "Exactly! What she thinks is best. What about what I think is best, Da?"

Tabitha could see this conversation going off track quickly and interjected, "Good. So, they both have some knowledge of your interest in botany. Then, this is the story we will tell them. You will say you visited the university to hear a talk from a famous botanist. Lily, what might such a talk be about that a medical student would also attend?"

It seemed as if Tabitha had hit upon a subject of genuine interest to Lily, who said, "The talk could have been about the current research on the medicinal benefits of plants. We can say it was given by William Turner Thiselton-Dyer. He is doing fascinating work researching medicinal plants found in the Indian subcontinent."

"Perfect," Tabitha continued. "We will say that you met Peter, a young medical student interested in the topic at this talk. You maintained a correspondence to talk about this subject. We will not mention politics, suffrage, or anything likely to inflame the dowager or your mother. You will be suitably contrite and acknowledge the impropriety of corresponding with such a young man and deep shame at lying about his gender. You will say that on your return to Edinburgh, you had arranged to meet Peter at another talk at the university and, when he hadn't turned up, had become worried."

As she spoke, Tabitha mentally ran through any possible loopholes in this story. Would the dowager attempt to confirm that these talks had taken place? Tabitha didn't think she would put herself to such trouble. Tabitha assumed this version of the story would be less inflammatory than the truth. She put the question to Hamish.

"Aye, they may no' be pleased. But Lily's fascination wi' botany has been kent for a lang time. Though such an interest is deemed improper for a lass, especially o' Lily's station, it's surely less scandalous than the truth," Hamish confirmed.

They rose to return to the drawing room with the story firmly in place. Just as Wolf was about to open the door, Tabitha put her hand out to stop him and turned to face Hamish and Lily walking behind them. "This story has to be believable. Hamish, make clear that you have expressed your displeasure. Lily, you must be suitably contrite. Be prepared for your grandmother to vent her disapproval of your behaviour in no uncertain terms. You must accept her words in shamefaced silence, no matter how outrageous. We must allow her to get it out of her system and not prolong the discussion more than needed. The more it is discussed, the greater the chance of holes appearing in the story."

Everyone nodded in acknowledgement, and they continued back into the drawing room, where they were received by a visibly impatient dowager countess, tapping her foot and cane in an irritable, synchronised rhythm. In a nearby chair, Jane appeared even less happy than when they had left. Tabitha suspected the dowager had spent the intervening time taking her impatience out on her cowering daughter.

"Finally! That took long enough. One can only imagine what exchange of confidences needed to take so long. Never mind the distress caused to those of us left behind. Why, Jane here has been beside herself with worry." At the mention of her name, Jane shrunk back in her armchair as if by doing so, she might disappear altogether from her mother's notice. Tabitha wondered if her sister-in-law regretted requesting her mother's help with Lily's coming out, no matter how dire the situation had appeared.

Tabitha, Wolf, Hamish and Lily took seats as the dowager continued to rant, "So, are we finally to be told what you discovered today? Most likely, it will be anticlimactic after such a melodramatic build up. Nevertheless, I confess myself more than a little curious as to what sits behind the shenanigans I've had to tolerate this afternoon."

At this point, Hamish rose and said to Wolf, "I need a whisky. Would yer care to join me?" Wolf nodded. "And Tabitha, a sherry for yer?" he offered.

"Laird MacAlister, while I wasn't included in that invitation, I will also avail myself of the libations at hand. Something tells me I may need to be well fortified," the dowager added.

Whisky was poured for Hamish and Wolf, and sherries were handed to the dowager and Tabitha. Finally, there was no more stalling for time. With a look from her father, Lily launched into the agreed-upon story. As expected, the dowager harrumphed as it was told, and with every sound of disapproval from her mother, Jane visibly paled and shrank further into herself. But the story was told without interruption.

When Lily was finished, the dowager put down her sherry. She pointed a gnarled finger at her daughter, "This is what comes of procreating with savages and then insisting on raising them beyond the reaches of civilised society."

Hamish ignored the insult, likely a version of one he had heard before. The dowager then continued, "University talks? Correspondence with some neer-do-well? This all went on beneath your nose, Jane, and you had no idea? Shame on you!" She then turned her attention from her terrified daughter to her granddaughter, "And as for you, Lily! To think that a granddaughter of mine could be so wilful and entirely lacking in any sense of decorum is just beyond the pale."

Tabitha reflected that it was entirely believable that someone related to the dowager was wilful and lacking a sense of decorum. The dowager then continued for a few minutes more about behaviour unbecoming of the granddaughter of an earl, focusing on what would be said about the dowager if news of such shameful conduct were ever to reach Lady Hartley's gossip-ready ears. As instructed, Lily hung her head and took the censure silently and with the most demure and contrite expression she could muster.

Finally, even the dowager seemed to have run out of outrage. She turned to Wolf, changing the subject abruptly, "So, now we know that this supposed young woman in distress, Petra, is, in fact, merely a vagabond who has importuned my naive granddaughter, I believe this investigation is at an end."

At this, Lily stood up, eyes blazing, all contrition forgotten, "It is not at an end. Peter is still missing. If the investigation is ended, I will again refuse to participate in any of your ridiculous debutante plans."

"Ridiculous, are they? And is that how you talk to your grandmother? If I am not wanted in this house, and my expertise is unwelcome, perhaps I should have Manning and Dobbs pack my things, and we can leave in the morning." This seemed to be a suggestion that was not unwelcome to Jane, and she visibly perked up. But she didn't know her mother well if she believed she would be released from her torturer that easily. The dowager continued, "However, unlike everyone else in my family, I know my duty and what is required of me. As painful it may be to stay, I will remain, and you will keep your word, young lady. I did as I was asked; I requested Lord Pembroke's help. That I was lied to in order to secure my assistance is a whole other matter."

Wolf could see this conversation was getting them nowhere and intervened, "Tabitha and I believe there may be something untoward in Peter's disappearance. By all accounts, he is a fine and upstanding young man training diligently to be a doctor. I'm sure we can all agree this is a worthy vocation." The dowager harrumphed but said nothing. Wolf continued, "I'm sure I speak for Tabitha when I say we will continue investigating and attempting to find this young man."

Wolf paused, then said with a hopeful tone, "However, Lady Pembroke, I can certainly understand why you feel compelled, as a matter of honour to disengage from the investigation." At least, that was what Wolf hoped the woman had been implying.

But Wolf was to be disappointed if he thought they could get rid of her that easily. Regardless of what she felt about the virtue of the investigation, the dowager could not countenance the thought of being excluded. It was clear her own high dudgeon boxed her in, and Tabitha could see the scheming woman's thoughts racing as she attempted to find a graceful way out of her self-imposed dilemma. Finally, alighting on what, at least seemed to her, like unassailable logic, the dowager proclaimed, "Let it never be said of Julia Chesterton that she retreats waving a white flag. Even though I'm unconvinced that this young man is worthy of my time and effort, I would never dream of withholding my wisdom and guidance from you, dear Jeremy. Not when I know how dearly you value it."

She simpered at Wolf as she said this last sentence in a way that nearly set Tabitha's eyes rolling again. It had been too much to hope that the woman would lose interest in the investigation. Or even better, go back to London. Tabitha resigned herself to the prospect of the dowager meddling in the investigation while simultaneously making outrageous judgments about the poor man they were trying to find.

CHAPTER 10

Dinner was a subdued affair that evening. Tabitha and Wolf felt it was best to let the family digest Lily's startling, if only partially true, news. Despite his promise of support, Hamish couldn't help but look at his daughter with disappointment. Based on her downcast eyes, Lily's contrition finally seemed genuine. The dowager had decided that, while she might be continuing her involvement in the investigation, Peter Kincaid was not worthy of dinner conversation and, instead, chose to hold forth on the latest London gossip she had received in an emergency telegram from Lady Hartley that morning.

"I'm not sure why anyone should be surprised, though," she said knowingly. "Viscount Sanders is the most notorious rake in London. The man lives at the tables and, heavens knows where he spends his nights." She clearly would have said more, but glancing at her granddaughter, even the dowager countess watched her words.

Tabitha had hoped they might have time to discuss their findings with Lily that evening. But after the dramatic revelation of the "truth" about Peter, it seemed wise to wait until morning and try to find time alone with the girl. There was no doubt that, at some point, the dowager would get over her outrage enough to remember her curiosity about what they'd discovered. Tabitha would prefer to speak with Lily before then. They needed time to consider how best to discuss their findings in the context of the highly edited story the dowager and Jane had been told.

In a brief, hushed conversation as they had gone up to dress for dinner that evening, Tabitha and Wolf had discussed how careful they would have to be with all the information they shared with the larger group. They might come across information that would easily expose the lies they had told about Peter.

"Well," Wolf mused, "given that it is highly likely we will find out more information about Peter's political activities, and that they may even be related to his disappearance, I think the best course of action will be not to try to hide whatever we find. I believe Peter's political leanings can be 'discovered' during our investigations, even while we maintain the fiction that they had nothing to do with how Lily came to correspond with the man."

Tabitha was sceptical, "Do you really think the dowager countess will believe the two are unconnected?"

Wolf considered the question and then answered, "Yes, I do. The story we told about how they met was so entirely shocking in and of itself that I don't believe it will occur to Lady Pembroke or Lady MacAlister that the truth is even worse. When spinning a yarn, it's important to stay as close to the truth as possible. The more complicated the lie, the harder it will be to remember and the easier for someone to pick apart."

Tabitha was amused, "Is that piece of wisdom from your thief-taking days?"

"No, from my cake-stealing childhood," Wolf admitted to her amusement. "When Mrs Brown, our cook, caught me in the kitchen with sticky fingers, or when our neighbour caught me stealing apples from his orchard, I learned to keep my lies simple. The more elaborate the lie, the less likely I was to remember it when I was inevitably dragged to my father's study by my ear."

"What lie could you possibly tell if you were caught with jam on your fingers and crumbs around your mouth?" asked Tabitha, fascinated by this brief glimpse into Wolf's childhood.

"You'd be surprised," he answered cryptically but with a grin on his face.

Realising she was getting no more details about the young Jeremy Wolfson Chesterton that evening, Tabitha conceded that his larger point was valid; stick as close to the truth as they could.

The following morning, Tabitha rose early. The dowager was a notoriously late riser, usually choosing to breakfast in her boudoir when at home. Tabitha bet that if she hurried to breakfast, she might find Lily alone. This decision was rewarded when she entered the breakfast room and found Lily sitting by herself, drinking coffee. However, the girl had just finished her last bite of toast and was getting ready to leave the table.

"Good morning, Lily. I'm glad to have caught you. We never had a chance to discuss what Cousin Jeremy and I discovered yesterday."

Lily immediately sat back down. Realising their privacy might be short-lived, Tabitha suggested, "Perhaps we might take another stroll in the garden. When we walked there yesterday, I noticed how many flowers were still blooming, despite the crisp temperatures. I'd love to learn more about the varieties of resilient plants you have here."

Lily's eyes lit up; there were few topics she'd rather talk about than the cultivation of resilient strains of plants. "Indeed, explaining my methods to you would give me the greatest pleasure. As you can imagine, resiliency is essential when growing botanicals for practical purposes rather than just decoration. In fact, Joseph Dalton Hooker's botanical explorations and taxonomic work have contributed greatly to the understanding of plant resiliency and their adaption to different environments. I have all of his books if you're interested in reading about his exploration and discoveries."

Tabitha could see the girl's passion for her subject could distract them if she wasn't careful and said, "Perhaps you might show the books to me later. But for now, I think a walk in the garden where you can point out the most resilient varieties while we discuss the investigation will suffice."

They agreed to fetch their coats and again meet in the

summer room. As Tabitha walked towards her room, she met Wolf coming down the hallway from his. She quickly and quietly informed him of the plan, and he agreed to join them, turning to retrieve his coat from his room.

Luckily, they didn't run into any other family members, and within a few minutes, Wolf, Tabitha and Lily were walking in the garden. Tabitha decided it was best to let Lily show them some plants before attempting to focus her attention on more important matters. The young woman happily gave them a tour of her favourite plants with long, elaborate descriptions of how she had cultivated strains for more resilience. There was no doubt Lily was both passionate and knowledgeable about botany, and Tabitha reflected on what a waste it would be if the girl wasn't allowed to pursue her studies and was indeed married off to the highest bidder.

Finally, after spending at least fifteen minutes looking at flowers and listening to Lily waxing lyrically about the vibrantly colourful pansies and their supposed use in treating respiratory conditions, skin ailments, and digestive complaints, Tabitha guided them back to the bench they had sat on the day before.

"Lily, as you know, we visited Peter's lodgings yesterday. We were able to search his room and…" Tabitha paused, still feeling guilty about reading Peter's private correspondence with Lily. "Well, we came across letters from you to Peter." Stealing a glance at Lily's face as she confessed, Tabitha was happy to find the girl was unperturbed by the admission.

"What could they have possibly told you that I haven't already?" Lily asked.

Wolf picked up the conversation, "Well, in a recent letter, you refer to a Mr Sinclair and call him Peter's benefactor. You say he'll be attending the dinner tonight."

"James Sinclair is Peter's mentor and benefactor. Peter was born in a workhouse and raised in an orphanage. Mr Sinclair was raised in the same orphanage. He started working down the mines at the age of eight." Seeing Tabitha's shock, Lily explained, "It wasn't until I believe 1841 or maybe 42 that child labour in the mines under the age of ten was banned. Peter told me in one of his letters that it was only last year that the age was raised to thirteen."

Tabitha's heart clenched at the thought. When Rat had come to live at Chesterton House, Tabitha had agreed that carrying messages, on occasion, for Wolf could be part of his duties. Wolf had interpreted that to mean he might use Rat to relay communications back and forth to some of his less-than-respectable contacts from his former life in Whitechapel. Much to Tabitha's horror, he'd even had the boy break into a house during their first investigation. The thought of Rat, or any child his age, let alone younger, performing the backbreaking, hazardous work of coal mining was heart-wrenching.

Wolf had once accused Tabitha of not considering and confronting the ugliness behind the industries that made her life so easy. On hearing Lily's words, Tabitha was uncomfortably aware that coal mining was one such industry. She had happily boarded the train to Edinburgh and revelled in the speedy trip. But she had never stopped to consider what it had cost the men and, apparently, boys, who had mined the coal needed to fuel that train.

Wolf could see that Tabitha had become distracted and guessed the cause. He asked Lily, "So this Mr Sinclair is a coal miner?"

The young woman laughed, saying, "Oh, James Sinclair hasn't been a coal miner for many decades. Somehow, he worked his way up through the mining business and is now one of Scotland's richest men. He owns more mines than Da does."

"How did he come to be Peter's benefactor?" Tabitha asked.

Lily continued, "From what Peter told me, once Mr Sinclair became rich, he created a scholarship at the Royal High School, one of the most prestigious schools in Edinburgh. Every year he would go to the orphanage to see if they had a boy deserving of the scholarship. When Peter was ten, he was interviewed by Mr Sinclair and awarded a free place at the Royal High School. Four times a year, he would visit Mr Sinclair's home for dinner to be mentored by the man himself."

"This Mr Sinclair sounds like a very generous man. Both with his money and time," Tabitha observed.

"Peter is a brilliant man," Lily gushed. "But all the brilliance in the world would have done him no service without a good education."

"Though, it seems Mr Sinclair was able to reach great heights without such an education," Wolf observed.

"But that's just it," Lily exclaimed. "He managed to get rich but didn't manage to do what he'd always wanted: to be an engineer. He told Peter that he had always been fascinated by machines of all sorts. With only a rudimentary education, it's a wonder he has even managed to rise as far as he has. He wanted to ensure that other boys like him could reach their potential. It's why he was thrilled when Peter told him he wanted to be a doctor. Peter won a merit scholarship to the University of Edinburgh. But Mr Sinclair provides a supplementary scholarship for his living expenses."

"From what you said in your letter to Peter, I take it that your father and Mr Sinclair are friends," Tabitha said. She was keen to meet this Mr Sinclair at the dinner that night. She had been thinking a lot recently about how she might do more to encourage the education of young girls and was interested to learn more about how other wealthy people put their money towards such philanthropic goals. James Sinclair sounded like a paragon of philanthropy and just the person to help guide her to do more with her wealth.

"I would say they have more of a business acquaintance than a friendship. But Edinburgh's high society is not large, and two successful colliery owners have much cause to interact. Father insisted he be invited tonight over Mama's strenuous objections," Lily added. "After all, Mr Sinclair, while very rich now, grew up in an orphanage and worked in a coal mine."

Tabitha finished Lily's sentence, "And your mother is worried about what your grandmother will think."

"Well, what she will think but mostly what she'll say. As you are very aware, Grandmama is not one to keep her judgements and thoughts to herself."

Wolf thought for a moment and then asked, "Is there something about Mr Sinclair's speech or behaviour that calls attention to his humble beginnings?"

Lily chuckled, "Well, there is. But as I said to Mama, you have to be Scottish to be able to tell the roughness in his accent and speech. Grandmama has said many times that we all sound like heathens to her. I very much doubt she can distinguish one accent from another. And even if she can, I am certain she makes no distinction between them."

Tabitha and Wolf acknowledged the truth of Lily's observation. As far as the dowager was concerned, society was stratified into the English aristocracy and everyone else, with perhaps some distinction given to the clergy.

Tabitha looked out at the garden, admiring the autumnal colours and blooms filling the garden. She turned back to Lily, and she asked, "Do you think Mr Sinclair might know anything about Peter's whereabouts? Why did you offer to speak to him about Peter?"

Lily didn't answer immediately. Tabitha and Wolf sat silently, allowing the young woman time to consider the question. "Peter admires Mr Sinclair greatly and is greatly indebted to him. However, I got the sense from some of Peter's letters that there has been some tension between them of late."

"What kind of tension?" Wolf asked.

"Ever since Peter's work for the Scottish Labour Party has become more public and vocal, his relationship with Mr Sinclair has become increasingly strained. So strained that Peter no longer receives money for his living expenses."

Now this was interesting, Tabitha thought. Of course, it made perfect sense that a man impassioned by the cause of workers' rights might come into conflict with an industrialist, particularly one who owned coal mines. She asked, "Do you know which of them ended their financial arrangement?"

"From the little Peter wrote of it, I believe it was quite

mutual. They had argued at the last of their regular dinners just last month. Mr Sinclair had accused Peter of hypocrisy, railing against industrialists but happy to take his money, nevertheless. Peter had agreed with him. I know that accepting money from Mr Sinclair had increasingly weighed on his conscience. Initially, he had told himself their arrangement was justifiable because he was studying medicine to better serve the poor. But that excuse was feeling increasingly thin, at least to his ears. He has an educational scholarship, so refusing Mr Sinclair's money would not impact his studies. It would just mean he would have to find another way to support himself."

Tabitha could imagine an idealistic young man's internal struggle over accepting money from someone like James Sinclair. Was this struggle anything more than a clash of ideas? She asked Lily that question, but the girl didn't have an answer. "Peter was a friend. Is a friend," Lily corrected herself. "But he also felt our relationship was one of student and teacher more than friendship. He felt his role was to educate me on the cause. It was only occasionally, in times of great distress, that his letters ever lapsed into more personal issues."

Tabitha was loath to invade Lily's privacy any more than they already had by reading her letters to Peter, but she had to ask, "Lily, is there anything in Peter's letters that you feel might help us locate him?"

"You are welcome to read them, Aunt Tabitha," Lily replied. "I know you still harbour a belief that my relationship with Peter is of a more intimate nature, but I assure you, it is not. And there is nothing in the letters that will convince you otherwise. I will have my maid put them in your room under your pillow. Given the story we have concocted for Grandmama and Mama, I have no desire for the letters to be discovered."

Tabitha and Wolf completely agreed with that sentiment. Those letters would blow apart their carefully constructed story.

CHAPTER 11

Tabitha wouldn't have time to read the letters until later that afternoon. They had decided she would claim a headache and retire to her room to lie down before the big evening soiree. That left the rest of the morning and early afternoon to continue their investigation. Lily had gone to her greenhouse to check on some hybrid plantings she'd been experimenting with, leaving Tabitha and Wolf out on the bench in the garden.

There was a real chill in the air, and Tabitha stamped her feet and rubbed her hands together to warm up. "Should we continue this conversation inside?" Wolf asked.

Tabitha shook her head, "I'll be fine for a few more minutes. It's so hard to ensure privacy in the house, and I'd like us to discuss our next moves before we return."

"Well, it's a given that we will talk to Mr Sinclair tonight. Of course, if he chooses not to discuss Peter, a genteel dinner party will hardly be the place to press him on the matter. But we can at least get the measure of the man. And perhaps we will get lucky, and he has information on Peter's whereabouts."

Tabitha listened to Wolf talk, but her mind was elsewhere. "We need to talk to Peter's friend, Louis. He must have some idea of any trouble Peter is in. Bear would certainly know if anything ever happened to you."

"True, but the very friendship between Peter and Louis makes me wonder. At least on the face of it, you have a studious, serious young man from humble circumstances whose best friend is a privileged, drunkard wastrel. I knew both kinds of boys then men at Eton and Oxford, and I never knew them to mix."

Tabitha always appreciated these glimpses into Wolf's younger life and asked, "And which were you? The diligent student or the wastrel?"

Wolf laughed, "Neither. No teacher would ever have called me a diligent student. However, I had neither the money nor the title to run with the wild crowd."

"So, which crowd did you run with?" Tabitha asked.

"Jack. At least at Eton, I ran with Jack Struthers. The youngest son of an impoverished marquis. With three older brothers, he had little prospect of inheriting the title. And it was well known that his father had gambled the estate dry. When I went to Oxford, Jack went to Cambridge. We lost touch, and as for friends when I was there, there was no one special. It wasn't the happiest time in my life, to be honest."

Tabitha reached out and put her hand on his arm, "I'm sorry to hear that."

Wolf looked down in silence for a few moments, reliving the loneliness of that time. "But then I met Bear, and a man could not ask for a truer friend." Wolf shook his head to dispel the sad memories, "We do need to find this Louis. There must be more to the man than we've been told. Let's hope he is concerned enough about his friend to talk with us."

Tabitha nodded in agreement and added, "We should ask Hamish what, if anything, he knows about Louis' father, Dr Trent. Why don't we go and do that now? It is too cold to sit out here any longer."

They returned to the house and ran into the butler, Dawglish, who informed them Hamish was in his study. The door to Hamish's office was closed. They knocked and entered on receiving a hearty hail. Hamish gestured for them to enter quickly and close the door behind them. "I'm hidin' from Lady Pembroke, ye ken. She's on the warpath, I tell ye!" he explained.

Tabitha took a seat and asked, "Is this general crankiness or is she in high dudgeon about something in particular?"

"Ah, ye see, Lily was tae go dress shoppin' the day, but she's disappeared."

"Well, that may have been our fault," Wolf confessed. "We wanted to ask her some questions, so we went to the garden. I believe that when she left us, she went to the greenhouse."

"That wouldnae surprise me. The lassie spends most o' her time there."

Tabitha considered for a moment what she wished to say and realised there would be no better time. "Hamish, while I have no wish to tell you how to parent your daughter, I must ask, do you know that she does not wish to marry? At least not yet. She wants to study botany."

"Aye, I ken fine. We've had enough quarrels o'er the matter. I cherish ma bairns and only seek what's finest for them. And for a young lassie o' Lily's station, matrimony and bairns are whit's for the best."

Tabitha wanted to tread very carefully. She didn't want to offend her host. But she felt she had to speak up on Lily's behalf. "Hamish, it's 1897. A new century will be upon us shortly. Things are changing, even for women. Lily is a highly intelligent young woman who is passionate about botany. Might you not consider allowing her to attend university?"

"Weel, wi' her grandmother involved noo, Lily has nae choice but tae tak' part in the season," Hamish said, but Tabitha felt there was noticeably less resolve to his tone. However, she acknowledged that the season would be happening no matter what. The dowager was now far too invested in her granddaughter's debut to allow any deviation from the plan. But a season didn't have to end with a marriage proposal. And Tabitha sensed Hamish would never force a husband on Lily.

Realising they needed to make the most of their time alone with Hamish, Tabitha changed the subject and asked, "Do you know a Dr Trent who lives in New Town?"

"Aye, in fact, he'll be joinin' us for dinner the nicht. Why?"

"I'm not sure it's anything, but Dr Trent's son, Louis, is Peter's friend. We'd like to talk to Louis and see if he knows where Peter might be."

This was a lucky coincidence, Tabitha reflected. Both men they wanted to talk to about Peter would be in attendance that evening. Tabitha just hoped they would have an opportunity to talk to them discreetly.

Leaving Hamish to hide in his study, Tabitha and Wolf found themselves at somewhat of a loose end; they felt they should be investigating, but had no leads to pursue.

"Perhaps we can use the afternoon most profitably by recreating your board," Wolf suggested. During their first investigation, Tabitha had created a makeshift board to pin notecards to. They had written every clue and question on a notecard and grouped them as connections were made. It had proven to be an excellent way to help them think about a case and keep track of all its threads."

"That's a good idea. But this isn't Chesterton House. We can't just requisition a painting, cover it with material and commandeer a room as our headquarters," Tabitha pointed out.

"Can't we?" Wolf countered. "Even though their motivations may vary, everyone in this house wants Peter found as soon as possible. There must be a small, rarely used room somewhere we could use as our base. That would also give us somewhere private to talk, away from prying dowager ears. It certainly can't hurt to ask." Tabitha agreed, and they set off searching for Jane to make the request.

The lady of the house was quickly discovered in the bright, sunny morning room, being browbeaten by her mother. In her own home, the dowager was notorious for arranging the furniture in her drawing room to put her visitors at a strategic disadvantage. A diminutive woman at barely five feet tall, the dowager sat upon a chair higher than any used by her guests. She ensured that by using furniture that almost seemed built for a nursery. It helped give the dowager a good viewing point out over the theatre of war which, as far as she was concerned, was any social occasion. But it also was uncomfortable as guests squeezed themselves into tiny chairs, adding to her strategic advantage and guaranteeing that all social calls were brief.

Somehow, even in her daughter's house, the dowager had replicated much of her battlefield advantage; she had taken the most throne-like chair in the room while Jane cowered on a dainty chaise-longue.

"Ah, dear Jeremy," the dowager said, ignoring Tabitha altogether. "Perfect timing. I was just reminding Jane that precedence must be observed tonight and that as the highest-ranking guest, you must accompany her into dinner, and Laird MacAlister will escort me. This seems to be something she has entirely forgotten."

Tabitha suspected that Jane's reluctance around this issue was primarily due to the lack of titles the rest of her guests held and her unwillingness to bring this to her mother's attention before she had to.

"Mama, we are not as formal here as you are in London," Jane stuttered.

"Well, perhaps you should be!" the dowager stated. "You are the daughter of an earl, Jane. It has been your duty these last twenty-odd years to bring some civilisation to these savages."

"Mama, we do not mix in the same society you do in London. Hamish has never felt comfortable in the more aristocratic circles. He considers himself a man of business and prefers to mix socially with the same."

"Pff! What nonsense," the dowager exclaimed. "He is a member of the upper class, is he not?"

"Yes, but, as I've told you before, laird is not an aristocratic title, and Hamish feels looked down on when mixing in higher circles." Jane was stuttering at this point, and Tabitha was worried she might burst into tears at any moment.

Wolf had nothing but the greatest sympathy for Hamish's point of view. Ever since ascending to the earldom, he had felt very uncomfortable mixing with those now considered his peers. He preferred to judge a man's worth on more than a title he had happened to inherit and certainly wished to be judged by more than that himself.

"So, let me see if I understand this correctly: you have

arranged the dinner tonight in my honour. Yet you have invited a group of people who are the second echelon of Edinburgh society. And I suspect that is being generous. Is that a fair statement, Jane?" The dowager's steel grey eyes, cold and hard as granite at the best of times, now glared so ferociously that Tabitha could see Jane's eyes filling with tears.

Feeling she must try and intervene, Tabitha said, "Mama, as you have pointed out on numerous occasions, Edinburgh is not London. Indeed, is that not why you made the great sacrifice to travel all the way up here to prepare Lily for her season?"

Tabitha knew that often the only way to distract the dowager countess from one rant was to divert her to a new topic of outrage. While she felt sorry for putting her niece in the line of fire, Tabitha felt sure Lily was hardier than her mother, so the sacrifice of one woman in favour of the other was justifiable.

"Indeed, and where is the chit of a girl? We were supposed to spend our morning visiting what passes for a modiste in this backwater, yet my granddaughter is nowhere to be found!"

The dowager continued, "I kept my side of the bargain, and I hope Lily does not believe that now you two are here and investigating, it is a fait accompli, and she may neglect her duty." The dowager paused, considered what Tabitha had said, and then continued in an even more strident tone, "And yes, as I have said more than once, Edinburgh is no London. Jane, as it is, I have serious concerns about this modiste." Her eyes raked over her daughter, wearing yet another dowdy, unflattering dress, "I do hope this woman is not the same one who makes your dresses. Because whoever that is has neither taste nor talent."

Jane flushed at the criticism and said, "I believe I already told you that this modiste has come highly recommended by Lady Williams."

"And who is this Lady Williams that I should trust her judgement? Will she be attending tonight so I can at least assess her sense of fashion for myself?"

At this, Jane flushed even more, "Unfortunately, Lady Williams is out of town and is unable to join us. But I assure you, she is considered very au courant within the highest social circles."

The dowager laughed out loud at this statement, "That one is considered au courant in Scotland is hardly something to boast of. And where fashion is concerned, you are hardly the person to judge; the dress you're wearing is barely above a potato sack. Perhaps it is for the best that our outing today has been delayed. I believe I must perform some due diligence of my own. I may need to telegram Lily's proportions to my modiste in London with instructions. We can always have last-minute alterations made once we are there." She paused again, "I'm not sure why I didn't insist upon such a strategy to begin with. That is what we will do. However, the girl will still need a few dresses for travelling and the days it will take to make alterations. We can afford to be less concerned about the quality as long as she's kept out of sight during that time."

Jane almost seemed relieved at this plan; all the responsibility for Lily's wardrobe would be taken off her shoulders. "What a wonderful idea, Mama," she said. "Lily certainly has clothes good enough to tide her over."

The dowager's eyes widened in amazement at such an absurd statement. "Good enough! She will be travelling in public with the Dowager Countess of Pembroke. Her clothes cannot be merely good enough. And" she added, "that presumes the unlikely scenario that her current wardrobe could even be considered good enough."

Taking pity on her sister-in-law, Tabitha intervened, "Mama, why do we not see how this evening goes? There may be ladies in attendance whose gowns you approve of. If there is, we can make inquiries as to their modiste of choice."

"Given that it appears that this dinner party will be comprised of the hoi polloi of middle-class Edinburgh society, I have no high expectations of encountering anyone with an appropriate sense of style. I doubt I will approve of anyone's gown." She paused, then added, "Including yours, Tabitha."

Tabitha was so used to this particular line of attack that she didn't even acknowledge it. However, she was worried that the dowager was right about that evening's guests. Or at least about her own likely assessment of them. She wanted to find a way to pour water on flames that she was at least partly responsible for igniting. If nothing else, she did not want to go full circle back to discussing the guest list for that evening. "Mama, perhaps I might escort you to this modiste after luncheon, and you can determine if she will do."

The dowager sniffed and said, "Under the circumstances, that will have to suffice. Jane, you will stay here. I do not wish this modiste, Madam Faubere, I believe her name is, to make assumptions about the level of quality we will accept based on your outfit." And with this statement, the dowager flounced out of the room.

That issue settled, at least for the moment, Tabitha still needed to ask Jane about a possible room. "Well, there is the library. Lily is the only person who makes regular use of that room." Tabitha agreed that the library sounded like an excellent idea. It was also not lost on her that the library was on the floor above and, therefore, not somewhere the dowager was likely to wander into during the day. When Tabitha explained about the board they used at home, Jane's eyes lit up. "I believe there is a board made of cork in the schoolroom that the children's tutor uses. Would that suffice?"

"I'm sure it would. I'm unsure why we never considered such a thing in London," Tabitha admitted.

Jane stood up, happy to have a reason to escape the possibility of her mother's imminent return and went to arrange to have the board moved to the library.

CHAPTER 12

Luncheon was mostly peaceful. This peace was broken by Lily's eventual reappearance almost toward the end of the meal. "Where have you been, young lady?" the dowager demanded. "Did you forget we had an appointment at the modiste this morning?" Not waiting for an answer, the dowager continued, "No matter. The delay gave me the opportunity to reflect on the unlikeliness of your mother's competence in selecting an appropriately fashionable dressmaker. Therefore, your Aunt Tabitha and I will visit to judge for ourselves this afternoon. However, we will still require your company so that your measurements may be sent to my London modiste."

Seeing the look on Lily's face, Tabitha intervened, "Mama, might I make a suggestion? My maid Ginny is an able seamstress. I'm sure she is more than able to take Lily's measurements."

Unwilling to let her granddaughter out of what she saw as a compulsory outing, the dowager hesitated to accept the offer. Tabitha continued, "After all, if, as you surely correctly imagine, this modiste is utterly unacceptable, might it not then be awkward asking her nevertheless to take Lily's measurements so another might make the dresses instead?" As it happened, Tabitha could well imagine how the dowager might not find it at all awkward.

"I'm still not sure why Lily should be rewarded for failing to meet this morning's obligation," the dowager said stubbornly.

Tabitha saw Hamish give his daughter a certain look. It seemed she had understood his meaning, and she said,

"Grandmama, please accept my sincere apologies. I became caught up in my studies." Seeing the objection forming, she quickly added, "Not that my studies are any excuse. I do understand that. Please forgive me. It will not happen again." The dowager harrumphed but said no more on the subject.

During a brief, whispered conversation as they left the dining room, Tabitha suggested that Wolf ask Ginny to talk to Lily's maid and ask her to bring Peter's letters to Wolf. She felt it best that they have a chance to read them thoroughly before talking to James Sinclair and Dr Trent that evening. Tabitha was resigned to a challenging afternoon with her mother-in-law and thought it best if at least one of them made some progress with the investigation.

The visit to the modiste turned out to be even worse than Tabitha had anticipated. The dowager countess had swept into the shop announcing, "I am the Dowager Countess of Pembroke, and I have serious reservations about whether your establishment is fit to dress my granddaughter for her upcoming London season." There had been no apologies for missing the morning's appointment nor attempts to frame her concerns in a manner less likely to offend. In fact, the dowager seemed to go out of her way to be as offensive as possible. Though Tabitha reflected, was that any different from the woman's normal conversational style?

Finally, some dress samples were produced and immediately pronounced, "Utterly unworthy of an earl's granddaughter." They were back in the carriage returning to Charlotte Square before even thirty minutes had passed.

The dowager spent most of the blessedly brief carriage ride crowing about her prescience concerning the inferior quality of any modiste selected by Jane. Truthfully, Tabitha had thought the dresses shown, while perhaps not the height of fashion, were certainly of sufficient style and quality for some travelling and day dresses. But having gone in determined to be right in her judgement, the dowager was predisposed to disapprove of everything she was shown.

"I hope your maid has been able to take accurate measurements," the dowager fussed. "Because our only option is to have my woman send dresses from London before we leave here. That won't leave her long to work, but, of course, she will prioritise my order." Tabitha had no doubt the woman was sufficiently browbeaten over the years that she had been dressing the dowager to recognise the impossibility of doing anything but to prioritise her order.

Overall, it had been a tedious, uncomfortable afternoon. Tabitha was very happy when they were back at the MacAlister home, and she could retire to her room. She only hoped that Wolf's perusal of the letters had yielded some useful information.

Entering her bedroom, she found Ginny puttering around the room, "Heavens, I'm glad you're back, m'lady," the maid said. "I've been waiting for you, refolded all your clothes, and have run out of things to keep me busy."

Tabitha was immediately alarmed. Seeing the consternation her words had caused, Ginny assured her, "Nothing is wrong. It's just that Thompson sent word that his lordship wanted to talk with you as soon as you returned. He's waiting for you in the library." Tabitha would have liked a few minutes to refresh herself, but she was eager to hear about the contents of the letters, so she hurried to meet Wolf.

True to her word, Jane had installed the corkboard on a table against a wall. Tabitha smiled on seeing that Wolf had taken on her usual task and had started writing up notecards and pinning them in groupings. Although, seeing them arrayed before her, Tabitha had to admit, they hadn't discovered much of use yet.

Wolf looked up as she entered the room and gestured that she should close the door behind her. He was sitting in one of a pair of green leather armchairs with the stack of letters on a small table next to him. Tabitha took the unoccupied chair and said, "I came as soon as Ginny told me."

"How was your afternoon?" Wolf asked.

Tabitha waved her hand dismissively, "Much as you would

imagine; it was a nightmare. I'd prefer to talk about anything else. Tell me what you've found in the letters."

"Well, for the most part, they are as expected. We've read the other side of the correspondence, and Peter's side matches what Lily told us; there seems to be nothing indicating a romantic entanglement."

Tabitha let out a sigh of relief. The truth of Lily's friendship with Peter was quite shocking enough. Tabitha and Wolf had encouraged the girl to tell a modified version of that story to the dowager and Jane. However, there was always an underlying concern that they might be inadvertently abetting a quite inappropriate romance.

Wolf paused, "Everything matched what Lily told us."

"But?" Tabitha asked, impatient to hear what he had discovered.

"It wasn't so much that the facts are different in Peter's letter, but rather how he expressed them. Or one of them, at least." Sensing that Tabitha's patience for a drawn-out story was wearing thin, Wolf continued quickly, "Lily told us that Sinclair called Peter a hypocrite for railing against industrialists and yet taking his money, and that argument caused the end of the scholarship. And that all seems to be true." Wolf paused and picked up the letter on the top of the pile, "But when Peter makes mention of it, he says," and Wolf began to read, "'It is for the best. I can no longer reconcile myself to taking his blood money.'"

Tabitha considered this briefly and said, "But didn't we already know this? Lily told us that Peter had struggled to reconcile his conscience to taking Sinclair's money and that his justification had once been that he would be able to help the poor as a doctor. Isn't this statement merely an acknowledgement that, ultimately, the two became irreconcilable?"

"Perhaps, but the phrase 'blood money' seems more than that. The way Lily told the story, Peter's dispute with Sinclair was a more philosophical difference of opinion. But this sounds more specific, something darker. Or am I reading too much into it?" Seeing Tabitha's reaction, Wolf questioned whether he had been too suspicious. Perhaps Peter's phrasing meant nothing beyond their original understanding of the falling out.

For her part, Tabitha reconsidered her initial dismissal of Wolf's claim. Blood money was a particularly strong statement. But then she considered the other side. After all, as Tabitha herself had considered just the day before, mining coal was a necessary part of a functioning industrial society. Yes, it was a dangerous job, but it needed to be done, and there had been various improvements to workplace practices in mines over the last hundred years. While they might not be enough, there could be no denying that conditions were improving for miners and, in general, the working class. Peter Kincaid was an idealistic young man fired up for his cause. Perhaps he refused to accept the sufficiency of slow-moving incremental change.

"It could be something, or it could just be strong words from a passionate man," Tabitha concluded. "Either way, we should add it to our new board. If I've learned anything from our two investigations, you never know when the smallest details will become important." Wolf agreed, and a notecard was created and pinned to the board.

Staring at the new notecard on the sparsely populated corkboard, Tabitha said, "Something we should discuss is how we should approach the two men we wish to talk with tonight. At this point, we have no real suspicions. We're not sure Peter has disappeared due to any nefarious cause. We certainly don't want to be heavy-handed in questioning the laird's guests."

Wolf agreed, but he had no suggestions as to their approach.

"I think we are getting ahead of ourselves," Tabitha concluded. "Why don't we get the measure of the men, engage them in drawing room conversation, and perhaps just drop Peter's name in at some point and see their reactions?" Wolf had no better suggestion, so with a rather unsatisfying plan in place, they each retreated to their rooms to dress for the evening.

Ginny had laid out a beautiful wine-coloured silk dress. It was the perfect choice, demure enough not to attract too much criticism from the dowager but beautifully chic and stylish enough to represent Tabitha's newly discovered personal fashion sense. She had a beautiful but simple red garnet necklace she had worn to her first ball with Wolf that would perfectly complement the dress.

Finally, with her hair dressed simply but elegantly, Tabitha took a final look in the mirror. Jonathan had been dead not much more than nine months, but it felt like a lifetime since Ginny's hardest task was artfully concealing the bruises and scrapes that Tabitha so often sported thanks to her husband's temper. It had been nine months since she had lived in terror of saying or doing something to ignite that temper. Contrary to what so many people in society had whispered at the time, Tabitha hadn't pushed her husband down the stairs. But she could not pretend any sadness at his demise. Like his father, apparently, Jonathan had been a brute, and Tabitha's world was certainly so much better without him.

And then there was Wolf. Had it only been a few short months since he had entered her life? There was that moment a few weeks ago when he seemed about to declare his feelings to her, and Tabitha had forestalled any proclamation. Not because she didn't have feelings for Wolf; there was an undeniable attraction which she felt sure was reciprocated. But Tabitha believed she could never trust a man enough ever again to put herself in his power. She was a wealthy widow now, with about as much independence and autonomy as a woman in 1897 could hope to have.

With her father dead, her fortune was hers to control. She was free to live where and how she liked. No one, no man, could tell her how to dress, when or how to speak, and most importantly, could have no legal right to raise his fists to her if he so chose. She believed, no, she knew, that Wolf was nothing like Jonathan. He had repeatedly proven that to her in so many ways. And yet, she could not bring herself to give a man, any man, that kind of hold over her again. A hold that, as his wife, was enshrined in the law. If being Wolf's wife was something she would forever deny herself, then what was there? Even though half of

London already believed she must be his mistress given their unconventional living situation, she was not prepared to make the malicious gossip a reality.

But then, there were those times when their eyes met, and he smiled at her. He had such an open, easy smile that lit up his already handsome face. There were the many times when he listened to her, really listened, taking her ideas and concerns seriously. While he still was inclined to try to protect her, he had begun to restrain himself when tempted to treat her like a delicate bloom liable to be blown away at the slightest gust. And he restrained himself because he took her seriously.

Whenever Tabitha caught herself having such thoughts, she would usually end with the devastating realisation that he would inevitably marry one day, if not to her, then to someone else. When that happened, she would have to move and lose her home. But, in reality, she would lose so much more than just a house. Shaking her head to dispel such gloomy thoughts, she focused again on the evening ahead. They had decided to divide and conquer, one engaging James Sinclair in pre-dinner conversation while the other tackled Dr Trent. Tabitha smiled at the thought of what a good team she and Wolf made. But no sooner had her lips turned up at the thought than she was brought back to her darker thoughts on what would happen when he married.

Finally, realising such ruminations were getting her nowhere, she made her way down to the drawing room. Luckily, she had not been so lost in thought that she was the last one down. That distinction was again taken by Lily, who blew into the room looking flustered just after Tabitha. Dressed in yet another drab, unflattering gown, at least the girl seemed to not have any twigs or plant matter in her hair.

"Aunt Tabitha," Lily whispered, "Will you and Cousin Jeremy talk to Mr Sinclair this evening?"

"That is the plan," Tabitha acknowledged. "We also hope to speak with Dr Trent."

For a moment, Lily looked confused but then said, "Oh,

yes, Peter's friend Louis' father. Why do you think he knows anything about Peter's whereabouts?"

"Well, he probably doesn't," Tabitha admitted. "But we wish to talk with Louis, and speaking with his father is a good start. I'll be interested to hear Dr Trent's view of his son's friend."

The dowager was already in the drawing room, seated, as she so often was, in the best chair available. From her battlement, she could both hold court and perform reconnaissance; she had a clear view of everyone entering the room but could also keep an eye on all the side conversations likely to happen. Tabitha doubted the perfect location of her chair was an accident; the woman always thought multiple moves ahead and was wily enough to arrange the board to her advantage.

With Lily by her side, Tabitha advanced further into the room towards the dowager. The old woman raised one eye as if critiquing her outfit. Tabitha assumed that the lack of a corresponding cutting comment could only mean that the old woman couldn't actually find anything to criticise. Looking around for Wolf, Tabitha found him leaning against the mantlepiece, talking with Hamish. He also caught her eye, but unlike the dowager, his face lit up with appreciation for how she looked.

As she often did during formal evening events, Tabitha noted how well Wolf wore evening clothes. He might not enjoy dressing in them, but that didn't mean he didn't wear them well.

"Ah, Tabitha, finally," the dowager's voice rang out. "And, Lily, tardy again, I see. It is hardly becoming of a young woman to keep her elders waiting regularly. I can only assume that, yet again, some plants took precedence." By the guilty look on Lily's face, Tabitha assumed that the dowager's guess had hit the mark.

The dowager held Jane in wretched captivity, seated by her side. While the elder Lady Pembroke derived no pleasure in her daughter's company, she nevertheless insisted on keeping her close at hand where she could function as part companion, part indentured servant and part verbal punching bag. Jane was such an easy target that Tabitha wondered why the dowager, a woman who could take down grown men with a single quip, really bothered. But then, Tabitha thought, there was probably something in having someone to practice on. The dowager certainly didn't want her vicious wit to dull while she was away from London.

Tabitha and Lily reclaimed their now regular seats on the sofa while waiting for guests to arrive. They didn't have long to wait, and by the time Tabitha had a glass of sherry in her hand, people had begun trickling in. It was to be a large formal dinner with thirty of, if not Edinburgh's finest, at least its middling to upper echelon sitting down for Scottish salmon and venison.

Protocol dictated that the guests should first be introduced to the dowager, who held court in queenly splendour, holding out a hand to each new guest to bestow a greeting as if a benediction, or more likely prefacing a royal command of "Off with his head!" Tabitha watched her mother-in-law in her element, doing what she did so well, assessing people within a moment's introduction and then cutting them down to size with a few well-placed comments. Comments said in such a silky-smooth voice that her victim was left momentarily stunned, unsure at first that they had just been insulted.

After Hamish had introduced each unsuspecting guest to his mother-in-law, he led them to Wolf, who greeted them with a far more sincere and benign welcome. Finally, they were led to meet Tabitha, some still battered and bloody from their encounter with the dowager and looking as if they needed nothing more than a stiff drink.

Tabitha was grateful to Hamish for ensuring they were formally introduced to his guests; it was a dinner in their honour, after all. And the introductions ensured that she and Wolf would have no doubt who James Sinclair and Dr Trent were. Sinclair was the first to arrive. He was a corpulent, ruddy-faced man who looked like he ate and drank too well, and to excess. If he had ever had a claim to good looks, those days were well behind him, and he now had a large, red-veined bulbous nose set in a pock-marked face. His eyes were the man's best feature; they shone with keen intelligence. Tabitha doubted he missed much.

As Hamish made the introductions, James Sinclair took Tabitha's offered hand and held it just a moment too long. While she had not felt her dress daring when she had looked at herself in the mirror, Sinclair now stared at her cleavage with such lechery that she second-guessed whether it was more outrageous than she had realised. It was obvious the man was taken with her, which left Tabitha with a dilemma; she and Wolf had agreed to decide in the moment which of their two targets was most appropriate for each of them to engage in conversation. There was no doubt James Sinclair would be very receptive to conversing with her. But would he be too receptive?

During their last investigation, Tabitha had been willing to allow a slimy German count, von Klezter, to flirt with her outrageously during a ball. She had even been willing to risk her honour and go to the man's house, where she almost certainly would have been ravished if not for the dowager's timely, absurd rescue. But she had been willing to endure such indignities because she believed von Kletzer was Melody's abductor. She was unwilling to put herself in a similar situation on Peter Kincaid's behalf.

Tabitha decided to postpone any decision until she had met Dr Trent. She didn't have to wait long to make such an assessment. Finally, an acquaintance pulled James Sinclair away, and Dr Trent was brought to her for introductions.

CHAPTER 13

Dr Richard Trent was as unlike James Sinclair as two men could be; while Sinclair looked like a man who enjoyed life to excess, Trent had the dour looks of a man who never enjoyed anything if he could help it. Tall, thin and grey. Grey hair, cold grey eyes, a grey pallor to his skin, everything about the man screamed puritanical disdain of anything enjoyable. Tabitha's initial judgment was confirmed when Hamish offered him a drink, only to have the man visibly shudder and say, "Need I remind ye, Laird MacAlister, that I dinnae indulge in the devil's fire?"

Hamish looked suitably chastened at the need to be reminded and said, "Aye. Apologies," turning to escape as quickly as possible. Confident that she was in no danger of being importuned by Dr Trent, Tabitha gestured to the now empty spot on the sofa beside her where Lily had sat before being called away by her mother to socialise with their guests. For a moment, it seemed that Dr Trent might refuse to join her. Perhaps he truly was a Puritan and believed her chestnut hair was close enough to the red historically associated with witches. As it happened, Tabitha could imagine Richard Trent heading up a witch hunt. He had that holier-than-thou look about him that seemed to be itching to find wickedness in those around him.

As he finally deigned to join her on the sofa, Tabitha wondered how such a man tolerated a son like Louis. Of course, he would not be the first overly strait-laced, strict father to have a child who rebelled in the most dramatic way possible. Tabitha was now more curious than ever to talk to him and decided to question the man sitting next to her. Wolf could tackle Sinclair. She tried to catch Wolf's eye to indicate her decision. However, he was deep in conversation with a plump, matronly woman who laughed like a hyena and seemed to find everything Wolf said terribly amusing.

Giving up on the chance for any unspoken communications with Wolf, Tabitha decided to make the most of her time with Dr Trent. He did not seem like a man much given to small talk, so she decided to plunge right in, "Dr Trent, I believe you have a son."

If Richard Trent was surprised to have Tabitha mention Louis, he hid it well. "Aye, I have a son, Louis. He is a medical student at the university. Or, at least, he is when he's sober and not whorin'," he added. Catching himself, he immediately apologised, "My deepest regrets for using such language, Lady Pembroke."

"Please do not trouble yourself, Dr Trent. I imagine having a child drawn to the less salubrious side of life must be a great challenge, and it is understandable if this leads you to use harsh language," Tabitha said in what she hoped was a mollifying tone.

Now that the topic of Louis' behaviour had been broached, Trent seemed happy to have a sympathetic ear in which to pour his tale of parental woe. "Ye speak the truth, Lady Pembroke. The boy is a constant challenge tae me. My wife, Jenny, died when he was but a wee bairn and I have tried tae be both mother and father tae the boy, but I fear I have failed tae instill in him any sense of decorum, duty or indeed morality of any sort."

Tabitha considered how much to reveal about what she knew of Louis and said, "Laird MacAlister told me that your son is a medical student. At least that must be a source of pride; your son following in your footstep?"

"Hah!" the man exclaimed, "Proud? Is that what I should be? My son is only studying medicine at the university because the alternative was tae bein' cut off and have tae pay his own gambling debts. As tae whether he might even graduate wi' a degree in medicine, well, that is entirely another matter. If I didnae have as much certainty of my Jenny as I do of myself, I would swear I was nay his sire."

The man's loquaciousness emboldened Tabitha to go further with her question. "As it happens, Dr Trent, I believe your son is friends with a young man whom Lord Pembroke and I are trying to locate. A Peter Kincaid."

As she said Peter's name, the doctor's eyes narrowed, and his mouth became a hard line before he answered, "Louis knows better than to bring any of his ne'er-do-well friends to his father's house. I believe I see Mrs Jackson comin' in an' I promised tae talk tae her about her bunions." With those last words barely out of his mouth, Dr Trent stood abruptly, bowed and took his leave. He left so abruptly that Tabitha had no opportunity to challenge this characterisation of Peter. So abruptly that, if she'd looked down for a moment, he would have been gone by the time she looked back up.

Tabitha pondered the man's words. He certainly had no problem disparaging his son to a total stranger. But the mere mention of his friend, who, by all accounts, was cut from a very different cloth than the dissolute Louis, had the man running away as fast as possible. It now seemed even more imperative that they talk to Louis Trent.

Across the room, Wolf had managed to get James Sinclair alone. He had also decided not to beat around the bush. "Mr Sinclair, Lady Pembroke, and I were summoned to Scotland because the laird's daughter, Lily, believed a friend, Peter Kincaid, has gone missing. I believe Mr Kincaid is also a friend of yours."

Sinclair snorted, "I dinna ken who characterised our relationship as a friendship, but it's nae what it is. Peter Kincaid is an ingrate who was happy tae be the beneficiary of my largesse when it suited him an' then turned an' bit the hand that fed him when it was nae longer convenient tae think aboot where that money cam' frae."

Wolf was interested in hearing Sinclair's version of this story and was curious at his choice of words. The man continued,

"I plucked Kincaid from a life o' poverty an' ignorance an' afforded him the best education Edinburgh can provide. I had him man and boy eat at my table an' benefit from my wisdom and experience. Then when he was admitted tae Edinburgh University tae study medicine, I couldn't have been prouder if he had been my own son, and I offered tae cover whatever expenses his scholarship didn't. I should add, it was an offer he was grateful tae take advantage of."

"He is lucky to have such a benefactor," Wolf said sincerely.

"Aye, a lucky man. But nae a grateful one. O'er the last year, he fell in wi' a bunch of radicals who filled his head wi' nonsense aboot the evils o' industrialists such as me. Peter Kincaid is a highly intelligent young man. However, he's also incredibly naive. He disnae understand the ways o' the world; he's happy tae hae coal in his fireplace tae keep him warm at night but thinks it's possible tae pull that coal frae the earth with nae risk tae life or limb."

Wolf nodded along with the man's narrative but kept silent. Sinclair continued, his already florid complexion becoming even more so as he warmed to his subject, "I was doon the mines as a young lad, and it was the makin' of me. It taught me grit and determination, and it made me a man. But now, there are age limits, and every bairn is tae get an education - what does a miner need with reading and writing?

"And as if that all doesn't make it hard enough for mine owners, now this new compensation act that was passed in the summer expects me tae bear the burden o' any worker foolish enough tae injure himself. But is that enough for Peter? Nae, it isnae! He wants tae restrict the hours that workers can spend doon the mine. And that's just the beginnin' o' it. And who does he think he's protectin'? When ye limit a man's workin' day, ye limit his wages. There was a time when a whole family could be earnin' a living doon the mine, bringin' hame their pay. But they went and put an end tae that, and now women cannae work doon there. What are those families meant tae do? Dreamers like Peter dinnae consider such matters."

Finally, Sinclair seemed to run out of steam, so Wolf prompted him, "And when you and Mr Kincaid fought, he continued to accept your money?"

"Nae! The lad's pride got the better o' him. He told me he could nae longer reconcile his principles wi' taking my money, and he threw my help back in my face. I dinnae know when I've ever been so disappointed in someone."

Sinclair paused, suddenly looking world-weary, even sad, "I never took a spouse, Lord Pembroke. I dinnae have any bairns nor an heir to inherit my business and fortune. There was a time when I regarded Peter as the son I never had, contemplatin' alterin' my will to bestow upon him a significant share. He would have become a man of considerable wealth and influence in due course."

"Did he know you were considering making him your heir?" Wolf asked.

"Aye, he had the audacity tae tell me that if he were tae inherit my fortune, he'd employ it in constructing hospitals and schools. Spoke as if I dinnae already contribute to philanthropic endeavours. As if creating jobs and driving industry has nae virtue in and o' itself. He's an arrogant young pup who thinks he alone knows how tae make the world a better place. Good luck to him, then. But he will nae be doing it wi' my money."

Wolf considered the man's words. It was clear he was still very angry at Peter Kincaid. He hadn't indicated that he knew anything about Peter's supposed disappearance. But then, why would he have had if they had fallen out? He decided there was nothing to be lost by bringing up the subject.

"Mr Sinclair, as I said, my cousin, Lily, believes Peter Kincaid to be missing, and she's asked us to investigate. While we were initially sceptical that this was any more than a young man spending a few days doing, well, what young men are prone to do, we now have reasons to believe that Lily's worries may be well-founded. What is your opinion?"

"Peter Kincaid is stubborn, wilful, and naïve, but he's also the most conscientious, hard-workin', serious-minded young man.

If it were that ne'er-do-well friend of his, Louis Trent, missing, I'd agree that it was likely nae more than whorin', drinkin', and gamblin'. But that isnae who Peter is. I cannae imagine what would be serious enough tae make him intentionally miss classes at the university." Sinclair stated this in a very matter-of-fact tone, showing none of the concern Wolf might have expected when talking about a man he had just described as the closest thing he had to a son.

The man continued, "And if your next question is tae ask if I know where he might be, the answer is, I have nae idea. I havenae spoken with Peter for a few weeks, ever since we argued. I dinnae know why he has disappeared nor where he might be. Now if you'll excuse me..." The man then turned abruptly and walked away. As he left, Dawglish announced dinner.

The meal itself was uneventful. Wolf was seated between the dowager and a very chatty matronly woman, Mrs Hillcrest, who monopolised Wolf, much to the dowager's irritation. Mrs Hillcrest was a founding member of Jane's sewing circle and regaled Wolf with many long and boring gossipy stories about the goings on of the circle's members. Luckily, Mrs Hillcrest was happy to carry on a one-sided conversation. So Wolf nodded occasionally, trying to look interested while his thoughts were taken up by his conversation with James Sinclair.

On the other side of the table, Tabitha was engaged in a more interesting conversation with her neighbour, the MacAlister's lawyer. Mr Arnold Frasier was a gregarious, cheery man who seemed to take genuine pleasure from his profession. He was also a history buff with the rare talent of bringing dry facts to life as he recounted stories of some of Edinburgh's more colourful historical figures.

The dinner was long as course after course was brought out. The food and the wine were of a high enough quality that it was hard to imagine even the dowager could find fault - though she would certainly try. Eventually, even Mr Frasier's stories started to wear on Tabitha. She hoped to find time to confer with Wolf about their respective conversations that evening, but she couldn't imagine when. The gathering was too intimate for them to be able to steal away and not attract attention.

After dinner, with everyone gathered back in the drawing room, Jane sat at the piano and began playing Chopin. Tabitha was pleasantly surprised to discover that her mousey sister-in-law was a marvellous pianist. Jane came alive at the instrument and played with all the passion and fire she lacked in other aspects of her life.

Left to her own devices, Tabitha would have chosen to sit elsewhere, but she had been summoned to sit beside the dowager. Curious about why her mother-in-law would suddenly be interested in her company, she waited to hear what the woman said. Initially, it was very little. When Jane finished her first piece, the dowager said rather too loudly, "At least Jane is musical. She has so little else to recommend her." Her words carried to poor Jane, who flushed with mortification.

When Jane launched into her next piece, the dowager said to Tabitha, rather more quietly this time, "And so what have you learned this evening about the elusive Mr Kincaid?"

Even if Tabitha had been inclined to share her observations with the dowager, she certainly wasn't going to discuss them in the middle of the drawing room in hushed whispers in front of the very people involved. Tabitha was amazed that even the dowager couldn't see the inappropriateness of asking the question there and then. Knowing the woman would not be easily put off, she said, "Dr Trent claims not to know Peter Kincaid." Luckily, the terseness of this answer deterred the dowager from further questions, and they listened to Jane's playing in silence.

It seemed the fashion in Edinburgh society wasn't for the long, drawn-out dinner parties that seemed so in vogue in London. Tabitha reflected that perhaps it was less about Edinburgh and more about the make-up of the guests, many of whom worked for a living and likely had to rise at a decent hour the following day. Whatever the reason, she was grateful when the last guest left long before midnight. Tabitha caught Wolf's eye, and he moved over to stand beside her.

"Do you think we can steal away and talk in the library before bed?" she asked.

Wolf nodded, "Why don't you make your way up now, and I'll follow in a few minutes. I would like to discuss our respective conversations and write notecards while they're still fresh in our minds."

CHAPTER 14

Fifteen minutes later, they were safely ensconced in the library. Wolf noticed a full decanter and glasses and was grateful when he realised the liquid was brandy rather than more scotch whisky. He poured them each a glass while Tabitha told him about her conversation with Trent. "Does Dr Trent know Peter Kincaid?" she asked as she wrote the same question on a notecard.

"The man had been positively chatty on the subject of his son's evil ways, but as soon as I brought up Peter's name, he clammed up and walked away quite abruptly. He talked about Louis' ne'er-do-well friends, which, from everything we've heard, is quite untrue about Peter."

Tabitha wrote the question on a notecard. Dr Trent's behaviour was odd, if nothing else, and she knew better than to pre-judge any potential evidence.

"There's no doubt that we have to track Louis Trent down, but I doubt his father will be much help in that quarter. What did you find out from Sinclair?" Tabitha asked.

"He's a man who is very proud of what he has made of his life and feels that if he had to struggle to pull himself from nothing, others should not get an easier time of it. He made it very clear what he thinks of all the labour laws enacted over the century. It's easy to see why he and someone with Peter's ideals would clash. Sinclair seems to have taken Peter's political activism as a very personal attack. He railed against Peter's naivety but mostly his ingratitude. He sounded very bitter."

Tabitha wrote notecards capturing the main points of Wolf's

narrative and then paused, tapping the pen against her lips as she thought, "Did he say anything that would indicate what Peter meant by blood money?"

"No," Wolf admitted. "But first thing in the morning, I want to send a telegram to my man of business, instructing him to dig into Sinclair's business dealings."

"We have multiple threads to tug on, but none of them seems more likely than any other to help us find Peter. Do we have anything here?" Tabitha had pinned all the notecards to the board, grouping them as made sense. Standing before the board, sipping on her brandy, she looked over their few cards, trying to see patterns. Turning back to Wolf, she asked, "What are our next steps?"

Wolf thought for a moment. A man like Louis Trent kept late hours. Even if they happened to find him home during the day sleeping off the night before, it was unlikely his father would agree to wake him to discuss an investigation he'd made clear he wanted no part of. "I need to ask Hamish where a man like Louis might spend his evenings gambling. Is this like London, and there's a club such as Whites? I assume so. Is this the kind of place a man such as Louis Trent would belong?"

Tabitha knew where this line of thought was going, and she was resigned if irritated; if such a club existed, Wolf would be visiting it without her. She realised this was not a case of his overprotectiveness towards her; these kinds of clubs did not permit women on the premises. While Tabitha briefly flirted with suggesting she don men's clothes again, as she had in their first investigation, she knew Wolf had never considered her disguise sufficiently believable.

Wolf continued, "However, visiting a club is not something I can do until evening, and even then, we can't be sure Louis will be there. But we have to start somewhere."

"And what do we do until then? I would like to find Peter and return to London as soon as possible. I miss Melody, and I worry that the longer she stays with Lord Langley, the harder it might be to persuade either of them that her home is Chesterton

House."

Wolf knew Tabitha felt deeply insecure about her place in Melody's life and affection. She had no legal ties to the child, who seemed inexplicably fond of the man who had abducted her just a few short weeks before. He wasn't sure what to say to put Tabitha's fears to rest. From the first moment she had suggested bringing Melody and Rat into the household and installing the adorable little girl in the nursery, Wolf had known the situation had the potential to be fraught. While he could never have anticipated that the danger would come from the direction of Langley House, he had always worried that something might happen to break Tabitha's heart.

"What are the dowager's plans for Lily tomorrow?" Wolf asked, if only as a distraction.

"Well, the matter of Lily's clothes dealt with, at least for now, I believe tomorrow is deportment and lessons in the who's who list of London society," she answered.

"What is wrong with her deportment?" Wolf asked, genuinely mystified.

"That is a good question. Lily was raised as a lady, educated by the best English governesses and seems, at least as far as I'm concerned, to be a charming, poised young woman. But, of course, my opinion on this hardly matters. I believe the dowager countess has decided that Lily's posture is unbefitting of the granddaughter of an earl."

Given that Wolf could imagine that was a direct quote, he didn't bother to question its inanity.

"I believe the real problem is that Lily is not sufficiently demure. She looks someone in the eye and holds their gaze rather than lowering her eyes and glancing timidly out from under her lashes. She speaks her mind and enters a room with purpose and confidence," Tabitha explained.

"And those are all bad things?" Wolf asked, genuinely confused.

"Well, they are not what is normally expected of a young woman coming out into society."

"Were you like that?" he asked. While Tabitha was always a picture of womanly grace and charm, she had a forthrightness, independence and inner strength that Wolf admired greatly.

"Ha!" Tabitha exclaimed. "Much to my mother's chagrin, I never perfected those skills. I believe it was one of the reasons she was so eager when Jonathan offered for me; she was worried that the longer I was out in society, the more chance there was that I would do something to embarrass her, making me unmarriageable."

Over the months since he had lived at Chesterton House, Wolf had glimpses into Tabitha's unhappy marriage to his cousin, Jonathan. He knew Jonathan had been a controlling, violent spouse, even if he didn't know all the details. Wolf couldn't even imagine how horrific Jonathan's behaviour must have been to cower the bright, vivacious eighteen-year-old Tabitha.

"So, what is the dowager's plan to correct these supposed faults?" Wolf asked.

"Honestly, I have no idea. But I'd rather be out of the house while these lessons take place. I'm afraid that if I'm at hand, it will be too tempting for the dowager to refer to me constantly as a cautionary tale as to where insufficiently thrown back shoulders and decorous behaviour can lead."

Wolf shook his head in bemusement, asking a question that was more rhetorical than anything, "Why does the dowager want Lily to behave more like Jane when all she ever does is berate her daughter for her lack of gumption? In fact, the person Lily most reminds me of is Lady Pembroke!"

Tabitha laughed and said, "For your sake, never mention that to her. Nevertheless, you are completely correct, of course. However, the dowager claims she was a picture of maidenly virtues during her season. But it is hard to believe she was anything other than some younger version of who she is today. However, she is a product of her time. We are almost at the turn of the century, but her views on how a woman should behave are stuck in 1850. At least as far as the rest of us are concerned, that is."

Tabitha was unused to seeing the dowager countess as a sympathetic figure, but as she spoke she thought about the similarities and the contrasts between the older woman and her granddaughter. "I hope that at some point, she will come to realise that Lily has big dreams because she can. Women can study now and go into science, even if the path isn't easy for them. Who knows what the dowager might have dreamed of doing in a world of greater opportunities for women."

Wolf turned back to the topic at hand, "I believe that our next steps should be to learn more about Peter's association with the Scottish Labour Party. It seems that his involvement with the party caused his rupture with James Sinclair. I know nothing of the organisation, but perhaps Lily can shed some light on the matter. I assume we will have to catch her early again tomorrow before her grandmother gets her claws into her. But I'd rather we didn't have to resort to sitting in the garden again first thing in the morning. It's getting a bit too chilly for that."

Tabitha agreed and suggested, "We have this library as our war room now, and we're reasonably confident it's enough out of the way to prevent any casual dowager drop-ins. I've noticed she is using her cane increasingly these days; for support, I suspect, rather than merely for its potential as a weapon. I hope that once she's downstairs, she'll be reluctant to climb the stairs again on the off chance of stumbling across gossip. Why doesn't Ginny deliver a message to Lily through her maid, asking her to meet us here before breakfast."

"Before breakfast?" Wolf asked.

"I'm afraid so. Even though the dowager is not known for being an early riser, she is on a mission, and we can't be sure that she won't expect to start polishing Lily as soon as possible. If she realises that we want to question Lily, she may insist on being part of the conversation, and we need to avoid that at all costs." Tabitha was as fond of her morning coffee as Wolf and added, "I'll have Ginny ask Dawglish to have some coffee and pastries sent up so you don't fade away."

"Talking of Dawglish," Wolf said. "Where is Manning? I know Lady Pembroke said she was bringing him with her to ensure her needs were met. I believe that was her wording. But I haven't seen him since we've been here."

The dowager's butler, Manning, had been falsely accused of murder and had spent a harrowing few weeks in Pentonville Prison. He'd lost a lot of weight during his incarceration and had seemed to age years by the time he was released. "Well, given that the dowager's fears of uncivilised heathens unable to even pour a cup of tea have been unwarranted, I believe she's encouraged poor Manning to view this trip as somewhat of a holiday. Certainly, the poor man could do with a rest." Tabitha explained. She continued, "Though, perhaps it would have been more appropriate to send the man off to the seaside on his own for a real rest, rather than dragging him to Scotland on the off chance she might need someone to open a door for her. But this is the dowager, and, as we saw, Manning is devoted to her. I'm sure he is as grateful for this 'holiday' as she would expect him to be."

It was late, and Tabitha tried unsuccessfully to suppress a yawn. Wolf suggested they retire for the night. There was nothing more they could glean from their conversations and observations that evening and Tabitha happily agreed.

Tabitha had asked that Ginny wake her early the following morning and had given her a note to slip to Lily's maid. She and Wolf had agreed to meet in the library at 8am, and as much as she was exhausted from the late night before, Tabitha dragged herself out of bed and dressed quickly. At home, the dowager was known for rarely emerging from her boudoir before 11am, preferring to breakfast and deal with her correspondence from the comfort of her bed. But who knew what time she might rise when in the midst of a military campaign. Having set her mind to the task of "improving" her granddaughter, she would be quite single-minded and efficient.

Entering the library, Tabitha was relieved that the ever-efficient Dawglish had already placed a pot of coffee and pastries on a side table. She wasn't sure she was ready to eat, but she needed some coffee to be useful to the investigation that morning. Wolf was already sitting in an armchair drinking coffee and happily munching his way through a pastry.

"I will say this for my cousin Jane, she keeps a good table," he commented. "These pastries are delicious." Wolf added, "Did Ginny manage to send a note to Lily?"

"Indeed, she did," Lily answered, entering the room.

Wolf stood and crossed to the door, closing it behind Lily. "I'm intrigued and yet delighted by all the subterfuge. What do you need of me?" Lily asked, crossing to the coffee, and helping herself to a cup.

"Your Aunt Tabitha and I need to not attract your grandmother's attention to our conversations. She is quite focused on preparing you for your season, providing a welcome distraction from any interest she might otherwise have in our activities."

"So, you believe that if she knew what you were doing, she would be less interested in 'fixing' me?" Lily asked, a dangerous gleam entering her eyes.

"Lily, need I remind you that it was at your request that we only told your mother and grandmother a partial truth about your friendship with Peter. If Lady Pembroke insists on becoming involved in our investigations, it will be impossible to keep the full story from her and effectively search for Peter," Tabitha admonished her niece. "Is it worth that sacrifice merely to save yourself from a few dull days of walking with a book on your head and being forced to memorise the family trees of London's best families?"

A suitably chastened Lily hung her head and answered, "No, of course not. You are quite right, Aunt Tabitha; it is not worth the sacrifice." But then, she raised her head, winked at Wolf, and added, "Well, probably not worth it. I reserve the right to revisit this decision after seeing what horrors Grandmama has in store for me today."

The girl was incorrigible, but Tabitha was also sympathetic. Lily was being forced to participate in an archaic ritual towards an end, marriage, in which she had no interest. She was being taken away from her botanical studies to learn the lineages of a group of people in whom she had no interest. And this entire endeavour was being overseen by the dowager countess, a woman not known for holding back on her vicious critiques. But, at least for the time being, they had a plan, and part of that plan was gathering more information while keeping the dowager countess otherwise engaged.

"Lily," Wolf began, "we want to learn more about Peter's involvement with the Scottish Labour Party. What can you tell us about it and the people with whom he was involved? Do you know how long he has been part of the organisation?"

"I know a little," Lily admitted. "When I first met Peter last year, he had just joined the cause. I believe he was first taken to a rally by someone at the university. He told me that he had never thought about politics before that point but that Mr Johnson, the speaker, ignited this flame inside of him.

"Peter's mother had been a maid in a fine house outside of Edinburgh. From what he understood, she had been accosted by one of her master's sons and had fallen pregnant. Once the pregnancy was evident, she was thrown out of the house without money or references. No one cared that the fault had not been hers. She ended up in the workhouse. Peter was born there, and then she left, presumably to try to find new employment. All he had of her was a letter explaining why she had to leave and wishing a better future for him."

Tabitha could well imagine the situation Peter's mother had found herself in. Whether a maid was a willing or unwilling participant in a tryst, she was usually blamed for any ensuing pregnancy. It was the rare master or master's son who took responsibility for his by-blows.

Lily continued, "When Mr Johnson talked about the inequalities in society, the different rules for the upper classes, the unfairness of a system that rewards some for the accident of their births and punishes others, he knew that this was a cause he had to be part of."

Lily's words made Wolf uncomfortable. He knew the truth of the unfairness she spoke of; he was a beneficiary of it. Despite his determination to use his sudden social elevation and unearned fortune to better the lives of those around him, he recognised that such efforts only went so far towards righting the wrongs of society.

"Do you know how we might find this Mr Johnson?" Tabitha asked.

"Actually, I do. There is a rally today. I would have attended, but clearly, I'm to spend my day doing something far more important instead," she said sarcastically. "It's in the Old Town, on Grassmarket. By the White Hart Inn."

"Wonderful! Do you know what time?"

"I believe it is early this afternoon. But if you plan to go, you must dress down as much as possible. And do not take the carriage all the way there. When I went to my first rally, I dressed in my plainest day dress." Given the state of Lily's wardrobe, Tabitha didn't think she would have had as much trouble blending in with the working masses as she seemed to think. But her point was well taken.

Putting her coffee down, Lily stood and walked over to the corkboard. She spent a few minutes reading all the notecards and then said, "Dr Trent denied knowing Peter?"

"He did. Quite vehemently, in fact," Tabitha told her. Now that the topic of Louis Trent had come up, Tabitha had to have her curiosity satiated, "From what we've heard about Peter and Louis Trent, they seem an odd pairing. In fact, Louis sounds like Peter's total opposite; dissolute, unserious about his studies, selfish and self-indulgent. Do you know how and why they became friends?"

"Da has known Dr Trent for many years. I wouldn't say he and Da are friends, but Da respects him, and our families socialise. Louis is a few years older than I am, so I don't know him well. But he has come to dinner occasionally, and your assessment of him is correct. He is a rake in every sense of the word. From what I've overheard recently, Louis has racked up huge gambling debts all around town. Dr Trent agreed to pay them only on condition that Louis attend medical school."

"From what we've heard, Louis may be enrolled, but that seems to be the extent of his university career," Wolf observed.

"Indeed, what Dr Trent thought he would achieve with such bribery is unclear," Lily agreed. "But as to how he and Peter became acquainted, I believe they met in one of Dr Trent's classes." Seeing the confused look on Tabitha and Wolf's faces, she explained, "Dr Trent teaches anatomy at the university. Apparently, even an unrepentant wastrel like Louis realised it was in his best interests to turn up for his father's lectures. He and Peter sat next to each other and struck up a conversation. As unlikely a pairing as they seem, they enjoyed each other's company and became friends. It was through Louis that Peter met Vivian."

"Vivian?" Wolf asked.

"Heavens, did I forget to mention Vivian? She is the woman Peter is in love with and hopes to marry," Lily exclaimed. On seeing Tabitha's eyebrows rise, Lily pointed out, "I did tell you that my friendship with Peter was purely platonic. He met Vivian Wakely just before I attended the rally and heard him speak; so, about a year ago. When we met and spoke, he admitted he was in love with a woman far above his station. But that, amazingly, his feelings were reciprocated.

"I did not know Vivian well, at the time. Again, she is a year or so older than I am, and our fathers do not get along, but her mother calls on Mama regularly, and Vivian often comes along. Once Peter had told me about their romance, I made an excuse the next time she and her mama visited and asked Vivian to join me for a stroll in the garden. I mentioned Peter and what he had told me, and she seemed so relieved to have someone to confide in. Shortly after, we left Edinburgh, but we corresponded regularly, and she shared all the details of their romance. Obviously, her parents have no idea. If they did, they would surely forbid her from seeing Peter again." Tabitha did not doubt this.

Lily continued, "She hopes that once he is a doctor, her father will view a marriage more kindly. Of course, Peter still has at least a year of medical school and must then do an apprenticeship. And that might take two years, maybe three. But Vivian is determined to wait for him. While she has not told her parents about Peter, she has told them she is unwilling to marry. Her grandmother left her a large fortune. When she is twenty-one and of age, she plans to introduce her parents to Peter and hopes they will accept her choice."

The entire tale sounded like wishful thinking to Tabitha, but she kept her cynicism to herself. However, she did ask, "When Peter failed to attend the rally and your meeting, did you ask Vivian what she knew of his whereabouts?"

"She is away in Inverkeithing visiting her sister, who is enceinte and now towards the end of her confinement. I didn't want to write and alarm her at such a delicate time. I hoped you and Cousin Jeremy would find Peter, and the letter would never need to be sent."

That seemed a reasonable enough plan, so Tabitha didn't push the topic further. But she did have one more question, "How are Louis and Vivian connected?"

"She is his cousin on his mother's side," Lily answered. "Louis and Peter were in Princes Street Gardens one afternoon, and Vivian was strolling with a friend. Louis introduced her to Peter. Apparently, it was love at first sight."

"Lily, it is possible that Peter has written to Vivian and that she knows where he is. I do appreciate why you've tried to protect her, but if we don't make significant progress soon, it may be necessary to contact her," Tabitha explained gently.

There didn't seem to be anything more they could learn from Lily. Tabitha wrote a notecard for Vivian and pinned it to the board. Lily watched and then stood to join her. "What an ingenious method," she said. "I wonder if I should adopt this concept for my studies." She noted the grouping of cards and continued, "I can see how this might help me better to identify patterns in my observations. So simple and yet quite ingenious." Tabitha blushed with pleasure; Lily might be only eighteen years old and naive and innocent in many ways, but she was also a scientist, and her praise meant a lot to Tabitha.

The notecards grouped and pinned, they all went down to the breakfast room. Wolf had impressed on both of them the importance of behaving as normally as possible so as not to cause the dowager to suspect they were sneaking around behind her back. Behaving normally meant eating in the breakfast room even though, thanks to the pastries, they may no longer be hungry.

The prudence of meeting in the library was confirmed when they found the dowager at the breakfast table far earlier than normal. She was ready and raring to go, announcing on their entry, "About time too! Where have you all been? It is almost 9am, Lily, and we have no time to waste."

They all sat down, and the footman poured more coffee for Tabitha and Wolf and tea for Lily. The dowager continued, "Lily, today will be mostly assessment. Of course, I have some idea how bad the situation is, but I need a fuller picture of what I have to work with." Narrowing her eyes and glaring at her granddaughter, she sniffed and said, "And that assessment begins immediately with the observation that you have an unfortunate tendency to roll your shoulders when dining. Your back must be rigidly straight at all times, and any movement comes only at the elbow. Watch me."

With this, the dowager lifted her teacup and brought it to her mouth. "Now you try," the dowager demanded. Tabitha could see the young woman's irritation and inclination to argue for the absurdity of such rules. Catching Lily's eye, Tabitha smiled and shook her head; Lily had no choice but to subject herself to these lessons and critiques, and, ultimately, she was better off doing as she was told with minimal debate on the topic.

Tabitha saw the moment the fight went out of Lily, and she resigned herself to her fate and did her utmost to drink from her teacup as instructed. Luckily, the dowager's attention was drawn away from her granddaughter's apparent inability to drink a cup of tea in a sufficiently ladylike manner by the arrival of Dawglish bearing letters for her and Tabitha.

The handwriting on both envelopes was identical, with the name and address of the sender engraved in the top left corner of the heavy-weight, quality paper; Maxwell Sandworth, Earl of Langley. Each woman eagerly opened her respective envelope. Inside each was a sheet of equally high-quality paper covered in the same sprawling handwriting as the envelope. But another sheet of paper elicited a gasp from Tabitha; it was a drawing from Melody with a few words written underneath. The stick-figure drawing was of a little girl holding the hand of a man with one hand and a dog's lead with the other. Under the drawing was scrawled, "Dear Tabby Cat, I miss you but am having lots of fun. Dodo says woof."

The dowager's picture was just of Melody and Dodo, and said, "Dear Granny, I miss you, and Dodo does too." Tabitha could have sworn the dowager's eyes were wet as she read her note from Melody. Assured that the little girl was fine, Tabitha quickly read Langley's letter. He had sent the same basic information to the dowager and Tabitha but was a smart enough man to know that it would win him points with the old woman if she received her own letter.

The letter mostly catalogued how well Melody was doing with her studies. This much was evidenced by the letter she had written. He also talked about her chess game and mentioned that he had started teaching her to play the piano. During Melody's last unauthorised stay with "Uncle Maxi", he had not been able to take her out of his house for fear of being seen. But on this second visit, he could take the child wherever he saw fit, so an entire paragraph was dedicated to their visit to the Natural History Museum.

It seemed the dowager's letter had included the same detail because she looked up from reading and announced, "I will have something to say to Langley when I return home. I was to be the one to take Melody to the Natural History Museum. In fact, if memory serves me correctly, I could not do so when planned because he abducted the child before I had a chance. And now he has the audacity to swoop in and take her before I could reschedule our visit. Tabitha, you assured me that my time with Melody would always take precedence over Langley's."

Tabitha sighed, there was no way to win this particular debate, but she did point out, "Mama, the museum is very large and endlessly entertaining for children. I'm sure that Lord Langley's trip there with Melody will merely whet her appetite for future visits with you."

The dowager harrumphed but said no more about it.

CHAPTER 15

After breakfast, Tabitha went to find Ginny to ask her to find Lily's maid, Grace, and ask her if she could borrow one of Lily's gowns, preferably the oldest one available. Luckily, Lily was as tall as Tabitha, and Ginny could work her sewing magic if necessary.

Wolf spent the rest of the morning composing telegrams to his solicitor and his man of business, asking them to look into Sinclair's businesses. He then composed one for Andrews, a London journalist he trusted and had previously shared news scoops with and received information from. He wasn't sure if stories about Sinclair's business would be of interest to London papers, but it couldn't hurt to ask. He also sought out Hamish, hiding in his study yet again.

Wolf had talked to Tabitha about how to approach Hamish with what he wanted to know. Like James Sinclair, Hamish had made much of his fortune from coal mines. Wolf didn't want to be heavy-handed when discussing workers' conditions down the mines and potentially offend his host. However, he wanted to understand whether Peter Kincaid's concerns were nothing more than the idealistic beliefs of a naive young man who didn't understand how the world worked. Or if his use of the phrase "blood money" might refer to some true rot in the Sinclair empire.

Tabitha had suggested that he approach the matter cautiously. Hamish was a gracious host and a loving father, but they had no idea how he was as a businessman. It was hard to believe he could be anything other than the jovial, kindly man they had experienced, but it was possible.

Sitting in the chair opposite Hamish, Wolf thought about Tabitha's words. He wished she was with him, but they'd agreed this was a conversation better had man to man. Given how infrequently Tabitha agreed that he should conduct a part of an investigation alone, he knew she must feel strongly that it was the best move.

"Wolf, how can I help ye?" Hamish asked.

"I hope I'm not bothering you," Wolf asked, gesturing to the pile of papers in front of the other man.

"Dinnae fash, what do ye need?"

"Hamish, I know that much of your fortune comes from coal mines," he began.

"Aye. My father diversified into coal mines when I was a wee laddie, and it's how he made the bulk of his fortune, ye ken. He'd inherited some land and a bit o' money, but he kent whit the future held. He could see the demand for coal driven by factories and steam engines. He had the opportunity tae acquire some mines at a bonnie price, and those were the first he owned."

Now came the part where Wolf had to tread carefully. He thought about the words he wanted to use and said, "Hamish, on inheriting the earldom, I also became the owner of many businesses throughout the country. I've been trying to understand more fully what my holdings are and understand the industries they're in. Frankly, it seems my cousin Jonathan was neither a good landlord nor a considerate employer. While many of the labour laws passed this century put certain obligations on him and men like him, it seems Jonathan walked as close to the lines those laws drew as possible. And, in some cases, may have crossed those lines where he believed he could get away with it. I have been doing my best to rectify these situations."

Wolf paused again. Hamish hadn't interrupted him, but his face had become quite stern, and Wolf was unsure whether that was at the thought of Jonathan's business practices or the idea that Wolf did not approve and was trying to reverse them. If

Wolf had hoped Hamish would make this conversation easy for him, he was disappointed.

Trying to prompt the man again, he said, "I know that the mining industry has been particularly regulated over the last forty or fifty years."

Unsure where he was going to go with that thought, Wolf was grateful that Hamish finally interrupted him, "Aye, and a good thing too. A colliery is nae place for a woman or a bairn. Doon ma mines, we go further than the law demands."

This was the opening Wolf had been waiting for. "It seems Mr Sinclair does not agree with you," Wolf said. "In fact, he made the case that in preventing young children and women from working in the mines, the government has taken away the opportunity for work that families need so badly."

"Hah! Aye, Sinclair was on that soapbox again, was he? I've heard him make that argument a hundred times. He's a fierce opponent o' ony government regulation o' the industry. I'm sure he told ye his thoughts on the workers' compensation laws and dinnae get him started on tae Coal Mines Act passed recently."

"Indeed, he did," Wolf acknowledged. "I take it you don't agree with him."

"Ma Da was a man much like James Sinclair, ye ken. Naethin' was mair important tae him than business and makin' money. There was a tremendous methane explosion at one o' his mines when I was a laddie, maybe nae mair than eleven years auld. I happened tae be wi' him at the colliery that day, and I mind watchin' them rescue the men and boys, some o' them ma ain age. I asked ma Da why bairns worked in his mines, and he told me the favour he was doin' them and their families by givin' them honest employment. But it didnae look like a favour tae me when I saw their battered, ruined bodies bein' pulled oot o' the mine that day."

Hamish paused, lost in memories for a moment, then continued, "I kent then that when I was in charge, I wad dae things differently, and I hae. The country needs coal tae function. The mines hae offered good jobs tae generations o' local men. But that disnae give us the right tae run those mines however we please."

Wolf was heartened to hear these words, but he had to ask, "If you believe this, how do you reconcile a friendship with a man such as Sinclair?"

Hamish laughed, "Ye're still a young man, Wolf. And ye're new tae the world o' business. If I shunned every man whose business practices didnae match mine, I'd never hae anyone tae share ma dinner table wi'."

Wolf wasn't sure he could make such compromises, but he kept that thought to himself. However, he had one more question, "How far do you believe Sinclair might go in skirting laws he doesn't agree with?"

Hamish paused again, considering the question. Finally, he answered, "Tae be honest, I'm nae sure. Because I ken his views on the industry are sae different frae mine, I try tae keep our relationship purely social. However, I hae heard some rumours ower the years. Naethin' solid, mind ye. But rumours o' corners bein' cut, some unsafe workin' conditions. Naethin' that could ever be proven."

Did Peter Kincaid hear some of these rumours and confront his benefactor with them? Was that the real cause of their falling out? Even if this were true, it didn't explain why Peter was now missing. But it might explain what he meant by "blood money".

Finally, Wolf asked Hamish about what club a gentleman such as Louis Trent might frequent.

"Ach, Louis Trent isnae a member of ma club, the New Club. From whit I heard, he does his gaming at a far less reputable establishment," Hamish answered.

Frustrated at this dead-end, but thanking Hamish for his time, Wolf went to his room. When Thompson packed for the trip, Wolf had the foresight to ensure his thief-taking outfit was included. Wolf wasn't sure what Thompson had been told by the rest of the staff about his new master's unorthodox prior career, but whatever he thought, he had packed the clothes without comment.

Wolf hadn't seen much of Bear since they'd arrived in Edinburgh. He understood his friend's unwillingness to subject himself to family meals with the dowager. But Wolf wanted the enormous man to join them for the rally excursion. So, on finding Thompson in his room, he asked him to track Bear down.

While Wolf had finally acknowledged his need for a real valet, he still felt uncomfortable having another person help dress and undress him. Sending Thompson off to find Bear gave Wolf the perfect opportunity to change into his thief-taking clothes unassisted. By the time Bear joined him, Wolf was putting on his well-worn boots.

Taking in Wolf's outfit, Bear said, "I'm assuming I should also change?"

Wolf nodded, "We're going to take the laird's coach part of the way and then walk."

"Walk to where?" Bear inquired.

"We're going to a political rally for the Scottish Labour Party," Wolf informed him.

"Are we? Then I'll make sure I'm armed. Who knows what trouble we might run into."

In truth, Bear's size was usually enough to deter most trouble, but Wolf knew there was no harm in being prepared for any eventuality. He had his revolver hidden in his boot.

Over lunch, Wolf and Tabitha had been careful to mention their outing that afternoon in the most casual of ways, so as not to alert the dowager that she might be missing out on the fun. She knew they were investigating Peter's disappearance. After all, that had been why she'd demanded their presence in Edinburgh. But as far as the dowager knew, there was no reason to believe anything nefarious might have happened to him. They wanted her to continue in that belief for as long as possible and had decided the best course of action was to tell her they were returning to the university to ask more questions.

As it happened, she had been so consumed with criticising everything Lily did, from how she held her fork to how much of the food on her plate she consumed, that the dowager barely noticed when they made their excuses for the afternoon.

Finally, having safely escaped the house without further scrutiny, Tabitha, Wolf, and Bear sat in the carriage as it made its way to the Old Town. After a brief discussion with the coachman about where he should let them off, they arranged for him to drop them on the Royal Mile, where they would then make their way on foot down the hill towards Grassmarket. The Royal Mile ran through the heart of the Old Town, sloping gently uphill from the eastern end near the Palace of Holyroodhouse toward the western end near Edinburgh Castle, connecting the two significant, historic landmarks.

CHAPTER 16

The cobblestoned Royal Mile was lined with shops, taverns, and homes. The architecture was a jumble of periods and styles, medieval, Renaissance, and some more modern buildings crammed next to each other. The buildings had narrow facades, stone or plaster exteriors, and distinctive Scottish, crow-stepped gables. The eclectic mix of tailors, inns, bookstores, and other small businesses stores were adorned with colourful signs advertising the delights within. But the Royal Mile was also lined with dangerously overcrowded tenement buildings.

Everywhere Tabitha looked, the streets were teeming with people; vendors hawking their wares, street performers, and children playing. They followed the coachman's directions and made their way to Grassmarket. The most notable aspect of Grassmarket was Edinburgh Castle looming over it. Tabitha took a moment to admire the fortification perched upon Castle Rock. The castle complex was a patchwork quilt of buildings from varying periods, some from as far back as the 12th century. Its imposing silhouette, standing guard over the city, was a reminder of Edinburgh's long, proud heritage even as it now watched over the poorest, most disenfranchised of its citizens.

A raised platform had been set up at the end of Grassmarket nearest the castle, and Wolf, Tabitha and Bear made their way down the cobblestone street towards it. A crowd had already gathered, some carrying banners, some flags. A band of musicians were on the platform playing, food vendors were to the side calling out their wares, and the entire rally had more of the feel of a carnival than of anything else. Of course, Tabitha had never been to a political rally, so she had nothing to compare it to. Lily had warned them to be careful not to signal their rank and wealth and, in doing so, had made the rally sound dangerous. But from what Tabitha could see so far, it seemed no more dangerous than the fairs held at Hampstead Heath. Which was to say, rife with pickpockets, but overall a scene of general merriment.

Luckily, Bear's presence was enough to warn off any would-be pickpockets, and the group stood off to the side in Grassmarket, observing the scene around them unbothered by anyone. They had been standing there a few minutes when the band ceased to play, and the platform started filling up with a variety of people. Some chairs had been placed on the platform, and there was some shuffling around as people chose which seat to take. Meanwhile, the crowd became restless, impatient for something more interesting to watch.

Finally, a tall man walked onto the stage. Before he even opened his mouth, he had a commanding presence. Indeed, when he held up his hand to the crowd, all the chattering ceased, and a stillness came over the many people who had now gathered in front of the platform. He stood there holding his hand out until the crowd was almost silent. Tabitha marvelled at how he had managed that without saying a word. A calmness radiated off him that seemed to influence the people standing before him.

Finally, the man spoke. Tabitha judged him to be perhaps in his early thirties. He was pleasant looking with piercing blue eyes. But the most remarkable thing about him was his voice; it was a deep, rich baritone with an almost singsong tone, which was quite hypnotising. Tabitha suspected the man would make a fine addition to a choir. Tabitha felt he could have been saying anything, and still could have beguiled his audience.

"Brothers and sisters," the man began. "My name is Angus Johnson." So, this was the man they had come to talk to. He continued, "A'm a workin' man, juist like yersel'. My faither was a workin' man, workin' doon the coal mines frae the age o' six. His mither, my granny, died in a minin' accident when my faither wis seven. His faither wis injured in a mine explosion an' lost his leg. They received nae compensation frae the mine owner, an' if it hadn't been for the pittance my faither an' his twa brithers brought hame frae workin' doon the mine, the family wid hae starved. They worked twal' oors a day, sometimes mair. My faither suffered fae miner's lung, an' by the time he passed at thirty-two, he could barely utter a sentence withoot wheezin' an' coughin'."

The man was a compelling storyteller, and Tabitha was caught up in his narrative. He spun a story of mine and factory owners getting rich off the backs of workers who barely made enough money to feed their families despite working long, back-breaking hours.

As Angus continued, the entranced crowd periodically cheered as he spoke of workers from industries ranging from whisky distilling, shipbuilding, textiles, and more, and the various injuries, illnesses and particular travails attached to each. Then he spoke of employers who were skirting the various laws passed to try to improve the lot of workers. He didn't name names, but as he spoke, the occasional jeer and comment would be thrown out from the crowd.

Tabitha wondered how many people in the crowd worked in the industries Angus was talking about. After all, even though it was a Saturday, only some industries gave half days. Whoever they were, the people in the crowd were sympathetic to Angus' tale. Sympathetic for husbands, brothers, fathers, and sons who worked in factories or down coal mines.

Tabitha looked out at the crowd and realised that these people were amongst those who enabled her life to be so comfortable with their daily labours. Yet, she knew next to nothing about the nature of their work or the conditions they endured. Listening to Angus' recitation of a catalogue of miseries supposedly endured by the average Scottish worker, she felt a pang of overwhelming guilt. She was so caught up in these thoughts that it was quite a shock when Wolf whispered into her ear, "Don't stop looking ahead, but I believe we're being observed."

Unsure what he meant, Tabitha whispered back, "What do you mean, observed?"

"I believe we have been followed here, and that person is now observing us," Wolf explained. His initial instinct had been not to say anything to Tabitha. But he'd been trying to share more with her and protect her less, so having told Bear this information, he knew he had to share it with Tabitha as well.

"How can you tell?" Tabitha asked. She knew that Wolf and Bear had an assortment of skills from their thief-taking days that she had no clue about until the moment it was revealed that Wolf could break into safes or pick locks. As soon as she asked the question, she realised that spotting someone following them was likely one such skill.

"I thought I saw a cab following us when we left New Town. But I wasn't sure. But that man over at the corner of the street there is trying too hard to be inconspicuous and, despite an effort at dressing down, his clothes are too clean and too obviously well-made." Wolf added, "Of course, I'm sure the same could be said of our efforts to blend in."

Wolf moved closer to Tabitha to continue talking as inconspicuously as possible, "Everyone else on Grassmarket is watching the stage, but he's watching us. And all he's done is watch us."

Realising she didn't want to be obvious in her observations and make clear to the man that his cover had been exposed, Tabitha continued to turn her head towards the stage but turned her eyes towards where she thought Wolf meant. It wasn't easy to keep her head from moving in that direction, but as luck would have it, as Angus Johnson became even more passionate in his speech, he began to walk the stage, and so it was not suspicious that she turned her head to follow his movements. When she did, Tabitha immediately saw who Wolf meant.

She wasn't sure the man would have stood out to her if she hadn't known what she was looking for. But now that she did,

Wolf's explanation made sense; the man wasn't dressed as a gentleman, but his attempts to dress as a working man were too perfect. The people surrounding him were dressed in worn, frayed, and sometimes even torn clothes. Clothes that hadn't been washed as frequently as they might be. These people had tired, care-worn faces, old beyond their years. Most people in the crowd appeared undernourished, and many looked sickly. But the man watching them had a ruddy, healthy complexion and looked well-fed and content. His clothes were clean, pressed, and while not fancy, they were not old and well-worn.

"What do we do?" Tabitha whispered.

"Nothing," Wolf answered. "Someone cares that we're investigating Peter's disappearance. That in and of itself is useful information. It makes it even less likely that he has merely left town for a few days. Now that we know we're being watched, we'll be careful, and we can use that information to our advantage."

This made sense to Tabitha, but still, she had to ask, "So, do we not talk to Angus today?"

"We might as well try to. Whoever is having us followed now knows the line of inquiry we're making. After all, we didn't come to a political rally in disguise for the fun of it. Whether we talk to Mr Johnson or not is irrelevant; our intention is clear."

And so, they stood and listened to Angus Johnson preach his gospel of workers' rights and reparations from the ruling classes while keeping a discreet eye on the man observing them. It was unclear how long they might have to stand there. Once Angus had finished speaking, would he stay on the platform for the rest of the rally? Luckily, this question was answered a few minutes later when he spoke one last rousing declaration of workers' empowerment and then ceded the stage to a far less dynamic speaker. Raising his arms as if anticipating a future victory, Angus Johnson walked off the stage to the cheers and claps of an adoring crowd. As soon as it was clear he was leaving the platform, Wolf indicated to Tabitha and Bear, and they made their way through the throngs of people to get nearer to the steps leading off the platform.

They were not the only people eager to speak with the fiery young orator, but after a few words of congratulations and slaps on the back, most people went back to listening to the next speaker or lost interest. Eventually, they wandered back to whatever they were supposed to be doing on a Saturday afternoon.

Bear's size and deceptively unnerving visage were usually enough to get someone's attention, and Angus Johnson was no exception. As the threesome approached, he looked over, startled at the enormous man coming in his direction. Wolf had much experience finding the right balance when using Bear's fearsomeness to his advantage and quickly strode out in front calling Angus Johnson's name.

"Mr Johnson, might we have a word?" he asked in as unthreatening a tone as possible. Bear's presence usually guaranteed a positive answer to this question, and this time was no exception.

"Aye," the other man said guardedly, unsure what this well-spoken Englishman and his giant friend might want with him.

"Perhaps we can adjourn to the establishment across Grassmarket," Wolf pointed to The White Hart Inn, "and I can buy you something to drink."

"Aye, I'll tak' a wee dram if ye're payin'," the other man said. Angus Johnson was a sharp man with good reason to be suspicious of strangers; his work for the Scottish Labour Party and his very vocal condemnation of the local mine and factory owners had made him many enemies. But despite his caution, he was curious as to what these fancy folks - because he didn't doubt that, despite their efforts to dress down, that's what they were - wanted from the likes of him.

The group made their way across Grassmarket, which took longer than it might have as people in the crowd congratulated Angus on his fine speech and wanted to shake his hand. Wolf noticed the man following them move away from his post, keeping a distance from them but determined not to let them out of his sight. Finally, they pushed their way into the inn, and Wolf led them to the saloon section. He felt uncomfortable enough taking Tabitha into such an establishment. He certainly didn't need to have this conversation in the public bar, which was full to bursting with working men, while the saloon was much less crowded. Wolf steered them towards a table that afforded the most privacy, and Bear went to the bar to get their drinks. Tabitha had declined a drink; it was early afternoon, and she couldn't imagine there was anything the White Hart Inn served that she could stomach so early in the day.

Finally, with whisky in hand for the three men, Angus Johnson asked, "Aye, it's all very pleasant, but why wad a fine talkin' Englishman like yersel' want tae buy a labour agitator like me a drink?"

Wolf took a deep breath, exchanged a look with Tabitha and said, "We want to ask you about Peter Kincaid." Whatever Angus Johnson had been expecting, the surprised look on his face made it evident that wasn't it. Wolf continued, "My young cousin, Lily MacAlister," he purposely left off the honorific, "is a friend of Mr Kincaid's, and she is concerned about his well-being."

"Is she now?" was Angus' only reply.

"Apparently, they have been corresponding about the various causes you and Mr Kincaid are fighting for and to which my cousin is very sympathetic." A raised eyebrow was all the response this got. It was unclear if Angus knew who Lily was or not, and so also not clear if any scepticism was about her rank or her gender. Or perhaps both. "Lily has recently returned to Edinburgh and was supposed to meet Mr Kincaid after a rally more than a week ago, but he never turned up. Lily became worried and asked me," Wolf paused, then added, "and my associates, to look into Mr Kincaid's whereabouts."

"Associates, ye say?" Angus asked, looking pointedly at Tabitha. "Let's begin wi' ye givin' me yer names; yer real names."

With another glance at Tabitha, which she answered with a slight nod, Wolf sighed and said, "I am Jeremy Chesterton, the Earl of Pembroke." Wolf pointed to Tabitha, "This is

Lady Pembroke." Wolf decided not to overcomplicate things by explaining his relationship with Tabitha, ending with, "And this is my private secretary, Mr Caruthers," he said, gesturing towards Bear.

"Shouldnae ye be o'er in New Town instead o' slummin' it o'er here on Grassmarket?" Angus asked sarcastically. "Aye, so lords are investigatin' fer the common folk now?"

Wolf sighed again. He should have known this wouldn't be easy. Somehow, during his thief-taking career, his obviously well-bred and educated voice and demeanour hadn't been too much of a hindrance. They hadn't gone unnoticed, but they'd often been an asset, enabling him to command a certain respect. But somehow, something had changed in the few months since he'd ascended to the earldom. Perhaps it was nothing more than having Tabitha by his side. Certainly, there was something in her bearing that even the drabbest, most worn dress could not bely; she was a lady of rank.

"I inherited the earldom quite recently," Wolf explained. "Before that, Mr Caruthers and I earned our keep as investigators."

"Aye, is that a fact? So ye want tae ken aboot Peter, dae ye?" Angus asked. But then, deciding he had tweaked Wolf's nose enough, he told them what they wanted to hear.

CHAPTER 17

Thirty minutes later, they left Angus Johnson at the inn, tucking into a pie and on his second "wee dram". They walked back up the hill to the Royal Mile, the man tailing them always keeping a careful distance away, assuming he was unnoticed. As they walked, they discussed what Angus had told them. It was clear that Peter's dedication to the causes espoused by the Scottish Labour Party was genuine and almost as passionate as Angus' own. Angus had called Peter Kincaid "a loyal foot soldier," if a little green perhaps. But what he lacked in experience, Peter made up for with a willingness to do whatever it took to fight the injustices of a system he felt had been stacked against him since conception.

"It's interesting that Peter seems to have felt himself a victim of the vagaries of life," Tabitha mused. "After all, someone might hear Peter's story and draw exactly the opposite conclusion."

"What do you mean?" Bear asked. He'd kept quiet throughout the conversation with Angus Johnson, but he'd formed his own opinion about the story the man had told. "He was the illegitimate son of a maid turned out of her home and job by the master who'd taken advantage of her. Abandoned by his mother, he grew up in an orphanage. I can see why he felt life had been unfair."

"And yet," Tabitha pointed out, "he was then plucked from that orphanage and given the best education possible in Scotland. He had the friendship of a wealthy man who continued to support him financially as he worked his way towards his chosen career. Indeed, he could have been Sinclair's heir and would have worked his way from an illegitimate child born in a workhouse to inheriting enormous wealth and influence. That Sinclair did not make him his heir seems to have been almost entirely Peter's choice. While he certainly started out life seemingly born under an unlucky star, he quickly became far more fortunate than most children, even ones starting off with a better chance in life."

"I suppose that's true," Bear conceded as they continued to walk back down the hill towards where they'd left the carriage earlier. Wolf wondered what the man keeping track of them would do once they were in the carriage. From what he'd seen so far, there certainly didn't seem to be much opportunity to find a hackney cab in the Old Town.

Tabitha began discussing the most interesting part of their conversation with Angus, but Wolf subtly indicated that the man was still behind them, albeit at a distance. "Let's wait until we're in the carriage," he said.

Finally, seated and on their way back to New Town, Tabitha said, "I believe we now have an idea what Peter meant by 'blood money', at least."

Wolf agreed, "It would seem to be the case. Certainly, Peter's suspicions that Sinclair was flouting the Coal Mines Act, putting in place insufficient safety measures, continuing to employ underage boys, pressuring workers not to report accidents and then falsifying records and bribing inspectors to cover it all up would seem a good enough reason to call any support he received from Sinclair by that name."

Tabitha chewed her lip, always a sign that she was thinking through a problem, "But how did Peter come to know this? Or did he merely suspect it? Did he have proof?" she wondered aloud.

"Certainly, Angus had no idea," Wolf said. "I think the bigger question is, did Peter confront Sinclair with what he knew or at least suspected? And if he did, does that have anything to do with his disappearance? If Angus is telling the truth, he didn't realise Peter was missing and knows nothing about any conversation he might have had with Mr Sinclair."

Bear added, "And why are we being followed? Certainly, that indicates someone is worried about our investigation." The other two nodded in agreement. They were mostly silent for the rest of the ride back to Charlotte Square; each lost in their reflections of what they'd learned from Angus Johnson.

Arriving back at the MacAlister home, Tabitha was barely through the front door when she was confronted by the dowager in high dudgeon, always something of which Tabitha was leery.

"Where on earth have you all been?" the old woman demanded. And then, only just noticing Tabitha's outfit, "And why are you dressed like that? Tabitha, don't tell me that Jane's utter lack of taste and style is rubbing off on you after only a few days. Heaven forbid!" Then noticing Wolf in his thief-taking outfit bringing up the rear of the group, the dowager narrowed her eyes and asked, "Have you been investigating without me?"

Tabitha sighed and answered patiently, "Mama, you were the one who asked us to investigate. And didn't we agree that you are too busy preparing Lily for her season to join us?" Tabitha wished for nothing more than to retire to her room, wash the dust of Old Town off, and change her clothes. She certainly had no desire to engage in the usual absurd brinkmanship with her mother-in-law.

"I'm not sure I agreed to any such thing. And even if I did, I assumed that only meant I would be sitting out the more mundane aspects of the investigation. But by the looks of you all, I believe I have been left out of high jinks."

Tabitha sighed again. There was no doubt that the dowager had previously been of use, particularly in their last investigation. And she knew it was futile to believe they could make use of the woman's particular skills only when it suited them and then expect that she would be willing to miss out on any aspects she deemed "fun".

Before Tabitha could formulate a suitable response, the dowager continued, "And while you were gone, a telegram arrived from Langley."

This news sent Tabitha into an immediate panic; why would Lord Langley be sending a telegram unless there was a problem with Melody?

Seeing the look on Tabitha's face, the dowager took pity on the younger woman. She said, "There is nothing wrong." Then she added, "Well, at least nothing is wrong with Melody."

So far, the conversation had been conducted in the vestibule, the front door still open with Wolf standing just inside it. The dowager indicated they should follow. All thoughts of changing her clothes crowded out by concern for her ward, Tabitha, Wolf and even Bear traipsed into the drawing room where Jane and Lily were waiting. Tabitha was happy to see a pot of tea and indicated to the ever-present Dawglish that she would like a cup. Then, seating herself on the sofa next to Lily, she said, "Mama, now please explain. Or better yet, where is the telegram?"

As it happened, the telegram was on the side table next to the chair the dowager had now claimed as her own whenever they were all gathered in the room. The dowager pointed to it, and Wolf took it over to Tabitha, who read it quickly and then read it again out loud, her tone one of both relief and bemusement.

"Mother arrived. Must leave home. Arriving Edinburgh today. Melody, Rat, and Dodo with me."

Looking over at Jane, Tabitha said apologetically, "It appears we are to be the cause of yet more guests descending upon you. I assume you know Maxwell Sandworth, Earl of Langley."

Jane nodded, "Mama and the earl's mother were friendly when I first came out, so I have a passing acquaintance with him. But why is he coming here, and who are Melody, Rat, and Dodo?"

There was so much to explain. Not the least of the explanation was the dowager countess' threat at the end of their last investigation to summon Lady Langley to London by reporting on the so-called alarming state of her son's house and suggesting his mother immediately rectify such an untenable situation. While Lady Langley might not care whether her son had been neglectful in decorating and maintaining his London home, the very idea that the Dowager Countess of Pembroke might spread such gossip throughout high society was enough to spur Langley's mother to abandon her pastoral peace in Cornwall and head to London.

Tabitha was actually surprised the woman hadn't arrived sooner. After all, the dowager had threatened to write to her more than three weeks ago. This was answered by the dowager's next comment, accompanied by a self-righteous sniff, "Why, I sent Fiona that letter more than a week ago. It certainly took her long enough to take action."

Noting the look of curiosity on Tabitha's face and correctly interpreting it, the dowager added, "Despite my threats, I held off sending the letter for a few weeks. Fiona Sandworth really is a crashing bore. All she can talk about are horses and dogs and hunting with horses and dogs. If I were the cause of her leaving that decrepit pile of rocks in Cornwall she calls an estate and making her way to London, I might bear some responsibility for entertaining her. However, once I knew I was coming to Edinburgh and would be out of town for at least a few weeks, I saw no reason to continue to spare Maxwell his well-deserved punishment, and I summoned his mother. Of course, it never occurred to me that he would turn tail and run. I should hand the man a white feather on arrival!"

Shaking her head at the absurdity of this explanation, Tabitha took over the conversation and explained, "My ward, Melody, a charming four-year-old girl, has been staying with Lord Langley while we're in Scotland. Dodo is her puppy, and Matt, otherwise known as Rat, is her brother." As she said this, Tabitha stole a glance at the dowager. When Tabitha had first introduced Melody to her mother-in-law, she had been sparing with details of Melody's life before coming to live at Chesterton House, merely saying she and her brother had been orphaned and that the children had nowhere else to go. At the time, the dowager had been so charmed by the little girl that she had, uncharacteristically, not asked questions. In particular, she'd never asked where the brother was. Clearly, more explanation was now going to be needed.

But before Tabitha could launch into an explanation that was both plausible but also sufficiently sanitised, the dowager said, "Jane, I know you're not a woman of the world as I am, but please don't have a fit of the vapours when I tell you that Melody and her brother, Matthew, are street children from Whitechapel. Matthew, called Rat by some, though not by me, is part of the staff at Chesterton House, and Melody is living in the nursery."

Before Jane could say anything, the dowager continued, much to Tabitha's amazement, "Melody is an exceptionally bright and charming child, and I expect her to be treated as any guest's child would be. And based on what I hear from Melody," and with this, the dowager looked pointedly at Tabitha. "Yes, from Melody. Did you really think she wouldn't tell me everything, Tabitha?" She continued, "Based on what I hear from Melody, Matt sounds like a very enterprising young man who did what he had to in order to keep his little sister safe. I very much look forward to finally meeting him."

Tabitha sat with her mouth hanging open. Truly, this woman never ceased to surprise. Just when Tabitha thought she could perfectly anticipate the dowager's likely response to a situation, her expectations were turned upside down all over again.

The dowager smirked, "Not only did you think you could keep this information from me, Tabitha, you thought my reactions so foreseeable that you are now amazed to find that I don't care about Melody's humble origins! Pray do not ever make the mistake again of considering me predictable." For once, Tabitha had to agree with the dowager; she really would never make that mistake again.

Of course, that still left the conundrum of Rat's place during their visit. Was he to be a guest of Laird MacAlister's? Was he to live and eat with the household staff? Somehow, this decision seemed more fraught away from the normalcy of life at Chesterton House. Surprisingly, the problem was solved by Bear, who said, "Rat can share my room and meals." Given Bear's own nebulous status in the Edinburgh house, it made perfect sense that he would take charge of Rat during that visit.

Sensing the last problem, Bear added, "Perhaps the lad can be responsible for the dog while we're here."

"A dog?" Jane exclaimed, finally reacting to the news of her unexpected visitors. News that threatened to make her mother's visit even more of a circus than it already was. "And why is Lord Langley coming here? Surely, he has multiple country estates he might retire to if he wishes to avoid his mother's visit."

Tabitha had a good idea why Langley was on his way to Edinburgh, but the explanation wasn't one she wished to share with Jane unless she had to. As it happened, Tabitha reflected, if she was correct, Lord Langley deserved some credit for empathy and common sense. If he had fled London to a country house and Tabitha had returned home to London suddenly, she would have suspected the worst of the man who had already abducted her ward once. But in fleeing to Edinburgh, he ensured she would not suspect him of foul play. Bringing Rat with him showed a degree of additional sensitivity she was surprised to credit the man with. It was clear Langley would go to great lengths not to jeopardise his continued afternoons with Melody.

Wolf's thoughts ran along similar lines. But he also had the idea that Langley might prove useful in this investigation. After all, Langley had been a peer for many years and was quite active in the House of Lords. He must understand any recently passed legislation better than Wolf did.

It seemed as if everything was settled, and Tabitha was taking a last fortifying sip of tea before leaving the gathering and finally going to her room to change. She'd just put her teacup back on its saucer when Hamish strode into the room waving his own telegram.

"Jane, Lily, ye'll never guess what! Uncle Duncan is comin' to visit." Surprised at seeing everyone gathered in the drawing room, he stopped short and looked around. "Am I interrupting something?"

Jane answered, her tone indicating that an already challenging day was about to become more difficult, saying,

"Tabitha has received a telegram, and it appears we are to have some additional unexpected guests."

Hamish seemed to not sense that his wife might be at the end of her tether and said cheerfully, "The mair the merrier. We hae plenty o' room."

Tabitha wondered how true that statement was. The house was certainly capacious and the staff extensive, but with the dowager, Tabitha, Wolf and Bear already in residence, and Langley, the children and presumably Mary on their way, would one more guest be the tipping point? If not for space, then for Jane's nerves?

As if she had suddenly realised a great hole in Hamish's story, Jane asked hopefully, "Isn't your Uncle Duncan off doing something in the Orkneys? Fishing? Hunting? Something to do with whisky, perhaps?"

"Aye, he's started his ain distillery, but he had a sudden need to come back to Edinburgh. He's sorry he couldnae give us mair notice, but he'll be wi' us for dinner the nicht."

From what Tabitha could tell, the prospect of an avuncular visit seemed to simultaneously fill Hamish with delight and Jane with dread. Lily seemed firmly on her father's side, clapping her hands, and saying gleefully, "Oh Tabitha, you'll love Uncle Duncan. And he's the only person who takes my studies seriously."

Well, that was one thing in the man's favour, at least, Tabitha thought.

Realising the situation was entirely beyond her control, Jane stood and said, "If we are going to be more for dinner, I must talk with the cook; Lord Langley's presence at our table requires at least one additional remove."

This last comment caused the dowager to glare at her daughter and demand, "Are you saying that the meals served to me so far have been less than would be served to Lord Langley? May I remind you that I am a dowager countess, and dear Jeremy here is himself an earl? I did not previously comment on the lack of meat in aspic or light game served at your table because

I assumed this was some quaint Scottish tradition, and I am nothing if not sensitive to the mores of other lands. But now I find out this omission was not the custom of a socially backward nation, but rather merely an indication of my unimportance as a guest in my daughter's eyes!"

Jane had the look of a deer come face to face with its predator, her eyes widened in fear, and from where Tabitha sat, it looked as if the woman was visibly shaking. Tabitha was about to step in and save the poor woman when Lily did it for her, "Grandmama, you're being so absurd. You're family, not a guest. And so is Cousin Jeremy. As it is, we've had more removes than usual when dining alone. Now, wasn't there something you wanted to show me in Debrett's about Lady Hartley's lineage?" With that, the young woman stood, took the dowager's arm, and led her out of the room.

Tabitha was truly impressed; not only had Lily sacrificed herself on the altar of the dowager's pride in her immense knowledge of the family trees of all the great and good, but she had done so with such finesse that the dowager didn't have time to protest. After waiting enough time for Lily to drag her grandmother into her father's study, Tabitha rose and left the room.

It was going to be a very interesting evening. If the timing of their train was any guide, Langley and his entourage would be arriving in a couple of hours. Who knew when Uncle Duncan would arrive. Tabitha needed to lie down and rest before facing the likely drama at dinner.

Left with Hamish as Jane and Bear excused themselves from the drawing room, Wolf asked, "Did I happen to get replies to my telegrams from this morning?" He knew that the few hours since he had sent them were unlikely to be long enough to allow his man of business and solicitor to look into Sinclair's holdings, but he was impatient to move the investigation forward. On receiving an apologetic no from Hamish, Wolf decided he might as well freshen up and change his clothes.

CHAPTER 18

Tabitha laid down for an hour but couldn't sleep. Angus Johnson's words, both during the rally and in the inn, kept running through her head. On Jonathan's death, Tabitha had become a wealthy woman, inheriting many of his non-entailed businesses. At the time, she'd been happy to leave her portfolio's management to Jonathan's man of business.

But now, Tabitha considered whether she had a moral obligation to become more involved. She knew she didn't own coal mines, but what other businesses did she have a financial stake in, and was she, however unwittingly, the kind of employer Angus had railed against? She knew that Wolf had his hands full just trying to understand and oversee the business and financial interests he'd inherited as part of the earldom. However, perhaps she might follow his example and ask her man of business to teach her about her holdings. Or at least to teach her enough that she could ensure any business contributing to her coffers had exemplary working conditions.

Having settled her mind over that issue, she returned to Peter's phrase, "blood money". Was that merely the hyperbole of an idealistic, passionate young man? Or had he discovered something and confronted Sinclair with evidence? For the first time, Tabitha considered the possibility that the young man they were searching for might no longer be alive. She hadn't liked Sinclair from the moment he'd leered over her. Wolf's description of their conversation at the laird's evening soiree had only confirmed that intuition. If Angus was correct, the mine owner had no qualms about flouting regulations and risking men's lives to increase profits. But how far would a man like that go to protect himself and his wealth?

Finally, realising she was too restless to nap, she got out of bed and rang for Ginny. After a long soak in the bath, she sat at the dressing table, looking in the mirror as Ginny styled her hair. Tabitha told Ginny all they had discovered that afternoon and was curious to hear what her sensible maid thought.

"M'lady, yourself and his lordship are good employers. You care for the people in your household and treat us all with respect and fairness. But you are not the norm. Perhaps, this Mr Sinclair is no worse than most are towards the people who work for them. You should hear the stories our Molly has to tell about the factory she works at," Ginny said.

Tabitha thought about Ginny's words. She knew there was much truth to them. Was that all Sinclair was doing? Cutting some corners here and there?

Ginny had been very excited to hear that Melody and Mary were arriving that evening. Ginny usually watched Melody when Mary had her afternoon off, and the two had become quite close. "Lady MacAlister still has children in the nursery and one, a little girl named Violet is not much older than Miss Melody." Another flower, Tabitha, noted. Ginny continued, "Miss Violet is six, so she will be a fine companion for Miss Melody while she's here."

Tabitha had told Ginny Bear's suggestion of how they might handle Rat's status while they were in Edinburgh. Ginny approved and said cautiously, "M'lady, I would never presume to tell you what to do, but…" The maid paused, and Tabitha could see in the mirror how uncomfortable the woman was.

"Ginny, I believe you know me well enough that if you have something to say, you realise you can say it. I trust your judgement, and your advice to me has always been invaluable."

Nodding in acknowledgement, Ginny continued, "I can't see how Rat and Melody's living situation can continue as it is. At least not for long. He's a smart lad. Very smart. In fact, from what I can tell, he seems to be leaping ahead in his studies with Mr James, the tutor. Certainly, having him in the same class as

Mary has become more difficult. He was learning his numbers with me for a while, but it wasn't long before I couldn't keep up with him."

The maid paused again. She had been thinking about this for some while, but now that it was time to say it, she wasn't sure how even a mistress as lenient as Tabitha would take to the impertinence of being told what to do by her maid. Seeing this hesitation, Tabitha assured her, "Ginny, just say whatever you have to say. I promise I will not be angry. I know you only have Rat and Melody's best interests at heart."

Finally, realising the truth in Tabitha's assurances, Ginny said, "Rat can be so much more than a groom or a gardener, and he should be given a chance to prove that. As your ward, Miss Melody will grow up to be a fine young lady. How can she come out into society while her brother is rubbing down the horses out back and digging up the onions?"

Ginny stopped speaking then and busied herself with Tabitha's hair. Tabitha didn't answer, not because she disagreed but because Ginny's words reflected her own concerns. Having Rat work as one of her servants while his sister was raised in the nursery had always been a short-term solution. In her heart, she realised that. But what was the alternative? Bringing Rat into the household as her ward and raising him to be a gentleman? Apart from anything else, Rat himself poohpoohed such an idea. And having not done so when the children first became part of her household, it was hard to envision how such a transition would now work, both for Rat himself and the rest of the servants.

Having said her piece, Ginny was content to let the subject drop. Despite a relationship with Tabitha that went far beyond what most lady's maids had with their mistresses, Tabitha owed her no answer.

Tabitha found herself dressed for dinner far earlier than usual. But she was also keen to be downstairs for Langley's arrival. Indeed, as she descended the stairs, she could hear a commotion in the vestibule and the sweet sound of childish voices. Hurrying down, Tabitha felt a rush of affection overwhelm her as she saw the little girl standing beside Langley, holding his hand. They made quite a large and noisy group between Langley, Melody, Rat, Mary and Langley's valet, to say nothing of Dodo and all their luggage.

As she descended the last few steps, Melody looked up, and the joy on her face at seeing Tabitha was the sweetest of sights. "Tabby Cat, I've missed you!" Melody rushed forward, and Tabitha bent down to catch the child and swung her up into her arms.

"I've missed you too, Melly," Tabitha said.

"I went on a train with Uncle Maxi, and he told me and Rat all about the places we saw along the way. And then, do you know what?" Tabitha couldn't imagine and, luckily, didn't need to guess before the child continued, "Uncle Maxi got the train driver to show Rat how it worked." At this, Tabitha looked over at Langley and raised an eyebrow. He merely shrugged. Tabitha wasn't sure she could ever bring herself to like or trust the Earl of Langley completely. Despite a kind of handsomeness, there was something off-putting about the man. However, she had to admit that he had revealed some surprising sides of his personality over the last few weeks.

Tabitha hadn't considered the train seating arrangements for Langley's gaggle of children and servants. But if she'd had to guess, she would have presumed that Rat had sat in the second-class carriage with Mary and Langley's valet. But apparently, that hadn't been the case, and he'd travelled in first-class luxury with Langley and Melody. Looking more closely at Rat, Tabitha realised he was wearing new clothes, ones more befitting of a young man sitting in first-class. Unsure what to make of this unexpected turn of events, Tabitha decided to let it go for now. It wasn't that she was unhappy that Lord Langley had been treating Rat as more than one of the servants. It was rather that, particularly in light of the conversation she had just had with Ginny, Tabitha was unsure what such preference meant for the future of Rat's tenure in her household staff.

Tabitha made eye contact with Rat, who was wearing a cap

that he quickly doffed and said, "Milady Tabby Cat," his name for her. "The train was so wonderful. I sat up front with the driver, and he showed me all the levers. Do you know they run the whole train on steam?"

Apart from the childish enthusiasm Rat showed, which was lovely, Tabitha noted something she couldn't quite put her finger on at first. Then she realised it was his speech. Born and raised in Whitechapel, Rat was a true cockney, and his speech always reflected that. Tabitha had never tried to correct his dropped aitches and Whitechapel patter because it helped him fit in with the other servants. But it seemed, in the few short days they had been away, Langley had taken some correction upon himself.

Since she had been hugging Melody, Bear and Wolf had drifted into the vestibule from wherever they'd been around the house. Tabitha was pleased to see Bear standing beside Wolf as she said, "Rat, I'm so happy to hear you enjoyed the train ride so much. I look forward to hearing about it all tomorrow. Perhaps over breakfast. But you've all had a long trip and must be tired and hungry. Mary can take Melody to the nursery, and you are to stay with Bear during your time here. If that is all right with you?" she added.

Rat grinned and said, "Ullo, Bear, wot's been 'appening?" A light touch on his shoulder from Langley and the boy corrected himself, "I mean, how do you do?" Langley nodded his approval. Wolf and Bear raised their eyebrows but did not comment.

Dawglish led Mary and Melody away, and Bear took charge of Rat just as Hamish, Jane and Lily appeared, drawn by the commotion. Hamish warmly welcomed Langley, and Jane was her normal timid self. Langley took her hand and kissed it, "Lady MacAlister, it has been too long. How well you look."

Jane blushed at his chivalry and said, "Lord Langley, I'm honoured you remember me. It's been a very long time since my debut." Emboldened by Langley's attention, Jane turned to Lily and said, "Let me introduce you to my eldest daughter, Lady Lily."

Langley was yet again all chivalry as he bowed over the young woman's hand, saying, "Lady Lily, you are as lovely as your mother was at your age." Tabitha almost rolled her eyes; she wasn't sure that was the compliment to Lily that Langley might have hoped.

Suddenly, a booming voice behind Tabitha said, "So, Maxwell, I see you have been run out of town by your mama with your tail between your legs." The dowager finished her descent down the last couple of stairs and pointed her cane, which she had decided to use as her weapon of choice that evening, in the new arrival's direction. "For shame! A grown man scared of his own mother. And you call yourself a member of British I–"

Before the dowager could finish that sentence, Maxwell had covered the short space between them in the vestibule, put his hand on her arm and said severely, "Lady Pembroke! Remember what we discussed."

At the conclusion of their last investigation, they had all, some more willingly than others, promised not to disclose what they knew of Lord Langley's work for British Intelligence. To the dowager, for whom secrets were a power she gleefully held over her victims in society, such a promise was torture. However, she was a woman of her word, and this reminder from Langley was enough to silence her. Or at least silence her on this topic. "Yes, well anyway," she muttered, momentarily thrown off her game by the censure, "my point stands; what kind of grown man can't share the same house as his mother for more than a day?"

Graciously ignoring the dowager's jabs at him, Langley took his hand off her arm and instead kissed her hand, saying, "It is equally delightful to see you, Lady Pembroke."

Langley then turned back to Jane and said, "I must apologise for imposing on your hospitality at such short notice. There were," he paused, then added, "extenuating circumstances." Langley looked at Tabitha as he said this, and she took that as confirmation that her assumptions about why he had chosen to flee to Edinburgh were correct.

"You are more than welcome, Lord Langley. I'm sure you

would like to freshen up and change before dinner. We will hold it until you are ready and will be in the drawing room."

The dowager harrumphed, "Holding dinner? I am a frail old woman and need regular sustenance. So, make sure you jump to it, Maxwell. Let us not add starving the elderly to your already long list of crimes," she added pointedly.

Dinner was a surprisingly uneventful affair. Lord Langley freshened himself up promptly enough that even the dowager couldn't complain of any delay to dinner. Despite the promise of Uncle Duncan's arrival for dinner, the man hadn't materialised by the time they were ready to sit down, and Jane, with a quick glance at her mother, suggested they not wait. This turned out to be a fortuitous decision as the man himself did not finally breeze into the room until dessert was served.

By the looks of him, he was somewhat the worst for drink, which might answer the question of his tardiness. Uncle Duncan was a near-perfect physical match for Hamish in about twenty or thirty years and probably many bottles of whisky later. Uncle Duncan had the same large gruffness as his nephew, but rather than red, threaded through with grey, his was a shock of snow-white hair. He had the same twinkly blue eyes and a wide, toothy grin. And he certainly had a similar, cheery personality to Hamish, Tabitha thought. If it wasn't all the drink.

Duncan barrelled into the dining room, announcing, "Nay fear, I've arrived. Apologies for being a wee bit late. But I was waylaid by some old friends as I left the station. It would have been rude to nae stop for a wee dram."

By the look of the man, it had been more than a wee dram, but Tabitha kept that thought to herself. The dowager was less inclined to such genteel blindness, declaring, "Apparently, good manners are not a thing in the wilds of Scotland. In London, even the most sauced of gentlemen know better than to arrive partway through dinner. Why, I was dining with Lady Willis recently, and even her husband, a man almost always in his cups, had enough grace to take himself off to eat in the kitchen when he arrived thirty minutes late from his club."

A lesser man, well perhaps a more sober man, might have taken offence at such a greeting from a total stranger, but Duncan MacAlister merely took the empty seat opposite Lily and said, "Ye're a wee fiery lass, eh? That's quite the sharp tongue ye have. I like it."

Uncharacteristically, the dowager seemed struck dumb by such a response. Was it the sheer gall of the man? Was it a response to being called a lass at her age? Whatever it was, Tabitha found the scene playing out over the dining table vastly amusing. There was no doubt Uncle Duncan would liven up their visit immeasurably.

After dinner, while sipping whisky with Hamish and Duncan, Wolf spoke of their need to talk with Louis Trent, and Dr Trent's seeming obstructionism. Hamish said that Richard Trent was a member of the Free Presbyterian Church, a particularly conservative breakaway branch of the Church of Scotland that promoted strict adherence to traditional Calvinist principles. As such, Dr Trent, a church elder, spent all of Sunday morning into the early afternoon at church. It went without saying that his wayward son did not join him. Hamish suggested this would be an opportunity to call on Louis Trent, who would likely be sleeping off his merriment from the night before. Hamish suggested that around noon would be the perfect time to find Louis out of bed but would leave them an hour or more before Dr Trent's return.

Over breakfast the next morning, Tabitha and Wolf discussed Hamish's suggestion and agreed it was the perfect time to talk with Louis without his father's interference. Hamish, Jane, and Lily were good churchgoing members of the mainstream Church of Scotland and had taken themselves off to services. The dowager, who was fond of saying she was more than capable of conversing with her creator from the comfort of her bed, had not yet descended. Sitting with them at the breakfast table were Bear, Rat, and Melody. And, of course, Lord Langley.

Over dinner the night before, everyone had taken turns filling Langley and Uncle Duncan in on the ongoing investigation into

Peter's disappearance, or at least the more sanitised version of it that the dowager and Jane had been told. Managing to take Langley aside before he retired for the evening, Wolf had indicated there was more to the story and suggested the man meet Tabitha and him in the library after breakfast.

Over kippers and Bannocks, which he was eating with gusto, Rat continued to enthuse about the train and the train-related facts Langley had shared during their ride to Scotland. Meanwhile, Melody kept up a running childish prattle about Violet, who ate her breakfast in the nursery. Apparently, the six-year-old Violet had a doll's house nearly as wonderful as the one the dowager had at her house for when Melody visited. The two little girls planned to spend the morning playing with it, and then Mary and Violet's nurserymaid, Allie, were going to take the children out to play in the large green space at the heart of Charlotte Square.

Finally, the children had finished their breakfast. Rat had gone to feed and walk Dodo, and Melody had happily skipped out of the room with Mary. Tabitha, no longer able to contain her curiosity, said to Langley, "You seem to have taken a particular interest in Rat."

Langley took his time answering, wiping his mouth with his napkin, finally saying, "The first evening the young man came to have dinner with his sister, I sat with them and observed a fine intelligence and intellectual curiosity there. Unpolished for sure, but there is no doubt the lad could aim far higher than a groom or gardener."

Tabitha was stung by the implicit criticism in the man's comments. However, she chose to ignore it for the time being. Instead, she said, "I completely agree. That is why Melody's tutor, Mr James, has also been working with Rat."

At the mention of Mr James, Lord Langley laughed derisively, "I believe I've made my feelings on this so-called tutor quite clear. But beyond the lad's education, what is your plan for him? Surely, you can see how untenable it is that Melody be raised as your ward to be part of aristocratic society while her brother is tending to your horses."

Langley's words were so similar to Ginny's the night before that Tabitha momentarily wondered whether the two had somehow discussed the topic, but she quickly realised their sentiments were similar because they were both correct. Tabitha could tell Wolf was about to leap to her defence, and she put a hand on his arm to hold him back, saying, "You are entirely right, Lord Langley. Indeed, you are not the first person to bring this issue to my attention. I am merely unsure what the appropriate corrective action is. Rat has made it clear he has no desire to move into the nursery with his sister and be raised as a gentleman. So, what is the alternative?"

Langley paused again and nervously tapped his fingers on the table. He had been planning this conversation for the entire train ride the day before, but now it was upon him, he was nervous about how to begin. As Tabitha feared, it was not lost on the man that she had no legal right to Melody and certainly not to the boy. However, despite his reputation, Langley was no monster; it was evident that Melody was happy at Chesterton House and responded to Tabitha as a mother figure. He was not the man to drag a child from a warm, maternal embrace. He was grateful for the afternoons he spent with the little girl, particularly given his ill-considered abduction of the child. The boy was a different matter.

Finally, he said, "The Crown has a great need for intelligent and courageous men. As you saw in your last investigation, the Germans are becoming increasingly threatening and their tactics evermore devious. I worry about Britain's ability to recruit and train sufficiently able men."

Tabitha narrowed her eyes and said with a warning tone in her voice that Wolf was astute enough to notice but which was lost on Langley, "So what are you suggesting? That you train Rat to be a spy?"

"Well, it's unclear what aspects of intelligence the lad might be best suited for, but I've already observed that he has some abilities that lead me to believe he might be perfectly suited for cryptology."

Wolf asked, "What do you mean by 'cryptology'?"

Langley patiently explained, "As you both observed in the case of Claire Murphy's death, it is common for those in the intelligence business to communicate using codes. The Germans do it, we do it, everyone does it. Over time, each side learns how to crack the other's codes, and so, they've had to become increasingly complicated. The science, well really the art, of creating impenetrable codes for our side and cracking the complex codes created by the other side is the field of cryptology. It has been my experience that, while elements of cryptology can be taught, a person either has an innate talent for it, or they don't."

Langley paused and then said directly to Tabitha, who was the one to be persuaded, "I believe the lad has such a talent. And that's rare."

Tabitha didn't bother to ask how Langley had assured himself of this fact, she was too torn as to the offer he was making. She didn't know much about how the intelligence services worked. However, she'd seen enough during their last investigation to realise the work was dangerous and that the people involved, on both sides, often operated with a situationally fluid sense of morality. Could she possibly condone throwing a child into this world?

She said as much to Langley, who answered, "Working down the coal mines is dangerous. Being a soldier is dangerous. A boy of his class might end up in all sorts of dangerous professions. Working for the intelligence services has its dangers for some, but for many, particularly cryptologists, it is a desk job, usually in an office somewhere in Whitehall. I am offering Rat a career that will immediately elevate him to at least the middle class. Surely that is a better opportunity for the lad than digging your garden? Perhaps we should ask Rat what he would prefer."

This last comment took some of the steam out of Tabitha's self-righteous anger. Langley was correct; she had no legal or moral hold over Rat. The decision was entirely his to make, and she had no right to make it on his behalf. But then, a more practical objection occurred to her, "The reason he agreed to become part of the household at Chesterton House was so he wouldn't be separated from Melody. What you are proposing would do just that."

It seemed Langley had anticipated this objection and immediately said, "Would it? Melody comes to me three afternoons a week, and they could spend time together then. And I suggest that Rat continue to eat with Melody in the nursery at Chesterton House in the evenings. This is more time than he currently spends with her, is it not? And, of course, he would be free to visit Chesterton House whenever he feels like it. His residence at Langley House would not be as a servant; he would be free to come and go as he pleases." This last sentence was said quite pointedly to Tabitha, and she didn't miss the subtle criticism. Finally, out of arguments, she conceded that the final decision must be Rat's.

The plan had been to retire to the library to discuss the case privately with Langley. But before they could adjourn, they were surprised by the earlier-than-usual entrance of the dowager countess. Over the previous few days, the wily old woman had developed a strong suspicion that she wasn't being given all the facts of the investigation. And she was certain she was being left out of aspects that she would enjoy. With the MacAlister family away for the morning, the dowager guessed that Tabitha and Wolf might use that time to include Langley in their schemes, and she had no intention of missing out.

Seeing Tabitha's face fall as she entered the breakfast room confirmed the dowager's suspicions, and she said, "You look particularly unhappy to see me, Tabitha. Could it be that you were hoping to induct Lord Langley into the investigation behind my back?"

This accusation was so close to the truth that Tabitha blushed and stammered, "Good morning, Mama. We were indeed planning to discuss Peter Kincaid's disappearance with Lord Langley. But no one was planning anything behind your back."

The dowager snorted her disbelief at this statement, saying, "I know I'm not being told the whole story. Jane is a dullard and cannot see that the tale we have been fed is made out of whole cloth. I'm insulted that you believed that I am similarly addled."

Tabitha and Wolf exchanged glances. It was surprising it had taken the dowager this long to question the story she had been given. However, that didn't mean they now had to tell her the truth. If nothing else, they had made a promise to Lily. Finally, the dowager solved the immediate problem for them, "It is clear I will not wrangle the full story out of you over tea and whatever this insipid swill is supposed to be," she said, gesturing to the entire breakfast buffet. As it happened, Tabitha found most of the Scottish breakfast foods very tasty. Even the black pudding, once she'd plucked up her courage and had a tiny taste.

Again, exchanging looks, Tabitha and Wolf came to an unspoken agreement that he would take the baton from her. "Lady Pembroke, dear Lady Pembroke," he added in the tone of almost an abject lover. As was so often the case these days, Tabitha had to resist the urge to roll her eyes. Wolf continued, "You are one of the inner circle who know of Lord Langley's, how should I put it? Lord Langley's covert career. Tabitha and I merely hoped to make use of some of his special skills."

Very clever, Tabitha thought. Make her feel special. Indeed, the dowager, as wily as she was, seemed entirely won over by Wolf's words and murmured, "Yes, well as you say, I do have very special knowledge of the inner workings of," and at this, she lowered her voice, "British Intelligence." As with so many statements made by the dowager, this was hyperbole, to say the least. The woman continued, "Which is why I believe you have made insufficient use of my expertise. Something I expect rectified immediately."

"What about your work with Lady Lily?" Tabitha asked innocently.

"Yes, well, that of course is still of high importance. As it stands today, I can't imagine taking the girl anywhere in London society. However, I plan to set her various tasks to work on. Not the least of which is studying Debrett's. This will free me up to be of aid to the investigation."

It was clear to Wolf that this was a battle they would not win. "Lady Pembroke, as it happens, Tabitha and I have an important visit to make this morning and would welcome your help." Tabitha quirked an eyebrow, but he ignored her and continued, "We need to interview Peter Kincaid's friend, Louis Trent, Dr Trent's son. However, Dr Trent has proved rather obdurate regarding his son's friendship with Peter, and we were hoping to find the son at home when the father is not. Lord MacAlister has informed us of the certainty that Dr Trent will be at church all morning and well into the early afternoon. Therefore, we were planning to visit the Trent home at noon." He added, "We wish to maximise the chance of Dr Trent being away from home and his son not being abed after his prior evening's cavorting."

The dowager snorted, "So you wish to catch the wastrel while the zealot father exalts in his piety?"

"Indeed. And it strikes me that your addition to the party is exactly what we need to induce the boy to talk." As Wolf said this, Tabitha's first instinct was to wonder what on earth he was thinking. But then, she considered, perhaps it was a stroke of genius. If anyone could strike fear into the heart of a potentially recalcitrant ne'er-do-well, it was the barely five-foot-tall, old woman sitting opposite her.

"So, you need me to come and terrorise the young man. Is that what you're saying?" the dowager asked astutely. If it was unclear if she was offended, her next statement put paid to such a thought, "That sounds like a marvellous way to spend a Sunday. I've always believed that rather than insipid platitudes mouthed to a deity who must certainly have better things to do with his time than listen, a more effective and efficient way to expunge wickedness from the world is by taking direct action. It will be my pleasure to lead such a charge."

Her enthusiasm for their outing was not the only worry Tabitha had. How could they effectively question Louis while avoiding the aspects of Peter's relationship with Lily they were keeping from the dowager? It was no matter now because the die was cast. They would just have to do their best to extract the information they needed while hoping that the dowager wasn't alerted to any inconsistencies in the version of the story she had been told.

Langley watched this exchange with some amusement, always happy when someone else was in the dowager's line of fire. However, he sensed that there were aspects to the investigation Tabitha and Wolf wished to discuss with him alone. It seemed unlikely that all three of them would be able to retire and leave the dowager countess behind. So, with an apologetic look at Tabitha, he said, "Pembroke, I believe you have some matters pertaining to the House of Lords you wish to discuss with me after breakfast. Is there a place to which we can retire so I can update you on some of the recent legislation?"

"Yes, Jeremy. Do take Maxwell elsewhere if you insist on discussing the machinations of a bunch of bumbling fools. I have no desire to have my tea and toast ruined with such inane conversation."

Tabitha realised what Langley had done. She knew it meant that not only would she be left out of explaining the investigation, but she'd have to continue to sit with the dowager. However, she acknowledged it was a sacrifice that had to be made. "Yes, Wolf. Why don't you go and discuss the 'legislation' with Lord Langley in the library," she said pointedly.

Recognising an escape route when he saw one, Wolf rose and left the breakfast room quickly, followed by Langley. Just as Tabitha wondered how she might also gracefully escape, Uncle Duncan burst into the room and sat beside the dowager. There were many other chairs the man could have taken, and the dowager expressed that thought, "Sir, I believe you might be more comfortable across the table where the toast and jam are within easier reach," she said with no attempt at subtlety.

The large, jolly man merely laughed, "Dinnae fash yersel' aboot me. I'll tak' a bonnie lass o'er a meal any day."

The look on the dowager's face as she realised what he had

said was priceless. It made up for any regret Tabitha felt at being left out of the conversation with Lord Langley.

"Mr MacAlister! That is no way to speak about my daughter-in-law," the dowager admonished.

"I wasnae talkin' aboot the younger Lady Pembroke. I was referrin' tae you, lass," the rascal said with a wink.

"Lass? Is that what you called me? How dare you speak to me in such a fashion, sir. I am the Dowager Countess of Pembroke!" the woman said with such indignancy that her voice shook.

"I speak as I find. Ye're a bonnie woman, and there's nae crime in sayin' sae, as far as I can see," Uncle Duncan said. If he was aware of the firestorm he had ignited with his words, he seemed not to care.

The dowager threw her napkin on the table, stood, and drew herself up to her almost five feet and said with the imperiousness that came from the inbreeding of four hundred years of aristocracy, "I find I have lost my appetite. I will retire to the drawing room where I hope to find peace and solitude." The last statement was directed very pointedly at Uncle Duncan, who still seemed oblivious to her meaning.

"I will finish my haggis and then join ye. Perhaps we may tak' a turn around the garden. I believe there are some fine trysting places," Uncle Duncan said, seemingly unperturbed by the fire-breathing dragon he had awoken.

Julia Chesterton, the Dowager Countess of Pembroke, was used to being feared. In fact, she cultivated this reaction in friends, family, and casual acquaintances alike. She was not used to her words of scorn and derision falling on entirely deaf ears. Was the man a lunatic? Perhaps a dunderhead? Whatever it was, she would waste no more of her time on him. She turned without any further words and stormed out of the room, slamming the door behind her.

Finally, Tabitha could not keep her laughter in any longer. Uncle Duncan looked at her chuckling away, and said, apparently in all sincerity, "What's sae funny, lass?"

"Wiping tears out of her eyes, Tabitha answered, "Mr

MacAlister, I don't even know where to begin."

CHAPTER 19

In the library, Wolf filled Langley in on all the details of Peter Kincaid's disappearance. Langley let Wolf speak without interruption as the younger man used their corkboard full of notecards to walk him through the information they had gathered and the suspicions they had formed. Langley didn't comment until Wolf indicated he was done.

Gesturing towards the corkboard, Langley started by saying, "This is quite ingenious." Wolf agreed and gave all the credit to Tabitha. Langley then asked, "What information can I help with?"

"We're not entirely sure," Wolf admitted. "I'm ashamed to admit that I don't know much about the workers' rights movement or the Scottish Labour Party."

"Well, I won't claim this as an area of expertise," Langley admitted. "However, the Prime Minister's Conservative government, quite predictably, views the movement warily."

"Even though they have been responsible for a significant amount of recent regulation favouring workers?" Wolf asked.

"Yes, even then. The Conservative Party favours maintaining the traditional order and views the labour unions and their ilk as disruptive elements. However, there is no denying that we live in times of unprecedented technological and social upheaval, and there have long been voices, often powerful and persuasive, within the Conservative Party itself, who recognise the need for at least some limited labour reforms."

The man continued, "The Labour Party is a nascent

organisation even within England. Its Scottish cousin is even less on the radar of Westminster and Downing Street. However, I have no doubt that this movement is gaining momentum, and we will hear ever louder and more strident calls for meaningful change as we cross into a new century."

The man paused, then choosing his words carefully, said, "This is not an area I am overly involved with. As you are aware, I have a particular focus on foreign threats rather than domestic ones. However, if the question you are skirting around is whether the British government might be behind this Peter Kincaid's disappearance, my informal answer is: I doubt it. From what you've told me, Mr Kincaid is small fry, even in local politics. It sounds as if this Angus Johnson is the real instigator, and I can't imagine why he wouldn't be the target. If anyone was," he added cautiously.

"Thank you, Langley," Wolf said sincerely. "That helps to shut off one likely avenue of investigation." Wolf wasn't entirely convinced he should trust Langley's word. He had no doubt the man would have no qualms about lying if he felt the situation warranted it. However, Lord Langley's demeanour and speech indicated no subterfuge, at least at the moment.

While they were in the library, Dawglish came in with a telegram for Wolf from his man of business. Quickly perusing its contents, Wolf explained to Langley, "I'm attempting to understand James Sinclair's business. My man explains it is a tangle of various holdings and associated companies. It seems Sinclair has his fingers in many pies beyond coal. He has been unable to dig up any specific examples of malfeasance by Sinclair, but does say that, in his experience, an industrialist who weaves such an elaborate legal and business web around himself usually does it to camouflage illicit activities."

Wolf pinned the telegram to the board and turned back to Langley, saying, "Having met the man, I can't say it surprises me to hear he may be less than scrupulously honest. He strikes me as someone who believes he pulled himself up by his bootstraps despite the odds, and that others should live by a similar philosophy of individual responsibility and self-reliance."

"I have met men such as Sinclair," Langley said. "They believe in the power of the free market to regulate itself without the need for government interference; as they call it, a laissez-faire attitude. I'm sure such a man is very dismissive of the recent Coal Mine act."

"Indeed. As he expressed it to me, his view is that if going down the coal mines as an eight-year-old boy was good enough for him, it's good enough for young boys today," Wolf admitted. "Given this, Angus Johnson's claim that Peter suspected, perhaps even knew, that his benefactor was flagrantly flouting the Coal Mines act and other recent regulations, is wholly believable."

Meanwhile, Tabitha had left the breakfast room in search of Rat. Having promised Langley she would discuss his offer with the boy, she wanted to waste no time in doing so. She finally found him in the garden with Dodo. It appeared he was trying to train the dog to sit and stay. To Tabitha's dog-sceptical eye, it appeared the excitable puppy saw this as merely another game. Seeing Tabitha approach, Rat stood up from the crouch he'd been in as he attempted to push the puppy's wriggling rear end down as he said, "Sit!"

"Milady Tabby Cat. What are you doing out here? It's nippy."

Tabitha agreed it was rather chilly and questioned why Rat wasn't wearing a coat.

"I've been running round with Dodo, like. It's keeping me warm," the boy explained.

"Perhaps we can leave Dodo in the kitchen and find a quiet spot to talk," Tabitha suggested.

"Am I in trouble? Should I not 'ave come with Lord Langley?" the boy asked nervously.

"It is nothing like that, Rat. I assure you. You are very welcome here and are not in trouble. Quite the opposite, in fact."

Tabitha led the boy through the house, leaving Dodo behind in the kitchen with Bear, who was sitting at the large servants' table. They found a cosy empty parlour, and she closed the door behind them as they entered. Tabitha took a seat and indicated that Rat should sit beside her.

Unsure how to begin, Tabitha finally decided to leap right in, "Rat, Lord Langley is very impressed with you. He believes you have great potential. Potential that will be wasted if you continue to be a servant at Chesterton House. He wishes to have you live with him, and he will educate and train you to be," she paused. She wasn't sure how to phrase Langley's suggestion. He hadn't indicated that Rat knew his own covert position, and she couldn't imagine how to explain Langley's plan without giving that away.

Finally, she said, "He wants to train you to work with him on behalf of the government."

"Wot, me?" the young boy asked wide-eyed. "Cor, I can't 'ardly read yet. Though I'm getting better. Why does a toff like him want to train the likes of me?" Tabitha observed that, in his excitement, Rat's speech had reverted.

"Lord Langley has had you solve some puzzles, I believe," Tabitha said. "Apparently, he was so impressed by how you did that he believes that, with hard work and determination, you might be able to solve far more important puzzles for the government. Puzzles that might, in time, enable you to be of service to Britain."

"Really? 'E thinks that?" the boy marvelled. "Ma and Pa would never 'ave credited it."

As he said these words, Tabitha sighed, realising the decision had been made. Moreover, in her heart, she knew it was the right decision. While she still had her doubts and fears, there was no doubt that this was an extraordinary opportunity, and she could not stand in Rat's way.

"I'm sure your parents would have been very proud of you, Rat. Even before you came to Chesterton House, you did your parents credit as you cared for Melody. This is a wonderful opportunity, and I'm glad you're interested in taking Lord Langley up on the offer. I'll let him know. We can work out the details before we return to London." Saying this made Tabitha remember the part of the plan that might give the boy pause.

"Rat, I'm not sure if this was clear, but Lord Langley expects you to live at Langley House with him. I would hope that Melody would stay at Chesterton House."

The boy thought for a moment before replying with a seriousness beyond his years, "Milady Tabby Cat, staying with you at Chesterton 'Ouse is the best thing for Melly, and being with 'Is Lordship is best for me. I can see that. And it's only a five-minute walk."

Tabitha sighed in relief that Rat wouldn't request that his sister move with him, "Indeed, it is a short walk. Lord Langley has suggested you continue to take your evening meal in the nursery with Melly, and of course, you will see her on her visits to Langley House."

Satisfied that this conversation had gone as well as possible, Tabitha released the boy to return to his attempts at dog training. Looking at the clock on the mantle, she realised the morning had disappeared quickly and that if they were to arrive at Dr Trent's home for noon, she should retire to her room and change out of her day dress.

CHAPTER 20

Hamish had informed Wolf that Dr Trent lived in Morningside, a neighbourhood approximately two miles from Charlotte Square. Morningside was an affluent neighbourhood favoured by successful professionals and academics. Tabitha noted its attractive architecture and abundant green spaces as the carriage approached it from across town. While the houses were not as grand as Charlotte Square or most of New Town, nevertheless, they reflected their inhabitants' prosperity and status.

It had been decided in the carriage that the dowager would lead the group as they knocked on the front door. The woman had never met a man she couldn't pulverise if she chose to; a butler would stand no chance against her. Indeed, Dr Trent's butler quickly realised he had met his match and showed them into the drawing room, saying he would alert Mr Trent to their visit.

The dowager looked critically around the room and sniffed, "Clearly, standards are lower in Scotland, for all things." Tabitha and Wolf didn't reply. In truth, the furniture was old-fashioned, and the room's colour scheme was overly dark, giving the room a somewhat oppressive feel. But everything was clearly of good quality. Rather, it was as if no one had given a thought to the room's decoration in a very long time. Since Dr Trent's wife had died more than twenty years before, Tabitha suspected no one had.

They sat and waited. And they waited. The dowager, apparently anticipating a possible skirmish, had brought her cane. She now tapped it impatiently on the floor. Finally, the door opened, and a dishevelled but handsome young man entered. He looked as if he had hurriedly pulled on a shirt that was only partially tucked in. The man wore no cravat or jacket, and his tousled hair and beard stubble spoke of a recent, unexpected exit from his bed.

Louis Trent seemed surprised at the apparent eminence of his guests. His butler had informed him that a strident older female was demanding to see him. But in Louis' world, this could have been anyone from the irate mother of a girl he had debauched to a tradeswoman come to claim her due. Normally, Louis would have brushed off such a visit and certainly wouldn't have dragged himself out of bed. However, Robertson, the butler, made it clear that he believed that if the master didn't descend to meet her, the woman in question would charge the bedroom.

Louis had no idea as to the identity of the tiny, terrifying-looking battle-axe flanked by the very pretty young woman. He took one look at her face and wished he could flee back to bed. Louis hadn't noticed Wolf when he'd first entered the room, but as Wolf rose and came forward with his hand outstretched, Louis found himself very curious about his male guest. His current attire notwithstanding, Louis Trent liked fine clothes and prided himself on wearing only the best tailoring, even when he couldn't afford it. So, he knew the man before him was wealthy; his clothes told that tale. But the man's hair was unfashionably long, and he had beard stubble almost as bad as Louis'. Who was he?

Louis' curiosity was immediately assuaged as Wolf introduced himself, "I am Jeremy Wolfson Chesterton, the Earl of Pembroke. This is my cousin-in-law, the Countess of Pembroke and finally," Wolf pointed towards the dowager, "this is the Dowager Countess of Pembroke." Louis was confused by the connection between these people, who shared a title, but he had only fallen into bed at 5am and hadn't had a cup of coffee yet. It was all he could do to keep his eyes open and form complete sentences. He shook Wolf's outstretched hand, bowed to the two ladies, then gratefully sank into a comfortable armchair.

Louis had no idea what his visitors could want from him. Perhaps they had intended to ask for his father. Yes, that made much more sense. He was about to suggest this when the scary old lady pointed her cane in his direction and demanded, "Young man! Do you think this state of dishabille is an appropriate one in which to greet visitors? Shame on you! Do you not know it is midday already? Far past time to still be in your bed."

Given that the dowager was inclined not to emerge from her boudoir until just before luncheon, Tabitha wondered at the lack of self-awareness necessary to criticise this behaviour in another. But she wisely kept this observation to herself. However, she did share a brief look with Wolf, which indicated his thoughts had moved in a similar direction.

Wolf realised that if he didn't take charge of the conversation, it might quickly spiral out of control as the dowager scolded Louis on the evils of his apparent lifestyle. They needed the young man's cooperation and so must save him from the dowager's haranguing.

"Mr Trent, we apologise for interrupting your sabbath." The dowager snorted, indicating her belief that Louis Trent's intentions for the day were anything but devotional. Wolf continued, "We wish to ask you about your friend, Peter Kincaid."

At this, Louis looked confused. "Peter?" he asked. "Why do you want to know about Kincaid, of all people?"

Tabitha wondered at Louis' phrasing and asked, "Why would Peter not be someone you'd expect questions asked of? Do you not realise he's missing?"

Louis Trent was a charming, roguish young man. Well, charming to everyone except his father. His good looks and happy-go-lucky personality had mostly provided him with an easy life, punctured occasionally by his father's proclamations of eternal damnation. Louis' maternal grandfather had been a moderately successful English industrialist and had provided

Louis with a gentleman's education at Harrow and Oxford. Louis had contrived to spend as much time away from his father as possible, taking every opportunity to take his holidays with the well-placed friends he made at school and then university.

If Louis could have found a way to support his lifestyle and not return to Edinburgh and his father's house, he would have. Unfortunately, the inheritance he had received when his grandfather passed away was quickly lost at the gaming tables, and he was forced to return as anything but a prodigal son.

Everyone who knew Louis found him to be a delightful child, irresponsibly generous with money he didn't have, and possessing an affability he did not inherit from his father. Falling under his charms was easy, but being a true friend to him was not. Louis was a master at self-inflicted wounds, laughing off setbacks that would have sobered a more sensible man.

Peter Kincaid was Louis' mirror image; serious, careful, and oppressed by life. Yet, somehow, the two had formed a bond. However, that bond was not based on mutually enjoyed activities; Peter had neither the money nor the inclination to gamble, drink, or whore. And so, it was common for days to go by when the friends' paths didn't cross.

Louis started at Tabitha's words, "Missing? What do you mean he's missing? And how are you connected to Kincaid?" Louis knew enough of Peter's background to realise that he was not someone whom earls and countesses would come looking for in the normal course of events.

Wolf answered, "My young cousin, Lady Lily MacAlister, is an acquaintance of Mr Kincaid." Tabitha and Wolf had briefly conferred before the ride to the Trent home, and before they were joined by the dowager, and had decided they would stick as closely to the truth as possible without revealing the political interests that connected Lily to Peter.

Wolf continued, "Lady Lily had arranged to meet Mr Kincaid when she returned to Edinburgh recently. When he failed to keep the appointment or respond to subsequent messages, Lady Lily became worried and asked me," Wolf paused then added, "and the two Lady Pembrokes, to make inquiries." Noting Louis' raised eyebrows, Wolf continued, "Before recently ascending to the earldom, I made a career of helping to track down people and possessions." If Louis Kincaid wondered what such a career might be, he pushed such thoughts aside. He was not a deep thinker and found that undue curiosity about other people's lives, motives, or ability to pay their debts at the tables usually brought on a headache.

"We were initially sceptical that Mr Kincaid had done anything other than disappear for a few days, as young men are sometimes wont to do when pursuing their pleasures." This would have been the point at which a more thoughtful man might blush, recognising the representation of how he often lost days at a time. Fortunately, Louis Trent was unencumbered by shame, remorse, or even mild embarrassment at his lifestyle. This alone was enough to drive his father to spend many extra hours on his knees each week in communication with his creator.

However, Louis was a good enough friend to interject with, "Peter Kincaid is not a man to lose days and nights to the more frivolous aspects of life. Wherever he has gone, he is not sleeping off a night of carousing."

Wolf agreed, "Indeed. We spoke to his landlady and the porter at the medical school, a Mr McDonald, who both spoke highly of Peter Kincaid and assured us that this was not behaviour in which the man would indulge."

Louis Trent smiled the lazy, mischievous grin that charmed the women and infuriated his father, professors, and creditors. "So, you spoke to Old Tom, did you? I'm sure the man had nothing good to say about me." When no one contradicted that, Louis added, "He's never forgiven me for the prank I played on him last year. Considers me nothing but a wastrel. I'm sure he told you he couldn't imagine why a fine young man like Kincaid would waste his time on a rotten apple like me."

Given that those were the exact words the porter had used, no one contradicted that either. Instead, the dowager, impatient to get to the part of the conversation where she could make use of interrogation skills that wouldn't have been out of place in the Spanish Inquisition, chimed in, "Yes, yes, all very well. You are clearly an embarrassment to your father and to his good name. That much is beyond dispute. But what do you know of this Peter Kincaid and his likely whereabouts? That is all we came for. I have a young woman whose readiness to greet society is almost beyond repair, and I cannot waste my time with this polite shilly-shallying."

Given that the dowager had insisted she accompany them when she could have been preparing her granddaughter for her season, this seemed an absurd complaint to make. However, Tabitha and Wolf were eager to cut to the heart of their visit. So perhaps allowing the old woman to move things along wasn't the worst idea.

The dowager's tone and stern expression were enough to make Louis Trent sit up a bit straighter and be even more eager to have his unexpected guests depart so he might return to his bed to enjoy a couple more hours of sleep before his father's return. "The last time I saw Kincaid, we walked with my cousin Vivian in Princes Street Garden."

"Yes, Vivian Wakely," Tabitha said. "Lady Lily told us there is an understanding of sorts between your cousin and Mr Kincaid."

"Yes," Louis confirmed, "they were sweet on each other from the first time they met. I usually chaperone their afternoons out. For herself, I believe Vivian would be happy to rendezvous with him alone. But Peter is far too good a man to risk any mark on my cousin's honour." As Louis said this, it was unclear whether he considered such restraint admirable or absurd. Perhaps both.

Tabitha continued, "We believe your cousin is currently with her sister. Do you think it's possible that Peter is with her there?"

Louis shook his head vehemently, "That is the last place he would go. Vivian's family knows nothing of their betrothal, and there is no doubt her sister would look unfavourably on a man with Kincaid's lack of family connections and fortune."

Wolf asked, "Is there anywhere else you believe Peter might

have gone to if he felt the need to leave Edinburgh?" He hoped Louis could also provide some insight into why Peter might have felt compelled to flee the city. However, he realised this line of questioning was likely the easiest for the half-awake Louis to answer.

Louis thought about the question briefly, then answered, "He used to talk about the orphanage he grew up in. If I remember correctly, it was in Stirling. Surprisingly, he had fond memories of his time there, particularly of the governor, some reverend or other. I can't remember his name for the life of me. But Kincaid looked up to him as almost a father figure. I believe it was this governor who suggested that James Sinclair provide Peter with his scholarship. I know he returned to the orphanage once or twice a year. He always spent Christmas there, at least."

Now they were getting somewhere. This was very useful information and seemed a likely place for Peter Kincaid to flee to if he felt he had to leave the city in a hurry. Unfortunately, Louis couldn't remember the orphanage's name or its governor. But how many orphanages could there be in Stirling? Wolf had already decided they would travel there the following day. He had considered trying to pinpoint the orphanage and then send a telegram. But he was worried this might make Peter merely flee Stirling. Better to have the element of surprise.

Louis desperately needed coffee and was suddenly ravenous. He considered calling for Robertson and asking him to bring refreshments. In fact, he reflected that he probably should have done that already and offered his illustrious guests at least a cup of tea. However, he desperately wanted this conversation to end and worried that offering food and drink would extend the visit.

"Mr Trent, I met your father the other evening at Laird McAlister's home, and I asked him about Peter. He said you knew better than to bring your friends into this house. He then left abruptly."

Louis' head was starting to pound, and he needed coffee more than ever. He could barely concentrate on the questions being asked of him. "My father is a strange man," was all he could summon the energy to say. When would these people leave?

Tabitha and Wolf were also eager to finish up the interview. Terrified to suggest otherwise to her mother, Jane had offered to postpone luncheon until their return. The unladylike rumblings coming from Tabitha's stomach suggested that their return should be sooner rather than later. But there was something else they needed to find out from Louis before they left. Tabitha asked, "What do you know of Peter's relationship with James Sinclair?"

Louis laughed dryly, "Sinclair! That crook. Peter came to rue the day he took a penny of the man's money. Even though it's hard to imagine how he would have received the education and opportunities he had without it."

"A crook? That's a rather dramatic claim to make, is it not?" Tabitha asked.

"Is it? Thieves are a dime a dozen in Edinburgh. There's always someone looking to pick your pocket. From what I've heard, Sinclair is just a rogue on a far larger scale."

Tabitha and Wolf waited patiently for the man to continue. The dowager, for whom this outing hadn't provided the opportunity for hand-to-hand combat she'd anticipated, was less patient. "Stop talking in circles, young man, and say whatever you must. I have neither the time nor patience to play these polite games."

These words struck the appropriate terror into Louis Trent's heart, and he got to the point as requested. "There have long been rumours of the lengths to which Sinclair will go to make coin. He has been very vocal in his opposition to the various laws passed over the last few years, which, at least as he tells it, are a financial burden to him and to his workers. Honestly, I can't remember his rationale for why the workers don't benefit from better working conditions and compensation for injuries. But Peter would tell me how it was often all the man could talk about at their dinners."

"So, Peter believed that Mr Sinclair was knowingly flouting

regulations?" Tabitha asked.

"As far as I could tell, he was doing so quite gleefully. It wasn't a topic that interested me much, so I tended to pay no heed when Peter got on his soap box about these things. But Vivian was always an avid audience for Peter's rantings, so I was forced to hear more of it than I would have chosen to."

Wolf could see they had likely gotten as much information from this rather vacuous young man as possible. But he had one more question, "Did Peter have any proof of these accusations?"

Louis squinted as he considered this question. "You know, we were together just before Vivian left town a week or two ago, and I couldn't help overhearing their conversation, no matter how hard I tried to ignore it. I do remember him saying something. Let me think for a moment about the way he phrased it." The man thought and then said, "It was something like, 'I will confront him with this and be done with his blood money for good.'" Louis sat back in his armchair, seemingly depleted by the energy expended in reflection on a boring conversation that didn't involve him, a pretty woman, or a bet on a horse.

If they had been inclined to continue to question the young man, the decision was made for them by the dowager who stood, pointed her cane at Louis and said, "Young man, I strongly suggest you change your ways. A life of dissipation, such as you are clearly indulging in, can have no good ending." And with that, she proceeded to walk out of the room. Tabitha and Wolf exchanged glances and then followed her.

CHAPTER 21

The carriage ride home had been taken up with the dowager bemoaning the youth of the day, interspersed with complaints about the previous Sunday's luncheon and her ardent hope that this one would follow a more typical English pattern. "We started with something called Cullen Skink. Have you ever heard a less appetising name for a soup?" the dowager demanded.

"How did it taste?" Tabitha asked.

"That's neither here nor there," the dowager stated indignantly. "How can one be expected to enjoy a dish knowing that is its name?" From this answer, Tabitha assumed the soup was far tastier than its name might imply and secretly hoped they would be served it during their stay. The dowager continued, "And then, we were served something called Cranachan for dessert! Cranachan! I didn't think it could get worse than Cullen Skink, but apparently, it could."

The dowager's complaints only made Tabitha and Wolf more eager to see what might be on the menu for this Sunday's luncheon.

Tabitha was happy the dowager's thoughts were directed away from the story Louis Trent had told. The dowager's pronouncements and prejudices would merely muddy the water. She needed time to reflect on the young man's words, and she hoped to steal Wolf away to the library that afternoon so they could discuss their thoughts and make notecards.

Tabitha's hopes about their meal were not disappointed, and the delicious Sunday roast lunch was prefaced by a very tasty

Cock-a-Leekie soup. The soup combined chicken with leeks and prunes and was a warm and satisfying starter on a rather chilly day.

Uncle Duncan was not present for luncheon. Apparently, he had taken the train that morning out to the village of Gullane to play golf at the "Honourable Company of Edinburgh Golfers," commonly known as Muirfield. The dowager had sneered about Scottish sports unbecoming of a so-called gentleman, but otherwise seemed happy not to have to endure the man for another meal.

It had been too much to hope that their morning visit wouldn't be a topic of eager conversation as they ate. Luckily, the dowager's replaying of their interview with Louis Trent negated the need for Tabitha and Wolf to contribute much. The dowager's recitation was a predictable mixture of self-regard and overblown melodrama; outrageous exaggerations of her role in extracting information from the man were interwoven with self-righteous sermons on the various evils of which she believed Louis an exemplar.

Finally, eager to move the conversation onto a different topic, Tabitha decided she had no choice but to sacrifice her niece. Casting the young woman an apologetic look and praying she would understand that Tabitha's actions were in the service of the investigation, Tabitha said, "Lily, how was your morning studying Debrett's?"

Wolf smirked, fully understanding Tabitha's ploy. Lily narrowed her eyes and shot Tabitha a look of irritation, then answered, "I believe I now understand the complicated history and lineage of the Duke of Marlborough."

The dowager immediately seized on this subject, "Ah, Marlborough. Yes, an unfortunate turn of events. While my usual stance is that it is always better to marry up, I would caution you to beware of men such as Marlborough, whose extravagant lifestyle and reckless spending has taken a ruinous toll on the family and its estates." The dowager thought for a moment and then added, gesturing around the room, "It is evident that a MacAlister inheritance is insufficient to mend the fortunes of such a man."

If Hamish took offence at this implied insult, he was wise enough not to show it. Tabitha was sorry that she had been the cause of the conversation pivoting to a topic likely both to annoy her niece and further insult her family. However, the dowager was now suitably distracted, and that was something.

A further benefit of Tabitha's attempt to change the topic was that the conversation was sufficiently distracting that the dowager decided she needed to spend the afternoon with Lily, laying out which other noble lines were to be avoided as matrimonial possibilities at all costs. No sooner had the last spoonful of the rich and delicious Dundee cake been finished than the dowager dragged a sullen Lily to the drawing room to continue her judgments on the great and the good, or otherwise, of English society.

The dowager safely ensconced with her reluctant granddaughter, Tabitha and Wolf intended to escape to the library. Before they did, Tabitha took Wolf aside and suggested, "Perhaps we should ask Hamish if he would join us. There were elements of Louis' story I would like to discuss with him. And he can also advise us about a possible visit to the orphanage."

Hamish hadn't been in the library since Tabitha and Wolf had taken it over as the investigation's command centre. As with most people who saw the board pinned with notecards for the first time, he was fascinated. As he always did, Wolf was happy to give all the credit for the ingenious idea to Tabitha and boast on her behalf about its pivotal role in helping them unpick the many tangled threads of their previous investigations.

While Wolf explained the board's utility to Hamish, Tabitha was busy writing up notecards for what they'd learned that morning. She had questions she wanted to create notecards for, but it made sense to vocalise those questions to Hamish and hear his response first.

They told Hamish the entirety of their interview with Louis Trent. Wolf said, "To hear Louis tell it, Sinclair boasted of his success circumnavigating recent regulations concerning his workers and the safety of the mines. Have you ever heard the man admit to such actions explicitly?"

Hamish sat in the armchair and tapped his fingers on his knee while thinking. "Honestly, I'm no' sure. The man kens my views on the topic are different than his, and I suspect he watches his tongue 'round me, somewhat. But ye met him. He's loud and boorish and boastfu'. I've certainly heard him make claims that I just wrote off as the words of a braggart."

Wolf felt they were going around in circles and asked, "Can you remember an explicit claim he ever made? Whether or not you believed it at the time."

"Aye, nae exactly, but there was an incident just a couple o' months ago. An explosion at one of his coal mines. Unfortunately, such things dae happen on occasion. But and I mind this clearly noo I think aboot it, Sinclair seemed tae almost crow aboot it in a maist unseemly way. We were baith at the New Club one evenin', sharin' a fine bottle o' claret wi' anither member, Paul Dwyer. Dwyer asked aboot the explosion, and Sinclair jist laughed and said there was naething tae ken noo. That he'd made sure o' that."

"But he didn't say more?" Tabitha asked.

"The man is ower clever for that. He says enough tae boast, but no' enough tae incriminate himsel'. He seems tae revel in bein' the mine owner who beats the system and regards someone like me as a dullard who rolls ower and accepts the regulations."

Wolf asked, "Is there anything else you can tell us? Anything unusual about how Sinclair runs his mines?"

Hamish thought for a moment and then said, "Aye, he does, makin' excessive use o' the tip or butty system." Seeing their confused looks, he explained, "It's when the mine owners dinnae pay the workers directly. Instead, they pay based on production. It's usually handled by a 'butty,' who oversees and pays the workers. The coal miners are nae paid a fixed wage by the mine owners or operators. The system used tae be far mair common, but it's fallen out o' favour o'er the years, at least wi' some owners. I dinnae use this system meself either. It's not the way I run things. It's important tae keep a close eye on how things are runnin' in yer colliery and how the workers are bein' treated and paid," he added.

Tabitha reflected on Hamish's words and asked, "So, you're saying that this butty system is a way for a mine owner to maximise profits by allowing unsafe working conditions, perhaps even using underage workers, while shielding himself from blame if anything goes wrong?"

"Aye, ye've hit the nail on the heid. The butty system takes the responsibility for stickin' tae regulations away from the colliery owner. Payin' only for the coal extracted rewards efficiency above all else. But there's nae doubt that it can encourage unsafe workin' conditions and exploitation o' workers. It's a system that has its downsides, that's fer sure."

Tabitha sighed. There seemed to be an abundance of gossip and speculation to indicate that James Sinclair played fast and loose with the regulations. The man seemed to have been careful not to provide any concrete evidence that could be tied back to him. But the fact remained that Peter Kincaid had indicated to Vivian and Louis that he had uncovered such evidence. What was it, and what might Sinclair have done to protect his reputation and business to prevent such evidence from being made public?

Tabitha articulated these questions as she wrote up more notecards. They then asked Hamish about travel to Stirling the following day. He told them the fastest way was to catch the train from Waverley station and then hire a carriage at the station in Stirling. They could be in Stirling in just over an hour if they caught the early train. As it happened, Hamish knew of the orphanage. It was one of several such establishments he was a patron of. He informed them that the governor's name was Reverend Stanley and that he would send a letter of introduction with them.

Assured they had no more questions for him, Hamish retired

to his study, hoping to hide from his mother-in-law and possibly have a post-lunch nap.

Left alone, Tabitha finished pinning and arranging the notecards on the board. Looking at them, Wolf admitted, "There's one more notecard to write."

"There is? What?" Tabitha asked with curiosity.

"The man who followed us to Grassmarket," Wolf said. "I've seen him again."

"You have? And you said nothing?" As always, Tabitha was irritated when she came to realise Wolf had sidelined her from an aspect of any investigation. "I thought we were beyond the point where you kept important details from me. Apart from anything else, this was information we should have had on the board days ago. The man has followed us multiple times, which needs to be factored into our investigation."

Wolf sighed; he knew she was right. In truth, he hadn't kept the information from her deliberately. Rather, he had noticed the man when they had left the house with the dowager that morning. On leaving the Trent residence, he had seen him again. Given that the dowager had been with them, it seemed unwise to bring the matter up in her presence. Since then, he hadn't had time alone with Tabitha until now. He explained this and saw that her anger soon dissipated. Instead, she asked, "Then the question is, who is spying on us, and why?"

"I've been thinking about that; the most likely person is James Sinclair. We know he walks a fine line, bragging about his successes in flouting the law while also remaining cagey enough about them that nothing can be pinned on him. If Peter Kincaid did uncover something concrete and Sinclair knows about it, it would be unsurprising if the man was not alarmed when we started asking questions. I even told him we were investigating Peter's disappearance."

"What do you suggest we do? Just continue to allow ourselves to be followed?" Tabitha asked sarcastically.

Wolf heard the edge to her voice and understood she wasn't entirely placated yet. Trying to defuse her irritation as much as possible, Wolf ignored her tone and answered, "I suggest we bait and then ambush the man."

"How do we do that?" she asked.

"Bear knows what the man looks like. I suggest that you and I go out in the carriage this afternoon and that as the man shows himself to follow, Bear apprehends him. We will then circle back around and can question him."

Tabitha considered this suggestion and pointed out at least one flaw, "Where will we question him? We can't drag him into the MacAlister home. Certainly not without the dowager inserting herself into the proceedings."

Wolf acknowledged the truth of her observation and suggested, "What about if we bring him into the carriage and question him there? Bear can join us; that usually is enough to scare most men into talking."

It was evident to Tabitha that this wasn't the first time Bear and Wolf had conducted such an interrogation. But she did wonder, "And what if he won't talk?"

Wolf laughed, "It's the rare man that can't be brought to speak by the promise of some combination of money and bodily harm."

"You're going to hurt the man?" Tabitha asked in a shocked tone. "There? In the carriage, in front of me?" She wanted to be involved in all aspects of the investigation. But she was not ready to be involved in this.

"Don't worry. It is highly unlikely it will come to that. Usually, one look at Bear and the threat of what he might do is enough." Then he paused and added gently, "You don't have to be part of this, Tabitha. I will not think less of you as an equal member of this investigative team if this is something you choose to sit out."

Wolf's evident and genuine kindness in making such an offer touched Tabitha. It was an offer unsullied by condescension or overprotectiveness. Instead, they were merely the words of a friend offering her a choice. But on reflection, she believed she could not shy away from the harsher realities of their investigations any more than she could hide from the harsh realities of the world she lived in.

CHAPTER 22

Tabitha and Wolf agreed that there was no time like the present for putting the plan into action, and Wolf called for Dawglish and asked him to find Bear and Rat and send them up.

"Rat?" Tabitha asked worriedly. "Why are we involving him?"

"Tabitha, we've had this conversation many times; the boy is sharp. Even Langley can see it. We don't know from where on the square this man is watching the house. Bear is far too conspicuous to send out. But Rat can leave through the back, go out to the square, and do some reconnaissance for us. If this plan is to work, it's imperative that Bear be in the right place in order to grab the man as soon as he breaks his cover."

"And that is all the boy will be doing?" Tabitha asked suspiciously.

"I promise," Wolf said with his hand over his heart.

A few minutes later, Bear and Rat were being briefed on the plan and their respective roles. Rat grinned, "It's just like the old days, m'lord Wolf." Tabitha didn't want to know too much about what the old days had involved for any of them, so she let the comment go.

Finally, with everyone confident of the part they were to play, Wolf and Tabitha went to gather their outerwear and asked Dawglish to call the carriage. Tabitha had a niggling doubt that the man might not choose to follow them on that outing, but she kept such concerns to herself.

While they were preparing to leave the house, Rat slipped out through the back garden and made his way back around to

Charlotte Square. Wolf had given the boy a description of the man following them, and it didn't take long for Rat to spot someone who looked like that man. He was just out of sight of the house if anyone was looking out of the windows, but with a clear enough view of its comings and goings. Wolf and Bear had told Rat that the man was not the most adept shadow they had ever witnessed. That their tail had been spotted so easily in Grassmarket was evidence that he certainly didn't rank next to some of the men they'd dealt with over the years. That it took Rat less than five minutes to find him confirmed this.

Stealthily, Rat slipped back into the house and found Bear waiting for him. Rat described where the man was and how he believed even someone as conspicuous as Bear could leave the house and observe the man's hiding spot without being noticed. Bear nodded and made his way out through the garden. Rat then went to the front of the house, where he found Tabitha and Wolf waiting in the vestibule. He nodded, and Wolf, in turn, had Dawglish open the front door. They wanted to make as much of a commotion leaving as possible and so talked loudly as they made their way to the carriage. At one point, just as they were about to get in, Wolf even shouted back to Dawglish to be sure and tell the laird they might not be home for dinner. If that didn't get the attention of the man following them, nothing would.

They got into the carriage, and the driver took off. They'd told him to drive around for at least five minutes and then start making his way back. "What if that isn't long enough?" Tabitha asked.

"If, for some reason, Bear wasn't able to grab the man as soon as he broke his cover, then he's not going to catch him this time, and when we return, we will just make a lot of noise about having forgotten something," Wolf explained.

Tabitha was very tense for the next few minutes. As the carriage made its way back to Charlotte Square, she anxiously looked out of the window. Mindful of prying eyes, both in the MacAlister home and the neighbouring houses, Wolf had suggested that Bear meet them down the side street that led up to the square once he had the man in hand.

As they made their way up that road, Tabitha was concerned that she couldn't see Bear. But no sooner had they approached the turn, than Bear materialised from an alleyway with another man held firmly in his meaty paw. The man was squirming, but Bear seemed to make no more effort to keep hold of him than if he'd been holding a trout wriggling on the end of a line.

Bear opened the carriage door and pushed the man in ahead of him. Watching the man's eyes widen in fear as he looked over at them, Tabitha turned and realised Wolf was pointing a gun at him. When had that happened? Bear clambered in next to the man and slammed the carriage door shut. Wolf had made clear to the coachman that he was to just drive around, ignoring any sounds from within the carriage until they knocked on the roof.

The carriage started moving, and Wolf said, "You know our names, yet we don't know yours. Let's begin by rectifying that."

The man seemed as if he was going to deny any knowledge of them, but Wolf flourished his weapon, and the man thought twice about such a tactic and said, "Easton. The name's Easton." He sounded as if he was from the north of England, but Tabitha couldn't place the accent.

"I'd say it's nice to meet you, Mr Easton, but we both know that isn't true." Wolf continued, "I have one very simple question for you, and before you refuse to answer or attempt to dissemble, let me be very clear about one thing: Lady Pembroke's presence in the carriage will not deter my large associate here from breaking your fingers, one by one until you have told us all you know." As if to confirm this statement, Bear loudly cracked his knuckles. Tabitha couldn't have explained why this was so terrifying, but even knowing how gentle Bear was in reality, she could understand the look of panic that suffused Mr Easton's face.

Certain that his threat was being taken seriously, Wolf asked, "Who hired you to follow us?"

Taking another look at Bear, who grimaced back menacingly, Easton quickly answered, "James Sinclair. I have no idea why before you ask. All I was told was that I was to follow you and report back on where you went and who you talked with."

Wolf thought about his next move and said, "This is what you're going to do: you're to say nothing to Sinclair. If you do and I find out, and I will find out, I will have no qualms about sending my associate here to finish the job I'm barely restraining him from doing now. And then it will be more than broken fingers." Easton winced at the thought, and Wolf, comfortable that the man was taking the threat seriously, continued, "You are to continue to pretend to do what Mr Sinclair has hired you to do, follow us." Tabitha raised an inquiring eyebrow.

Wolf said, "I'm assuming you send a report back to Sinclair at the end of every day?" The other man nodded his assent. "Good. You can wait out here every evening and my boy will bring out a report for you to transcribe and submit. You will send word of nothing but what I tell you to say. Is that clear?" With another scared look at Bear, who growled back at the terrified man, Easten nodded.

But the man's evident fear of Bear wasn't enough to convince him entirely, "Sinclair is a ruthless man. If he finds out I'm lying, my life won't be worth living."

Bear cracked his knuckles again and then grabbed one of Easton's fingers, applying just enough pressure to make clear what would come next.

"Then you better make sure he doesn't find out you're lying. Trust me, my friend here can cause far more pain than Mr Sinclair," Wolf assured him. Easton just nodded.

"Good," Wolf said, knocking on the carriage's roof and indicating that Bear should shove the man out of the door before the carriage came to a standstill.

"Bear, can you take care of this? Send Rat out every evening with some concocted list of mundane activities that we've supposedly been up to." Bear nodded. Wolf paused, "It is clear Sinclair has an idea that we are investigating him. It will look suspicious if his spy suddenly starts to report an utter lack of activity on our part. So, throw in a few tasty morsels to make it seem as if we're asking around but have no idea what we're looking for. Use your creativity."

They rode on silently for a minute or so while Tabitha processed the encounter. Finally, as they rounded the corner to return to Charlotte Square, she asked, "Why are you leaving him in place?"

"Because we know who he is," Wolf explained. "If he is exposed, Sinclair will realise we're onto him and may even substitute him for someone better at his job. This way, we control what Sinclair gets to hear." Tabitha was impressed by this logic. She had much to learn about conducting a professional investigation.

CHAPTER 23

Tabitha and Wolf had been very discreet at dinner that night, both about their afternoon's adventure and their plans for the following day; they had no desire for the dowager to take it upon herself to join them.

The next morning, they rose and breakfasted early, running into only Langley, to whom they briefly recounted the previous afternoon's situation with Easton. Langley raised his eyebrows at the story but said nothing. Tabitha reflected, given that Lord Langley had hijacked the dowager's carriage and held Tabitha and the old woman at gunpoint a little more than a month ago, their behaviour was hardly something he was in a position to criticise.

It was not much past 8:30am, and Tabitha was about to go and gather her outerwear for the ride to the train station when the breakfast room door opened, and the dowager entered, dressed as if ready to go out for the day. Tabitha and Wolf exchanged glances, hoping against hope that this wasn't what it looked like.

"Mama," Tabitha ventured. "You are breakfasting early. And you look as if you're heading out this morning."

The old woman sat opposite Tabitha and took the cup of tea the footman poured. She added two sugars and stirred them slowly, all the while not taking her eyes off Tabitha, finally tapping her spoon against the side of the cup and placing it on the saucer. She lifted the cup to her lips and drank a fortifying sip, then replaced it and patted her lips with her napkin. All the while, she said nothing. Tabitha and Wolf sat in fearful anticipation, hypnotised by the mundane sight of a woman drinking a cup of tea.

Finally, the dowager said, "Nothing readies one for the morning like a strong cup of tea. It is particularly welcome after the troubled sleep I had last night." She paused, eyeing her prey with all the skill and cunning of a big game hunter.

"I am sorry to hear you slept poorly, Lady Pembroke," Wolf said, not as attuned to the warning signs as Tabitha. She knew they were being set up to walk into a trap and wished she could warn Wolf. But she knew the sharp-eyed old woman would notice even the most subtle attempt to communicate nonverbally.

"Are you sorry, Jeremy? Are you?" the dowager murmured.

"Indeed," he replied.

Warning bells were blaring, and Tabitha desperately wanted Wolf to hear them. The dowager never called him anything but 'dear Jeremy'. How could Wolf not realise the snare being set for him? But the man blundered forward, not realising the danger he was being lured towards.

The dowager continued, "Do you know why I had trouble sleeping, Jeremy?"

Yet again, her tone and use of his name without its normal term of endearment were warning signs to which he seemed oblivious. Finally, the look on the dowager's face alerted even Wolf that perhaps all was not well. Tentatively, he replied, "No, Lady Pembroke. I don't."

At this, the dowager reached for a slice of toast and began buttering it. Slow, languid strokes of the knife across the bread, back and forth and back and forth. Then, just as the tension was almost unbearable, she brought the knife down with a thwack to cut the toast in half. The noise was hardly particularly loud or jarring, but Tabitha was so on edge by this time that the sound made her jump.

The dowager said, "Everything alright, Tabitha? You seem a little nervous. What on earth would you have to be nervous about?"

"Am I?" Tabitha stuttered, amazed that she was utterly undone by the woman doing nothing more than eating her breakfast.

"As I was saying," the dowager continued. "I had trouble sleeping because something was nagging away at me. Some concern that I was still being kept out of the investigation." Tabitha and Wolf couldn't help but exchange guilty looks. The dowager saw them and smiled, a feline smile of sadistic pleasure as the couple before her twisted and turned, impotently trying to find an escape.

The dowager continued, "And so, I thought a book might help me fall back to sleep. I assumed that even a heathen such as the laird must have some decent, English books in his library. I made my way down there, and what do you think I found?"

Given that it was clear what she'd found, Tabitha and Wolf assumed this was a rhetorical question and didn't answer. Needing no reply, the righteous indignancy of the dowager's tone was growing, "I found evidence that you have been hiding away to discuss the investigation without me. And even worse, evidence that, as I suspected, I have not been told the entire truth of this investigation. And from what I could piece together, you are sneaking away this morning to investigate the orphanage this Peter Kincaid grew up in."

Tabitha wasn't sure what to reply, but she was saved from having to answer as the dowager waved her butter knife at them and said in her most strident tone, "Don't bother to deny it. The hour you are breaking your fast and your garments speak more truly than any words."

It was unclear what the right answer was at this point. It was obvious the woman had read the notecards and knew everything. In hindsight, Tabitha reflected that they should have asked for a key to lock the library. But regrets would not help this situation, and Tabitha was sure that platitudes and empty apologies would not work this time either. Instead, she bypassed any explanation of their behaviour and said bluntly, "We are catching the 9:15 train. I assume you'll be joining us. We were just on our way to gather our things and we'll meet you in the carriage which should be outside by now."

The dowager looked quite taken aback by Tabitha's response. She hadn't expected such a frank acknowledgement of her accusations and had no reply other than one of her signature harrumphs. Tabitha and Wolf took this as verification that she intended to join them and hurriedly left the room before the dowager realised she had more to say.

No one said much in the carriage. The dowager was in a state of high dudgeon. This state was, in fact, her perfect harmonic balance, allowing the use of her full range of most favoured emotions: aggrieved yet self-righteous, outraged yet vindicated. Tabitha, who had seen this show too many times, was determined to ignore the old woman. Yes, they hadn't told her the full story of how Lily and Peter had met. But for the rest, the dowager had asked them to drop everything - no, demanded that they do so - in order to investigate because she was too busy with Lily. That she had lost interest in preparing her granddaughter for her season in favour of inserting herself into the investigation and then realised the full extent of what she had chosen not to be a part of was not something Tabitha felt inclined to apologise for. Certainly not the kind of grovelling, abject apology the dowager most enjoyed.

For his part, Wolf knew better than to insert himself into this argument any more than he already was.

Finally, settled on the train, the dowager grew bored of the silence. She realised she wouldn't get her desired response from Tabitha or Wolf, so she decided to put her justifiable vexation aside for now. "What is the plan, Jeremy?"

It wasn't lost on Tabitha or Wolf that, while the dowager was now talking to them, he was still demoted from 'dear Jeremy'. However, hoping that the dowager's more conciliatory tone boded for a thaw in hostilities, Wolf answered, "We believe that the first determination to make is whether Peter Kincaid is in residence at the orphanage. If not, does this Reverend Stanley know where he might be? True to his word, Hamish had written a letter of introduction to the reverend, and Wolf had this safely in his inside jacket pocket.

"And how do we determine if the man is dissembling?" the dowager asked with an enthusiasm that suggested she hoped for an opportunity to flex her muscles and utilise some of her most favourite interrogation techniques. It was not lost on Tabitha or Wolf that the dowager had brought along her cane for the outing. Whether this was as an aid to walking or a precaution in case of an attack from the flank was unclear.

"I think that's a determination best made in the moment, Lady Pembroke," Wolf suggested.

"Indeed. However, I believe we need a code word so we can communicate our beliefs on the matter. What about crumpets?" she asked.

"What about crumpets?" Wolf asked, confused.

"Jeremy, do keep up. We could use crumpets as our code word. If one of us believes the man is being less than honest with us, we will say crumpets."

"How will we unobtrusively inject the word crumpets in a sentence?" Tabitha asked, truly mystified.

The dowager sniffed, "I'm sure I would have no trouble doing so. But, if you believe such subterfuge is beyond your capabilities, feel free to make a better suggestion."

Neither Tabitha nor Wolf felt the need for any kind of code word. They were able to read each other's facial expressions well enough that they normally knew the other's thoughts during an interview. However, apart from the dowager's insistence on choosing such a word or phrase, there was the real possibility that without one, she would blurt out her feelings on the reverend's truthfulness. Tabitha thought for a moment and then said, "We should talk about the weather. This is Britain, and the weather is always an appropriate topic of conversation at any point."

"What's there to say about this dreary, grey Scottish weather?" the dowager asked.

Tabitha tried hard not to roll her eyes, "Perhaps you might

comment on its dreariness and ask the reverend if it is likely to last for the rest of your stay," she suggested.

"Tabitha, the day I resort to inane chitchat about an inclement day will be the day you know I'm truly in my dotage." The woman paused, then conceded, "But perhaps I can make an exception this once."

The rest of the trip passed peacefully enough. The dowager had still not explicitly brought up the topic of how Lily had really met Peter. Tabitha thought about what they'd put on the notecards; had their deception been obvious? It was possible the dowager's anger was merely focused on being left out of the investigation, as evidenced by the corkboard in the library. Of course, without tipping their hand, there was no way of being sure. They would just have to wait and see. It was wholly possible that leaving them in this state of nervous uncertainty was the point; she always did enjoy her revenge served cold.

The 9:15am train was an express, and they arrived in Stirling in just over an hour. Wolf easily found a carriage for hire outside the station, and within five minutes they were at the orphanage. Wolf paid the driver to wait, and they descended. The orphanage was in a Georgian-era house that had been made over to the reverend's philanthropic endeavours thirty years before when the last inhabitant of the house died childless. The building had clean lines and a restrained, symmetrical design.

Tabitha wasn't sure what to expect in an orphanage. Her only knowledge of such institutions came via *Oliver Twist* and, as such, wasn't the best advertisement for the care of orphaned children. The Dulwich house that Tabitha now ran with the support of her friend, the Duke of Somerset and Bear's mother, Mrs Caruthers, was not an orphanage. However, it did provide shelter, education, and care for children with nowhere else to go. Tabitha knew that the girls at the Dulwich house were loved and nurtured and hoped the same was true of the children in this house.

As they had at Dr Trent's home, Tabitha and Wolf exchanged glances and agreed that they might as well make use of the dowager and let her lead the charge. Of course, was there ever an option to do otherwise?

CHAPTER 24

The sturdy oak front door was opened by a stern-looking housekeeper. With her grey hair scraped back in a severe chignon and keys jangling off her belt, the woman could not have looked more the part. Tabitha's first impression of sternness was reinforced when the woman spoke. Without waiting for them to announce themselves, she said firmly, "Ach, we've got nae time fer well-meaning visitors the day. Ye'll need tae make an appointment, aye."

There were moments when Tabitha gave thanks for the dowager. Albeit few and far between, when they happened, they did help her view some, if not all, of her interactions with the woman in a slightly kinder light. This was one of those moments. It seemed as if the housekeeper was about to close the door without even allowing them to respond to her unfriendly greeting. However, before she got a chance, the dowager wedged her cane into the frame preventing the door from being closed.

"An appointment? Do you know who you are talking to?" the dowager asked indignantly.

The housekeeper was a tall, sturdy woman who loomed over the diminutive countess. However, the dowager had never let such an imbalance prevent her from imposing her will. Not waiting for the housekeeper to answer, she demanded, "You will inform the Reverend Stanley that the Dowager Countess of Pembroke is here to speak to him. Now." Interestingly, the dowager felt no need to use Wolf's title as additional reinforcement. It seemed she was correct in her assumption that Wolf's title was merely gilding the lily when, after a moment's pause, the housekeeper unwillingly stepped back to allow them to enter. She turned and led them to a room off the hallway, saying gruffly, "Have a seat, and I'll let the reverend ken he's got visitors."

The dowager was used to receiving all the courtesies she believed due to her title and personage. She certainly wasn't accustomed to being talked to as dismissively as the housekeeper had. The woman had deposited them in the front room and abruptly left. No offer of refreshments and no concern for their comfort. "For shame! I have rarely encountered such rudeness and lack of servility," the dowager huffed.

They all took seats in the sparely decorated room and waited. Anything more than a minute or so would have been more than the dowager would have found acceptable. As it was, it was at least five minutes before a short, rotund, harried-looking man in his later years, wearing round, thick-glassed spectacles, shambled into the room, muttering to himself. From Louis Trent's description of the reverend as a mentor to Peter Kincaid, Tabitha and Wolf had expected a man of a more imposing demeanour.

The reverend started as he entered the room as if he hadn't been alerted to their presence, saying absent-mindedly, "Ah, yes, Mrs Rawlings said I had visitors." He shuffled over to the dowager and put his hand out, saying, "You must be the woman Mrs Rawlings warned me about."

Reverend Stanley's tone on making this observation was one of such innocent joviality that even the dowager was hard-pressed to summon any real indignation. However, unconvinced that she wasn't being talked to disrespectfully, even if she couldn't quite put her finger on it, she narrowed her eyes and stared suspiciously at the little man. "I'm not sure what there was to warn you about. Your housekeeper met us with a rudeness and lack of deference that I certainly would never tolerate from a servant. I merely put the woman in her place."

Looking bemused, Reverend Stanley asked, "What woman? What place? I'm sorry; I feel I'm missing something. Why don't

I ring for some tea and scones? I believe it is as important to nourish the body as it is the soul."

The dowager was quite peckish and would have welcomed a drink and something to eat. However, as a woman with steadfast views on the role of the clergy in society, she could not let this almost heretical statement stand. "Reverend Stanley are you suggesting that sustenance is next to godliness?" she challenged. "I will have words with the Archbishop of Canterbury the next time I see him about the blasphemous teachings being promulgated by his clergy."

The reverend blinked a couple of times, and his eyes darted to Tabitha and Wolf, hoping they might help extricate him from this doctrinal quagmire that he had fallen into headfirst without warning or even understanding.

Realising that, as was so often the case, the dowager's intransigent indignation was distracting them from the task at hand, Wolf came forward, shook the reverend's hand, and introduced himself and Tabitha. They all sat, and Mrs Rawlings, finally rectifying her previous negligence of her guests, brought in a tea tray and poured a cup for everyone. The dowager took her cup with a haughty sniff, saying, "About time too." Mrs Rawlings pursed her lips at this criticism, then left the room.

Finally, Wolf was able to get to the point of their visit. He explained how they came to be investigating Peter Kincaid's disappearance and why they believed the man had not merely left Edinburgh for a trip. There seemed no reason to withhold key information from Peter's friend and mentor. However, Wolf was cognisant that they still didn't know how much the dowager had gleaned from her perusal of the notecards about Peter's political affiliation. Therefore, Wolf held off speaking directly about the man's ties to the Scottish Labour Party. Instead, he spoke about Peter's growing concern for the conditions in coal mines and his subsequent break with James Sinclair over the issue.

When Sinclair's name was mentioned, the reverend put down his teacup and ruefully shook his head, saying, "Yes, that was very unfortunate. I had counselled Peter to show his benefactor some grace; the man has been nothing but generous to this orphanage and in particular to Peter. While I have no doubt that a man who has risen to his heights from such humble beginnings likely has a forceful personality and perhaps even exhibits a certain ruthlessness in his business dealings, nevertheless, through his philanthropy he has shown himself to be a man who cares about the plight of the most overlooked members of society." The man paused and considered what Wolf had said, "So you believe Peter is missing?"

He said this with such a seeming lack of guile that Wolf immediately suspected Peter would not be found in this house. But he answered, "Yes, Mr Kincaid has been missing for more than a week. We were hoping that we might find him here, but I'm guessing that is not the case."

The reverend shook his head sadly, "Unfortunately, it is not. And if your next question is to ask if I have heard from him, the answer is that I last received a letter from Peter a few weeks ago. However, there was something about that letter that concerned me and perhaps makes rather more sense now." At this, the reverend stood and disappeared from the room, leaving his three guests exchanging confused glances.

Well, Tabitha and Wolf exchanged glances. The dowager said, "Just when I thought this man's behaviour and that of his household couldn't get any ruder, he just ups and walks out with no explanation. I've a fair mind to run the archbishop to ground and complain. It is clear to me that the man is too consumed by his theological controversies and is neglecting his management duties."

Tabitha had the strongest doubts that the Archbishop of Canterbury was either interested in or responsible for Reverend Stanley's, albeit absentminded, behaviour. But when the odd little man hadn't returned after a few more minutes, even she wondered if the reverend's actions were beyond mere mild eccentricity.

Finally, just as the dowager was becoming so impatient that

Tabitha thought she might explode, the reverend came back into the room, holding some papers. "Apologies for the delay, but in Peter's last letter he entrusted some papers to me. He told me he had uncovered something of the highest importance, and I was to keep these safe. And well, I'd quite forgotten where I'd put them for safekeeping and had to dig through quite a few desk drawers before finding them under the house accounts, of all places."

Her irritation with this man at a boil, the dowager erupted, "Well, get on with it, man; what do they say? I never thought anyone could be worse than Lady Willis at getting to the point, but I swear you are shredding my last nerve!"

If the Reverend Stanley wondered who Lady Willis was that he should be so unfavourably compared to her, he was wise enough, or perhaps so discombobulated by his guests, that he said nothing. Instead, he answered, "I have no idea what they say. Peter never gave me leave to read them; he merely asked me to ensure their safekeeping."

The dowager shot him a look of utter bewilderment that anyone would conduct themselves according to such principles. She certainly couldn't imagine any circumstances in which she would be given such supposedly important papers to hold and wouldn't read them as soon as she could.

Wolf asked, "Would you allow me to read the papers? I realise you consider yourself to have been entrusted with them, but they may help us find Peter."

The reverend nodded and handed them over. He hadn't been explicitly instructed not to show them to anyone; it had just never occurred to him that it was his place to read them. He handed Wolf a packet of papers. As Wolf flicked through them quickly, Tabitha could see he was confused by what he was looking at. It took all of the dowager's much-vaunted self-control not to snatch the papers from Wolf's hands. Tabitha did worry that if he didn't relay their contents soon, the old woman might throw good manners to the wind and grab at them.

Luckily, the reverend, probably keen to make his escape as

soon as possible, suggested, "Perhaps I should leave you alone to peruse them. Would you care for more refreshments?"

They assured the man they had all they needed and allowed him to beat a hasty retreat. Finally, with the room to themselves, even Tabitha was impatient to hear what the papers said.

"In truth," Wolf admitted, "I'm not sure." He moved his chair to sit between Tabitha and the dowager. He brought a side table over, placed it before them, and laid the papers out.

"Jeremy, what are we looking at? This seems to be a ledger of some sort with what seems to be a list of place names. Besides the absurd names the Scots have given their towns, what is so shocking about that?" the dowager asked.

"Indeed," Tabitha agreed. "Do you see something that we don't, Wolf?"

He shook his head and said, "I believe we must persuade the reverend to let us take these papers to show Hamish. Hopefully, they will make more sense to him." Wolf stood and rang the bell, hoping to either summon Reverend Stanley himself or at least the dour housekeeper.

As luck would have it, the reverend returned a few minutes later, whether summoned by the bell or not. Again, on entering the room, the reverend seemed startled as if he'd forgotten he'd left his guests sitting there, not fifteen minutes before. "Ah, yes, very good, very good," the absent-minded man said, seeming finally to remember who they were and why they were sitting in his front room.

"Reverend Stanley, we have looked at the papers Peter left with you, but we're unable to understand their importance. We believe we must take them for Laird Hamish MacAlister, my cousin-in-law, to look at. Will you allow that?" Wolf asked. At this, he remembered Hamish's letter in his pocket, withdrew it, and showed it to the reverend.

"Yes, Laird MacAlister, a very generous man. Of course, I can have no concerns about such an upstanding citizen being privy to this."

Wolf beckoned the reverend over and asked, "What's written

in these ledger entries looks like place names. Are they familiar to you?"

The reverend walked over to the papers and looked at where Wolf was pointing. Moving his finger down the page as he read, the reverend said, "This is a list of collieries, as far as I can tell. Look, Bannockburn is less than three miles from here."

Wolf considered this information. It was still early in the day; perhaps they should take the hired carriage and visit Bannockburn. They had no real idea what they were looking for, but it couldn't hurt to try to talk to some locals and get a feel for the place. He assumed that Sinclair owned this colliery. Perhaps they might even be able to talk to some of his workers.

CHAPTER 25

The carriage driver was happy to take them to Bannockburn. The ride there gave Tabitha more of an opportunity to appreciate the glories of the Scottish countryside. The rolling hills and gentle, verdant valleys of the lowlands were dotted with farms, interspersed with woodlands with the occasional castle ruin off in the distance. Despite the dowager's earlier gripes about the weather, it was now a chilly but mostly sunny day. Sheep and cattle grazed lazily in the pastures, and labourers worked the fields. It was an idyllic landscape scene that would have brought Tabitha a sense of tranquillity under other circumstances.

However, any peace Tabitha might have been inclined to find in their trip's pastoral beauty was quashed by the dowager's incessant complaining for most of the ride. She spent the first ten minutes replaying her outrageous treatment by the insubordinate housekeeper who had almost slammed the door behind them as they left. While Tabitha had also found the woman's attitude unhelpful at the very least, she was disinclined to indulge the dowager's need to dissect the woman's every word and action for any other motive than a general unpleasantness.

Receiving no response from Tabitha or Wolf to refuel her indignation against Mrs Rawlings, the dowager moved on to the reverend. She added to the litany of charges against the man she wished to bring up with the Archbishop of Canterbury. In truth, despite his absent-minded eccentricity, Tabitha had found the Reverend Stanley quite charming and helpful, so this line of bombastic rhetoric also quickly burned itself out.

"Really, the two of you do not make good travelling companions," the dowager complained. "Is this how you conduct yourselves during investigations when I am not around?"

Unwilling to say anything to relaunch the dowager's crusade against Reverend Stanley and his housekeeper, Tabitha said, "Mama, I am merely considering what we learned this morning, and I suspect Lord Pembroke is as well."

"What did we learn? We have a bunch of papers that don't seem to tell us much. That's about it," the dowager stated confidently.

Tabitha verbalised the thoughts she'd been trying to work through instead of listening to the dowager's diatribe for the past twenty minutes, "Well, we learned that Peter Kincaid is not with the Reverend. So where is he? We also learned that whatever those papers mean, Peter was concerned enough to need to get them out of Edinburgh. I believe we must assume that those papers are connected to James Sinclair's business and came into Peter's possession somehow."

Wolf agreed, "From everything we now know about Peter's recent break with Sinclair and his talk of 'blood money', it appears he discovered something, and I believe those papers are the key to uncovering what."

"Where is this elusive young man? That's what I want to know," the dowager demanded. "It is extremely inconsiderate of him to disappear in this manner."

Tabitha hesitated but then said what had been on her mind since it became evident Peter wasn't in Stirling, "Is it possible he's not just missing?"

Wolf had considered the same thing and answered, "I believe we have to consider the possibility."

"What possibility? Stop talking in riddles and speak plainly, Jeremy."

"The possibility that Peter Kincaid is dead," Wolf patiently explained.

"Dead? Well, that would certainly make this investigation more exciting, wouldn't it! This was all starting to feel rather pedestrian, coal mines and workers' rights. Who can really muster up much enthusiasm for such topics? But murder, well, that just makes the whole trip up here worthwhile," the dowager said with a callousness that made Tabitha gasp. Even for the normally self-centred old woman who was almost always oblivious to the woes of others except as they might provide fodder for gossip, this was an appallingly unfeeling and uncharitable statement.

Unwilling to feed the dowager's macabre increased interest in Peter Kincaid, Tabitha nevertheless couldn't help but ask, "Is it possible he's been dead all this time, and no one has realised?"

"Well, who is there to realise such a thing? His best friend didn't even know he was missing, he'd fallen out with his mentor, and his betrothed is out of town," Wolf pointed out grimly.

When he laid it out so bluntly, it was clear to Tabitha that if Lily hadn't had an appointment to meet Peter and worried when he failed to turn up, it might have been weeks before anyone else noticed he was missing. If he hadn't returned within a week or two, his landlady would have sold his belongings and rented out his room. At some point, his self-absorbed friend Louis might have wondered something. But at what point would he have roused himself to do something about it? Once Vivian returned to town, it was likely that she would have raised the alarm. But how long might that have been?

Wolf continued, "I think that when we return to Edinburgh, we should ask Hamish to make inquiries with the Edinburgh City Police to see if any unidentified corpses have been discovered over the last couple of weeks." Tabitha nodded in solemn agreement.

The dowager, unable to contain her morbid excitement with even the minimal decorum, her eyes gleaming, asked, "So, our theory is that Peter Kincaid discovered some incriminating information about James Sinclair, who then killed him?"

Of course, that was a possible scenario, but like Tabitha, Wolf was reluctant to keep the dowager's gruesome pot boiling. Instead, he said in a measured tone, "Let us not jump to conclusions. We don't even know that Peter Kincaid is dead. And even if he is, we don't know that he has been murdered. It's entirely possible he got run down by a carriage or drowned in a river." Seeing the dowager's eyes still gleaming at these new grisly possibilities, he added, "Or he's still alive, and we just don't know where to find him."

"Well, where's the fun in that?" the dowager said sulkily.

Ignoring the unfeeling old woman, Wolf continued, "And if we do discover that Peter was indeed killed, we still have no evidence that the quarrel he had with James Sinclair was anything other than the heated conversation we have been told about. While a certain amount of theorising can be helpful in an investigation, it's also important not to get too far ahead of the facts. Particularly before accusing a powerful man of murder," he said, staring pointedly at the dowager.

The woman pouted and said, "If I'd wanted to spend my day with boring, sticks-in-the-mud, I would have stayed home and listened to Jane blather about her sewing circle or her children or her cook's arthritis."

Luckily, they had arrived at the colliery before this conversation could further spiral. Located not far from the village of Cowie, the colliery consisted of various ugly structures and buildings. Tabitha didn't know what all the equipment was, but some very large structures looked particularly imposing and forbidding. Wolf explained that he believed this was the winding gear used to lower and raise the workers in and out of the mine. The colliery was a hub of activity and noise as men went about their work. The winding gear, steam engines and other machinery all added to a cacophony of loud, harsh noise with a rhythmic clangourous chugging sound over the top of it all.

The atmosphere was heavy with an acrid odour of smoke, and fine grains of coal dust filled the air causing Tabitha and the dowager to bring their handkerchiefs to their mouths and noses. Intellectually, Tabitha knew coal mines were a necessary part of the industrial machine that drove trains, fuelled factories, and warmed homes. She knew the mines brought employment and relative prosperity to the neighbouring towns and villages. And yet, for all that, it was a bleak, depressing place, and she had only seen above ground. Tabitha couldn't imagine working in such a place day in, day out. Breathing that foul air all day and having all the beauty of the surrounding countryside blotted out by the smokestacks and the fumes emanating from them.

CHAPTER 26

None of the men milling around the colliery seemed to take any notice of the carriage and the well-dressed threesome that had descended from it. Looking around in frustration, Wolf said, "Tabitha, I think it best if you and Lady Pembroke get back in the carriage while I try to find someone to talk with."

As disinclined as Tabitha usually was to be left behind, the smell, noise and foul air were so bad that she quickly agreed. "I'll ask the driver to take us outside the colliery gates, perhaps even down the road. If you don't mind?" she added. Wolf readily agreed, and the ladies resumed their seats in the carriage which then pulled away.

Wolf continued to look around for someone who looked like they were in charge and finally saw a man dressed less shabbily and covered in less coal dust than the others. He walked over to the man who looked him up and down and said, "A'm no' quite sure whit ye're efter, but this is a warkin' man's domain, no' a gentleman's haunt."

Ignoring the man's taunt, Wolf said, "I have a few inquiries to make about the running of the colliery. Are you the right person to speak with?" During the carriage ride, Wolf tuned out the dowager's ramblings and considered his approach for gathering information at the mine. There was a ruse he and Bear had used successfully in the past that he thought might just work now; they referred to it as 'the interested purchaser' strategy.

Every iteration of the ruse had variations based on the given situation, but the underlying plot was always the same:

a wealthy industrialist was doing due diligence on a potential purchase. Back in their thief-taking days, it would have been unbelievable that Wolf or Bear was the wealthy would-be purchaser, but they could usually clean themselves up well enough to pass for his men of business. Wolf had considered whether he might now play the man himself, but considered whether such a fabulously wealthy person would be conducting his own research. And without the trappings of an earl's carriage, it was harder to make the case that Wolf was such an eminent personage. However, his fine clothes and bearing would be even more impressive as such a man's employee; if the man of business dressed that well, how much grander must the man himself be?

In thinking about the backstory for his pretend employer, Wolf decided the man was an American. Why an American industrialist might want to buy a Scottish coal mine was neither here nor there; it was doubtful the mine manager would pick apart the story's logic to that extent. Wolf thought an American might strike more awe into a potential future employee. Certainly, any unusual questions and requests could be shrugged off as one of the many oddities attributable to Britain's wealthy but crass cousins across the Atlantic.

Wolf ascertained that the man he was speaking with was the overman, just one below the colliery manager. He told the wealthy American industrialist story and asked if there was a place they could talk. In his experience, talking with someone senior enough but not the most senior person was often the most fruitful conversation. Such a person was usually ambitious and often had their sights set on their manager's job. They were often happy to expose this manager as lazy, dishonest, incompetent, or all three.

Seeing the man's uncertainty, Wolf added in a hushed and conspiratorial tone, "Mr Rutgers has questions about the running of this colliery, and I'm sure he will be very receptive to any recommendations I might have about changes in management after his purchase." The overman, Mr Charles, licked his lips in avaricious anticipation of the salary increase he could expect with the colliery manager job and indicated that Wolf should follow him into a low building on the edge of the property.

The building seemed to be mainly used for storage, but at the back, there was a small room with an equally small table and two chairs. Fergus Charles took one, and Wolf took the other after closing the door.

"So, Mr? Sorry, I didn't get ye name," the man asked.

"Tobias Smith," Wolf said. This was the name he always used when playing such a part. He'd found that using the same nom de guerre ensured he was comfortable answering to it and never forgot who he was supposed to be. "I have come up from London on behalf of Mr Rutgers, of Pennsylvania, the United States of America, to perform due diligence on a number of collieries he has an interest in purchasing."

"What makes ye think it's for sale?" Fergus asked.

"Mr Charles, it has been my experience that everything is for sale, for the right price. Mr Rutgers has a very strong interest in diversifying both geographically and functionally. He believes the demand for coal will only grow exponentially, and he hopes to dominate the industry on both sides of the Atlantic."

Wolf had no idea how plausible a motive that was, but he suspected that if he didn't know, neither did Fergus Charles. To gloss the story with a fine sheen of additional plausibility, Wolf said, "Ours is not to question the business wisdom of the tenth richest man in America. Why, the stories I could tell you about the industries the man has entered, much to the amusement of his fellow industrialists, only to have the last laugh when he dominated that key market a few years later."

Wolf paused, then added in his prior conspiratorial tone, "And he never forgets the people who helped him as he moved into those industries. Mr Rutgers is a very loyal man, and there's many a man across the eastern seaboard whose purse is much heavier every week because he had the good sense to be an early friend to Jeremiah Rutgers."

His eyes gleaming with greed, Fergus asked, "How can I be o' service to ye, Mr Smith?"

"Mr Rutgers has not become the successful businessman he is today by cutting corners. He has his concerns about this colliery. He has heard rumours of higher-than-average accidents, for example. And then, on looking through the books and in discussion with Mr Sinclair's bookkeeper, it seems this mine does not have as many men in its employ as I would expect."

Fergus licked his lips, and his eyes darted from side to side as he thought. Wolf understood the man's calculation: tell the unvarnished truth and risk jeopardising the sale, lie and risk being penalised for the dishonesty when the new owner realises the truth. Fergus Charles wasn't a book-smart man, but he was cunning and considered the choice ahead of him. To help nudge him towards full disclosure, Wolf added, "And I'm sure it goes without saying that anything you tell me will be treated with the greatest confidentiality."

Fergus made his decision, "Aye, Bannockburn is a rich seam, one o' the richest I've ever laid eyes on. We've barely scratched the surface o' the black gold that lies waitin'. With the richt manager in place, this colliery could be the jewel o' the lowlands."

"And I take it that right manager would be you?" Wolf suggested.

"Aye," the other man said, and then he began to tell his tale.

In many ways, the story he told was, in its broad strokes, mostly what they already knew or suspected; James Sinclair snubbed his nose at government regulations, ran an unsafe mine, and used child labour. He staffed his mines almost entirely through the butty system. Paying for yield encouraged faster coal extraction and incentivised the workers to prioritise productivity over their safety. Fathers who brought their underage sons to work at the mine could reap even more of the system's rewards. And James Sinclair could keep at an arm's length from all the unsafe and illegal practices, with the plausible deniability provided by the lack of direct control over the workers.

However, while the butty system had advantages for a mine owner, the lack of direct control also meant inconsistent quality, ultimately impacting the business' reputation over time. The miners working for the butty did not have the same loyalty to the pit and its owner, often moving around, working for the highest bidder. For all his accumulated business savvy, it seemed James Sinclair didn't understand the value of prioritising long-term gain over short-term profits.

But Wolf still had one more thing he needed to understand; the practices described were immoral, and in many cases, they were illegal, but nothing stood out as warranting the name 'blood money.' Wolf again pressed on the question of accidents at the mine.

"Aye. Aboot a few months ago, there was a particularly bad accident - twenty men and nine young lads, maist under ten, were maimed or killed."

According to Fergus, the local functionary of the Mines Inspectorate had been bribed to look the other way at the labour practices at Bannockburn. Still, a journalist from The Scotsman had come sniffing around after the accident, which had alerted some of the Inspectorate's higher-ups. From the rumours Fergus had heard, Mr Sinclair had paid some hefty bribes to make the problem disappear. Yet another example of Sinclair paying a price for chasing short-term profit, Wolf thought wryly. At least he finally understood what Peter Kincaid meant by 'blood money'. He still didn't understand the papers sent to the reverend, nor how Peter had got hold of them, but it was obvious what the crime was that so upset Peter that he refused any more scholarship money from Sinclair.

Keen to return to the carriage and get back to Edinburgh, Wolf asked a few more meaningless questions and assured Fergus Charles, "Thank you for your candour, Mr Charles. It is evident that this mine has great potential if it were only run honestly and effectively. It is also clear to me that you will be playing a pivotal role in helping Mr Rutgers turn this colliery around once he is the owner, and I will be making a recommendation to that effect. Thank you for your time and honesty." And with that, Wolf took his leave.

Wolf found the carriage waiting just down the lane from the colliery. The carriage driver had assured them that it was quicker for him to take them to St. Ninians railway station to get the train back to Edinburgh. It would still take at least twenty minutes, and the two ladies were far too impatient to hear what he had found out to wait until there were all on the train.

Wolf told them all he had learned from Fergus Charles. Tabitha was horrified; while they had heard speculation that James Sinclair employed underage workers, confirming this and hearing how many children had died in the recent accident was horrifying. However, there was still one question they didn't have the answer to: was this worth killing Peter Kincaid over?

"I don't see why not," the dowager said confidently. "If Mr Kincaid had some kind of evidence, what might a man such as Sinclair not do to prevent it from becoming public?"

Tabitha thought about this. On the surface, it certainly made sense. But something didn't quite sit right with her, "Why do we believe Sinclair would care enough? After all, it seemed that he could always find someone higher to bribe when necessary. And he's been quite Machiavellian in his use of the butty system to ensure he can deny any knowledge of what was happening. Whether or not this muck would finally stick to James Sinclair, he strikes me as the kind of man who always believes it will roll off him." Wolf thought she made a good point. The dowager was determined to be contrary, so they debated the topic for the rest of the ride to the station, and most of the train ride back to Edinburgh.

CHAPTER 27

Arriving back in Charlotte Square, the dowager determined she had investigated enough for the day. Their trip to Stirling hadn't offered her the opportunity for the hand-to-hand combat she so enjoyed and instead had delivered only a couple of rather lacklustre skirmishes. Having prepared herself for the heat of a battle she was then denied, the dowager had a need for an aggressive confrontation. She decided to satiate this need by finding Jane and berating her for whatever transgressive behaviour felt the most appropriate in the moment.

Tabitha and Wolf were relieved to find they did not have to manufacture a reason to exclude her from their plans for the afternoon which began with talking with Hamish. Finding the man in his study, Wolf gave him a full description of their conversations with Reverend Stanley and then with Fergus Charles at the colliery. He ended by handing over the papers Peter Kincaid had left in the reverend's care.

Hamish spent ten minutes silently examining the papers while Tabitha and Wolf waited patiently for the man's observations. Finally, Hamish put them down and said, "Aye, ye see, this seems tae be a record o' bribes paid tae various mine inspectors. From whit I can see, there's a standin' amount paid tae each man, and then a bonus paid fer specific incidents at the collieries. So, the entry ye pointed oot concernin' Bannockburn seems tae refer tae the horrific accident frae a few months ago that the overman told ye aboot. I suspect that when such a high-profile incident takes place, additional money needs tae be spread aroond tae ensure that the Mines Inspectorate didnae dig too deeply intae the cause o' the explosion, ken?"

Wolf felt he had to ask, "As a fellow mine owner, does this all shock you, or is it common knowledge that such things go on?"

Hamish sighed, "When the Mines Inspectorate was first established back in 1842, it had very few inspectors, especially compared tae the sheer number o' mines. O'er the years, things hae improved, but they're still understaffed and overworked, ye ken? There are various tools at the inspectors' disposal tae penalise owners who dinnae comply wi' regulations, includin' fines, closin' o' pits, or even possibly imprisonment. But a' these measures tak' a lot o' time and a lot o' effort tae prove and enforce. It may often be easier tae tak' a bribe and look the other way. I'd like tae be able tae tell ye it doesnae happen, but, sadly, I'm sure it does."

Tabitha thought about Hamish's words, "I'm assuming that if this bribery had been revealed, there would be serious consequences for the inspectors involved and for James Sinclair."

"Aye, fer sure. This isnae somethin' Sinclair would like revealed."

"If we wanted to talk with James Sinclair, where do you believe would be the best place to find him?" Wolf asked.

"Aye, the man has an office on Princes Street. He's fond of bragging that he's in it frae the crack o' dawn till the gloamin', so I've nae doot ye'll find him there," Hamish said.

Before they left Hamish in peace, Wolf asked if he could help them find out if any bodies fitting Peter Kincaid's description had been discovered recently. Hamish said that the Chief Constable of the Edinburgh City Police was a member of his club and he'd be happy to send a note to the man.

"Ye micht want tae visit the mortuary as well. If Peter had been taken tae a hospital and passed away, he'd likely end up there, and the police wouldnae hae been notified." Hamish told them they'd find the Edinburgh City Mortuary located on Surgeons' Square, near the Royal College of Surgeons of

Edinburgh.

"Aye, in fact, ye ken the chief pathologist there, Dr Trent." Under normal circumstances, Wolf would have been happy to make use of such an acquaintance, but he doubted Dr Trent would be inclined to help. Hamish promised to send the note to the Chief Constable immediately. Still, he couldn't guarantee as speedy a reply.

Realising that with the dowager otherwise engaged, it was the perfect time to sneak out of the house and visit the mortuary, Tabitha and Wolf wasted no time gathering their outerwear and summoning the carriage.

The Edinburgh City Mortuary and Post-Mortem Rooms, to give its full name, was a rather dreary-looking building. The very look of it made Tabitha shiver. She couldn't imagine working here day in and day out. But she could certainly imagine that if there was anyone made for such an austere working environment, it was Dr Richard Trent. In fact, the more she thought about it, the more it made complete sense that the man chose to work with the dead rather than cure the living.

By this point, Wolf was quite accustomed to turning to his advantage the absurd reverence with which most people viewed the aristocracy. This day was to be no exception. The front of the mortuary was dominated by a large archway leading to a courtyard. Wolf presumed that this was how the bodies were brought in by cart. Entry to the archway was controlled by a Mr Archibald McKay, known to his friends as Archie.

Archie McKay had been watching over the mortuary for thirty years. While, in truth, few people attempted unauthorised entry, Archie was proud to say that, if they had, he would have prevented it. Having spent the last thirty years with not much to do all day but admit the carts and occasionally turn away someone normally looking for a different building, Archie had used his time to reflect deeply on the human condition.

All manner of men and women passed him over the course of a day, and he watched many a domestic drama play out on the streets in front of him. But the one thing Archie had never experienced in those thirty years was a couple of toffs descending from a fancy carriage, approaching the mortuary, and asking to speak to the superintendent. While even the aristocracy had to deal with death, it was never expected that they would come in person to identify their relatives. Instead, they would typically send a representative in their stead.

Archie puffed up his chest in eager anticipation of a conversation that he could regale Mrs McKay with that evening. Approaching the porter, Wolf slipped on the haughty, entitled persona that he so hated but which undeniably was effective when dealing with members of the working class. Without the preliminaries of a greeting, he launched in, "I wish to speak to the superintendent. You may tell him the Earl of Pembroke is awaiting the pleasure of an interview."

Archie didn't have much hair left on his large, round head, but he tugged at the few stray hairs he could grab hold off in deference to the surprising, grand visitor. An earl! Of all people. That was a turn up for the books, if ever there was one.

Too in awe to say anything more, Archie merely mumbled, "Aye, of course, sir. Your lordship, I mean. Jist follow me, and I'll tak' ye tae him."

Mr Lachlan Murray, the superintendent, had his office just off the courtyard, affording the man a good view of all the comings and goings in his fiefdom. Lachlan Murray took great pride in running an exemplary institution. Sir Henry Littlejohn himself, the Medical Officer of Health, could have made an unannounced visit and would have found nothing of which to disapprove.

Such was the confidence Lachlan Murray had in his management of the mortuary that even the announcement by that dolt McKay that an earl would like a word didn't ruffle his feathers. Instead, he smoothed down hair that was already as smooth as his excessive use of pomade could achieve, and said in his most officious tone, "Ach, and ye've left an earl waitin' in the hallway, hae ye? Whit are ye thinkin', man? Bring him in."

Lachlan Murray had never met an earl before. He hadn't even met a baron. However, he had an opinion as to what such a person should look like, and the man before him fit the picture well. Perhaps his hair was a little longer than Lachlan would have expected of a man who could well afford to have his hair cut every day if he so chose, but his manly figure and handsome visage were all Lachlan might desire in his ruling class. And the lady accompanying the earl was all that a noblewoman should be.

Wolf entered the superintendent's office and took a chair without being asked to. Tabitha followed him. During a previous investigation, Wolf had done his best impersonation of his grandfather, the old earl. The old man's every move and word had communicated that he had better things to do and people to see than whomever he was with at the time. He had looked disdainfully down his aquiline nose when talking to almost everyone. Wolf crossed his legs, mimicking the old earl's languid manner. Tabitha had not been present for Wolf's previous performance as "The Earl of Pembroke" and found it highly entertaining. This was even better than his brief performance when they had visited the medical school.

The superintendent hurried around his large oak desk and bowed to his illustrious guests. He would not dare to presume to offer his hand to shake, but he wanted the earl to feel the full force of his deference.

"I am the Earl of Pembroke, and this is the Countess of Pembroke. What is your name, sir?" Wolf asked imperiously.

"Murray. Lachlan Murray, at yer service, yer lordship and ladyship. How can I be o' help?"

In the carriage on the way to the mortuary, Wolf and Tabitha had discussed the story they would tell. Deciding to stick as closely to the truth as possible, they agreed to say that they were searching for a friend of their young cousin's and were now concerned that he might be dead. This was now the story Wolf briefly gave to the superintendent.

"Can ye describe this friend and gie an approximate time when the body might hae been brought in?" Lachlan asked.

Wolf gave the few details they knew about Peter Kincaid from

Lily's description, "He is a young man of middling height, brown hair and eyes, perhaps twenty-two years of age, or so. He has been missing for almost two weeks."

This description probably fit many men in Edinburgh. However, Tabitha suddenly remembered something Lily had mentioned in passing; Peter Kincaid had a heart-shaped birthmark on his right cheek, just below his ear. She mentioned this, and the superintendent perked up. "We keep detailed records o' all the bodies brought in, includin' any distinguishin' marks. If the young man ye're searchin' for ended up at the Edinburgh City Mortuary, he'll be in my records," Lachlan McKay said with great pride. If there was anything Lachlan felt justified in congratulating himself on, it was record-keeping.

Standing up, he left the room for a few minutes, then returned and said, "Aye, I've asked Mr. Peters, our secretary, tae bring in a' the records from the last twa weeks for young men. It may tak' a wee while. Can I offer ye tea and refreshments while ye wait?"

Two cups of tea and a rather stale scone later, a reed-thin, pale young man entered the room holding some files. Seeing the surprise on their faces at the small number of records, Lachlan explained patiently, "We file by gender and age in cases where we dinnae ken the identity o' the deceased. As ye'd expect, we dinnae get mony young men o' the age ye described. Mostly older folk and bairns." He took particular pride in this filing system of his own devising. It had rarely proved useful, but he had been sure that one day it would be, and he was satisfied beyond words that day had finally come.

He took the files from the young man and scanned them, finally pulling one from the limited pile. "I believe this may be ye' man," he said with a grand flourish as he handed some papers to Wolf.

Wolf read what seemed to be a post-mortem report. Much of the report was incomprehensible to him. Apart from anything else, the handwriting was atrocious. He returned the papers to Lachlan, saying, "Mr McKay, can you help me understand what is written here?"

Lachlan glanced over the papers, then said, "Aye, this is quite a simple case. The hospital that sent the body tae us had nae record o' who he was, but it seemed he died o' influenza."

"Is it common for you to be sent unidentified bodies?" Tabitha asked.

"Aye, not common, but it happens. If a man stumbles in delirious wi' fever and dies shortly after, we may never ken who he was."

"And the medical examiner was sure this man died of influenza?" Wolf asked. "It's just that we talked to a porter who seems to have been the last person to have seen Mr Kincaid, the man in question. And he said nothing of the man exhibiting any signs of illness."

"If Dr Trent said that's what he died of, then there's nae doubt," Lachlan said firmly. He had no great love for Dr Richard Trent, finding the man stern and unyielding. But his distaste for the man personally had no bearing on his confidence in his competence. In fact, he was certain that, merely in virtue of being the medical examiner at an institution of which Lachlan McKay had oversight, Dr Trent must excel in his field.

"Yes, Dr Trent is the medical examiner here. We did know that" Tabitha said, almost as much to herself as to Lachlan.

"Dae yer ken Dr Trent?" Lachlan asked. Of course, it was no surprise that Dr Trent mixed in loftier circles than Lachlan McKay. Nevertheless, he was surprised that the unlikeable doctor found himself in the company of earls.

Wolf waved his hand dismissively, "That is no matter." Then he thought and asked, "Do your records say which hospital the body was sent from?"

Lachlan looked back and forth, "It disnae say." As it happened, this was just the kind of sloppy record-keeping that Lachlan abhorred. Lachlan sighed. Usually, the medical examiner had a technician working beside him who filled out the final report on behalf of the pathologist. But the appalling handwriting in this report made clear it had been written by Dr Trent himself, not a man who would take well to any criticism of his administrative duties. Lachlan commented on this abnormality but seemed untroubled by it.

Tabitha and Wolf exchanged glances. They had things to discuss, but it seemed as if they had got the information they had come for, and there was nothing else to be gleaned from the autopsy report. But Tabitha did have one more question, "What happened to the body after the post-mortem?"

"All unclaimed bodies are sent tae the medical school, where Dr Trent puts them tae use in his classes," Lachlan explained.

Their questions answered, Wolf stood, gave a few brief words of thanks, and abruptly left the room with Tabitha on his heels. Lachlan McKay watched them go and thought contentedly that if he died tomorrow, at least he could say that an earl and a countess had borne witness to the superiority of his filing system.

CHAPTER 28

Tabitha and Wolf didn't talk much during the carriage ride back to Charlotte Square. They were both deep in thought. While they hadn't heard of any influenza outbreak, given the crowded, unsanitary living conditions in the tenements of the Old Town, it was only to be expected that infectious disease be a common cause of death.

Tabitha was incredibly sad to have proof that Peter Kincaid was not missing but rather dead. She knew that Lily would take the news very badly, and then there was Vivian Wakely, Peter's betrothed, to think of. To have a young man, in the prime of his life, with so much promise ahead of him, die young was heartbreaking. Of course, Tabitha knew young people who had been taken long before their time; her mother had lost a child to scarlet fever when Tabitha was still a baby, but she found Peter's death particularly tragic.

Back at the MacAlister home, they shed their outerwear and headed for the library by unspoken consensus. There had been no opportunity to write up their findings from the morning, and so, after Wolf had rung for refreshments and poured himself a large glass of brandy, they sat and divvied up the task of writing up everything they had learned that day.

They pinned the notecards to the corkboard, and Tabitha regrouped some until satisfied. Then she sat down with a cup of the tea Dawglish had just delivered in her hand and asked, "Didn't Dr Trent recognise Peter when he performed the autopsy? He claimed not to know him, but Lily told us that Louis and Peter met in Dr Trent's anatomy class. Is it possible he didn't remember one of his students?" She wrote these questions on cards and pinned them to the board. "I wonder how long ago the class was?" Another question for the board.

As Tabitha was pinning the last notecard, they heard the door open. Tabitha spun around, hoping the dowager wasn't descending upon them. She was happy to see that the visitor was Lily. Well, she was happy until she remembered the sad news they had to share.

"I haven't seen you both all day," Lily said. "I know Grandmama has returned. She's been torturing Mama for hours. But the two of you seemed to disappear again. Has there been any progress towards finding Peter?"

Tabitha looked up at the young girl and said gently, "Lily, come sit next to me." Looking towards Wolf and then the brandy decanter, she indicated he should pour the young woman the stiff drink she was certain to need.

"What's wrong, Aunt Tabitha?" Lily asked, her eyes wide with alarm. "Has something happened to Peter?"

Tabitha pulled the younger woman down beside her and embraced her, saying, "Lily, I'm so sorry to have to tell you this, but Peter is dead."

Lily pulled back, confusion and disbelief suffusing her face, "But he can't be. How do you know?"

Wolf handed her the glass of brandy and said gently, "We went to the mortuary. An unnamed man fitting Peter's description, including the birthmark, was brought in two weeks ago. He died of influenza."

"Influenza?" Lily asked incredulously. "Peter wasn't old or otherwise sick. How could he have died of influenza?"

"Lily, you didn't know him well or for that long. You have no idea if he had underlying health issues. Just because he appeared to be a healthy young man doesn't mean he wasn't vulnerable to sickness," Tabitha explained. "It is the season when influenza hits particularly hard. It can take people very quickly." Lily was crying now, and Tabitha just held her and stroked her hair.

Finally, her sobbing subsided, and Lily asked, "So is that it? Is the investigation over?"

That was a good question. Wolf and Tabitha looked at each other and then at the board. Wolf said, "The investigation into Peter's disappearance may be over, but it seems he uncovered something which we believe we need to continue to pursue."

As Lily's sobs finally abated, Tabitha asked, "I am curious about one thing Lily; you said that Peter and Louis Trent first met when they were both attending one of Dr Trent's anatomy classes. Yet Dr Trent acted as if he had no idea who Peter was when I spoke with him. Furthermore, he was the doctor who performed the autopsy on Peter's body yet did not amend the record to reflect the corpse's identity. How long ago was this class, and was it possible it was so large that Dr Trent didn't realise Peter had been his student?"

Lily thought about the question and said, "Well, Peter told me about Vivian when I first met him about a year ago. And I do remember that he and Louis had recently met. I'm sure Dr Trent teaches a lot of students. It's certainly possible that he just didn't remember Peter." And then she paused and seemed to be puzzling over something. She said, "Cousin Jeremy, you never returned Peter's letters to me."

Wolf slapped his head, "Apologies. We have been rather distracted."

"No, it's not that," Lily explained. "I just want to check something in one of them."

"Let me go to my room and retrieve them now."

It took barely two minutes for Wolf to rush to his room, pull the letters from the desk where he'd been keeping them, and return to the library. He handed the letters to Lily, who shuffled through them, looking for the one she wanted.

Finally, pulling it out, she perused it quickly and read, "While walking in the park on Saturday, chaperoned by Louis as always, we had a somewhat worrying encounter with his father, Dr Trent. It appears Dr Trent prefers to walk rather than take a carriage - apparently, he feels to do otherwise is to tempt the sin of sloth. He was taking a shortcut through the park, and we almost ran right into him. While I had interacted with him in his lectures, I had never talked one-on-one with the man; he is rather intimidating. Louis introduced me, and I wonder if Dr Trent suspected anything of the nature of my relationship with Vivian. Certainly, she was very tense and quiet during the encounter with her uncle and for the rest of the afternoon. I tried to discover the cause of her disquiet, but she merely shook her head and said it was nothing."

Lily put the letter down, "Then he went on to describe the pamphlets he was helping Mr Johnson write about the cause of universal suffrage. The letter was from six weeks ago."

"So, there seems to be no doubt that, even if Dr Trent didn't remember Peter from his class, he had been directly introduced to him only six weeks ago," Tabitha noted. "Why lie, and why not correctly identify the corpse?"

Lily shook her head sadly, "I don't know, but does it matter? Peter is dead."

Tabitha stood and went to the board, rereading all the notecards. Then she turned and said to Lily, "I believe we must visit Vivian at her sister's home." Seeing Lily about to object, she raised her hand and said, "Lily, if nothing else, Vivian must be told that Peter is dead. Such news cannot be delivered by letter. And if her family should now hear about the betrothal, what difference would it make? Peter is gone. But there is no reason why they need to know. You will come with us, and we will say that we have news that we felt needed to be told to Vivian in person. Hopefully, her sister and brother-in-law will be too consumed by the impending birth to bother themselves with what that news is."

Lily nodded, realising the truth in Tabitha's words, "Yes, she must be told, and I am the only person who can break such news to her. I see that. Will we go tomorrow?"

"Yes, as early as we can." Tabitha paused, turned to Wolf, and asked, "What on earth can we tell the dowager that might deter her from joining our party?"

"I don't know. Why don't we think on it and tackle that

problem later or in the morning," he answered.

When Tabitha entered the drawing room before dinner, she saw that Uncle Duncan had returned from his golf outing, which had turned into an overnight trip. Tabitha was amused to see that he had insisted on sitting next to the dowager, who looked as if there were an unpleasant smell just under her nose. While Tabitha was disinclined to provide any possibility of relief for the dowager, nevertheless, she couldn't resist going over to learn what Uncle Duncan was saying that caused the woman to look as if she had a rotten piece of fish in front of her.

"Y'ken, the day before's golf game was positively dreary. Dull swings, tedious putts, and utterly uneventful. I merely wandered about the greens wi yawns aplenty. I couldnae bear tae listen tae Malcom's boastin' aboot his game any mair. Claimin' every swing was as smooth as silk, and his putts were like magic. But truth be told, we all ken his game was nought but a fluke, and he was just lettin' his ego run wild!"

At this point, the dowager threw all her years of breeding to the wind, put her hand to her mouth, and yawned. Another man might have been insulted or at least taken the not-very-subtle hint. But Uncle Duncan had a lot of experience boring others about golf and could not be deterred. He continued, "And sae I had tae stay anither day tae prove it was nae but a fluke. And lo and behold, the man lost his nerve entirely, and his game was a disaster."

The dowager noticed Tabitha approaching and called out, "Tabitha, dear." This endearment in and of itself was evidence of how desperate the dowager considered the situation, "Do join us. Or even better, why don't you take my seat and let Mr MacAlister regale you with his charming adventures in hitting a little ball with a stick."

Again, the sarcasm was entirely lost on Uncle Duncan, who chuckled and said, "Nay, dinnae flee, lass. I've other tales that ye might enjoy far mair." And with that, the man positively leered at the dowager and winked.

Suddenly, Tabitha had the wickedest but most inspired idea.

She took an empty chair near the incorrigible man and said, "Uncle Duncan, there is something I wanted to ask of you. Lily and I must take a train trip tomorrow to deliver some unfortunate news to her friend. Unfortunately, due to some estate business that has just come up, Lord Pembroke is unable to escort us. I wonder if you might be so good as to chaperone?"

The dowager narrowed her eyes and asked suspiciously, "What is this news and who is this friend?"

Tabitha had determined that she would admit to the news of Peter's death if necessary, but she preferred not to reveal this information if she could help it. She was sure the death would make the investigation all the more intriguing to the dowager and make it less likely she'd be prepared to be left out of the outing. Hoping to put the old woman off, she answered, "The friend is a Vivian Blakely. I'm not sure of the particulars, but Lily feels it's important she deliver this news in person, and, of course, I offered to accompany her."

"Aye, I'd be delighted to accompany ye. A day out, flanked by twa bonnie lasses, what could be grander?" Uncle Duncan answered. Then turning to the dowager, he said, "Will ye join us, Lady Pembroke? Maybe ye and I can share a seat on the train, and who kens what else might come tae pass."

This last part was said in a tone of such outrageous flirtation that the dowager merely sniffed loudly, stood, and then turning to Tabitha, said, "Enjoy your trip. I will not be joining you. I believe I would rather spend my morning with Jane's woeful sewing circle than spend it in this man's company!" And with this, she stormed off.

"She's a spirited bonnie lass. It makes the taming all the mair worthwhile," Uncle Duncan commented, chuckling.

Accompanying Tabitha into dinner a while later, Wolf asked, "What was that kerfuffle with Uncle Duncan about?"

Tabitha whispered, "Let's just say I have guaranteed that the dowager will not join us tomorrow." She added, "Unfortunately, a sacrifice had to be made; you also will not be joining us."

"I won't?" Wolf asked.

"No, but Uncle Duncan will."

Suddenly, Tabitha's cunning ploy became clear, and Wolf chuckled appreciatively.

"In that case, I believe I will pay a visit to James Sinclair," Wolf said. "Even if Peter died of natural causes, there's no doubt that Sinclair's business practices are rotten to the core. He's having us followed; that's not something a man with a clean conscience does. I want to hear what he has to say. And I'm curious to see how he reacts to the news of Peter's death." Divide and conquer seemed like an efficient plan, and Tabitha agreed.

CHAPTER 29

The train ride to Inverkeithing wasn't long, and Uncle Duncan was a charming and entertaining companion. Lily was rather subdued; the news of Peter's death and her realisation that she would now have to break this news to her friend weighed heavily on her. But even Lily managed to smile at some of Uncle Duncan's tall tales.

The train was to go over the Forth Bridge, which crossed the Firth of Forth, the estuary that included the River Forth. Tabitha was excited to experience this recently built wonder for herself. Over breakfast, Hamish had told her what a feat of industrial engineering the bridge was. He had described its three cantilever towers which supported the high train tracks. To hear Hamish proudly describe the bridge, it was a magnificent testament to Scottish innovation and industrial prowess.

Tabitha looked out of the window eagerly, wanting to catch the first view of the bridge. Finally, just as Uncle Duncan concluded a rather inappropriate story about a drunken game of golf that went awry, she caught her first glance of the majestic bridge, an imposing sight on the horizon. As they came closer, she marvelled at how its red-brown steel trusses formed an almost delicate, intricate lattice pattern against the crystal-clear blue sky.

They had crossed the bridge almost before she knew it, and soon pulled into Inverkeithing, a charming harbour village. Uncle Duncan managed to find transportation to Vivian Wakely's sister's house, which was a mile out of the village.

While Uncle Duncan arranged their transport, Tabitha had

suggested to Lily that he not accompany them to call on her friend. "Your Uncle Duncan is a very amusing man, but perhaps not the person whose presence is best suited to the conversation we need to have with Vivian."

Lily laughed wryly and replied, "Perhaps we can suggest that he wait for us here in Inverkeithing. I see a charming inn across the way, and I'm sure he will need very little encouragement to stay there until we return." As she suspected, Uncle Duncan proved very amenable to the suggestion that he enjoy a wee dram or two rather than accompanying the women.

Reverend Gordon and his wife, Annabel, Vivian's sister, lived in a sturdy-looking, rather plain house. Lily informed Tabitha that the home was referred to as a Manse because it was the reverend's official residence serving the local community of the Free Presbyterian Church of Scotland.

"So, Vivian's family belongs to the same church as Dr Trent?" Tabitha asked.

"Yes. Vivian's maternal aunt was Louis Trent's late mother. My understanding is that Dr Trent met his wife through the church, and the families have both been deeply involved in it for many years. Vivian's father is a church elder like Dr Trent," Lily explained.

Pulling up at the house, Tabitha asked the driver to wait and said they would pay him for as long as it took. Lily knocked hesitantly at the door, which was opened by a jolly-looking housekeeper. Lily quickly told their agreed-upon story.

"The mistress gave birth last night, and the hoosehold is in a right tizzy, but I reckon Miss Vivian is in the kitchen. I'll let her ken ye're here," the housekeeper said, leading them into a large, sunny room at the front of the house.

In a short time, the door opened, and a young woman, whom Tabitha assumed was Vivian Wakely, entered. She was petite and looked like a porcelain doll; perfectly even features, a rosebud mouth, and bright blue eyes framed by thick, long lashes. To complete the doll-like illusion, Vivian had golden ringlets hanging loosely down her back. She smiled when she realised Lily was one of her visitors, and it was a smile of such sweetness that Tabitha's heart broke to think they were about to be responsible for that smile disappearing.

"Lily, what a lovely surprise," Vivian said. The housekeeper followed her into the room, bearing a tray with tea and a delicious-looking fruit cake. Vivian came forward and embraced Lily and then turned to Tabitha.

"Vivian, this is my Aunt Tabitha, the Countess of Pembroke," Lily said, introducing the women.

"How lovely to meet you, Lady Pembroke. Are you visiting from London?" Vivian sat next to Lily on the sofa.

Tabitha and Lily exchanged glances; now they were here, they were unsure how to begin. They waited for the housekeeper to leave the room and close the door behind her. Then, Lily took Vivian's hand and answered for Tabitha, "Aunt Tabitha and Cousin Jeremy have been involved in some investigations of recent. I asked them to come to Edinburgh because," she paused, then tried again, "well, because...I don't know how to say this, Vivian. Because Peter went missing."

Vivian's delicate porcelain skin lost its bloom as she paled and asked worriedly, "What do you mean he went missing? Has he now been found?"

Lily looked at Tabitha, who gave the slightest of nods to indicate the need to deliver the sad news and not drag the moment out any longer. Lily grasped Vivian's hand tighter and said, with her voice cracking, "Peter is dead."

Vivian gasped and pulled her hand from Lily's, "No! This is impossible. Why have you come to tell me such lies?" Tabitha shook her head again; Vivian had to be allowed her initial reaction, whatever it was. When Lily didn't answer, Vivian continued, "Peter cannot be dead; I won't believe it's true."

Then she started to cry great heaving sobs. Lily put her arms around her friend and held her, comforting the other girl much as Tabitha had comforted her the day before, tears streaming down her face. "I'm so sorry, Vivian. I wish it weren't true. But there is no doubt."

The crying lasted some time. Neither Tabitha nor Lily said anything while the young woman processed her shock and grief. Finally, as the sobbing began to subside and passed into hiccups and sniffles, Tabitha poured tea for everyone and pressed a cup into Vivian's hands. The woman drank her tea and said in a quiet, pained voice, "Tell me what happened."

"As Lily said, Peter went missing. Lord Pembroke, Lily's cousin, and I began to search for him. When there was no sign of him anywhere, we resigned ourselves to the possibility he had died somehow. We visited the mortuary, and they have a record of someone matching Peter's description, including his rather unusual birthmark, having died of influenza about two weeks ago, just after the last known sighting of Peter. The body was unidentified, but there seems little doubt that it was him."

"Influenza? That's what Peter died of? How is that possible? He wasn't a frail old man or a sickly child," Vivian exclaimed, mirroring Lily's thoughts the day before.

"The autopsy report seemed quite conclusive," Tabitha assured her. "In fact, it was Dr Richard Trent, your uncle, who performed the post-mortem."

"Dr Trent?" Vivian asked. "And yet he didn't identify Peter? How can that be?"

The young woman was still highly agitated, but there were questions they needed answers to, and Vivian's words had struck at the heart of one of them; how could Dr Trent not have recognised a young man he had met a mere six weeks before?

"I had the same question," Tabitha acknowledged. "I know that Peter had been in Dr Trent's anatomy class last year, but Lord Pembroke and I assumed the class was large and so perhaps it was understandable that Dr Trent wouldn't have known all his students by sight. But Peter had written to Lily describing how you and he had been walking in the park with Louis when you had run into Dr Trent, and they had been introduced. He didn't believe Dr Trent had suspected anything of the feelings between you and Peter, but it seems unlikely he wouldn't have remembered a friend of his son's."

"But he did suspect something," Vivian exclaimed. "In fact, he threw the fact in my face when he, when I, well…" the young woman struggled for the right words.

Lily laid a hand on Vivian's arm and said, "There's no rush, Vivian. Take all the time you need. You've had a terrible shock."

Vivian shook her head and replied, "I just don't know how to explain this well. Perhaps, I should start at the beginning. Lily, as you know, my father is an elder in the church with Dr Trent. Our families have worshiped side-by-side for many decades. Dr Trent is not a blood relative, but we children always referred to him as uncle, out of respect. About two years ago, I began teaching Sunday school to the youngest children in the congregation. Dr Trent's particular responsibility was overseeing the spiritual education of the congregation, and he would often sit in on my classes and provide guidance to the children and became something of a mentor to me."

The woman paused and then looked away as she said, "One day, after class, he stayed behind and said he had something he wished to speak to me about. I assumed he had some advice for me on my teaching. So, as instructed, I went and sat beside him. He took my hand, which I believed to be the affectionate gesture of an uncle, and then before I knew it, he was making inappropriate advances towards me. He told me how much he had come to admire me and spoke of my beauty and compassion. I did not know what to say; in truth, I was in shock. Here was a man I had always looked up to spiritually, who had always treated me like his own niece, and now he was whispering words of love in my ear. To be honest, I felt sick to my stomach."

Neither Tabitha nor Lily wanted to interrupt Vivian's story, but Lily reached out and clasped her friend's hand. Vivian continued, "He must have interpreted my silence as consent because he suddenly reached out and grabbed me violently and then began thrusting his tongue into my mouth. I tried to pull away, but he held me too fast. Finally, I managed to struggle out of his embrace and pulled away from him. And then he just laughed and said that a little maidenly hesitation was only to be expected and was even quite enjoyable."

Vivian shuddered at the memory. "As he said that, he stood and left the room, leaving me shaking with shock at what had just taken place. After that, I made every effort not to be alone with the man."

Tabitha had to ask, "Was there any repeat of this incident?" She was horrified by the story Vivian had told. It was abhorrent to her that a young, innocent woman should have to fend off the groping of any man, let alone a man who held such a position of authority and respect in her church.

In reply, Vivian nodded her head, "Yes, twice more. And each time, the assault was more violent and the liberties he sought to take with my person more distressing." At this, Vivian began to cry again.

Lily exclaimed, "Did you never tell anyone? I cannot believe your father would not have defended your honour against such attacks."

"At first, I was in shock. And then I was too ashamed. The second time he came upon me alone, he pressed himself against my body and told me that he knew I secretly wanted his advances. He called me, well, I'm not sure I can tell you what he called me; it was so terrible." She paused, then said, "He called me a wicked temptress of a whore, who had been making eyes at him since I was barely out of the nursery. He told me he had watched how I batted my eyelashes at him and licked my lips, and he had known what I wanted. How could I speak of such things to my father? I felt I must have behaved as Dr Trent claimed, even if I hadn't realised what I was doing."

"Vivian, I don't believe that's true," Tabitha assured her. "It was nothing more than the justifications of a wicked, wicked man."

Vivian didn't look convinced by Tabitha's words. She continued, "Just over a year ago, my father called me into his study and told me he wanted to talk about Dr Trent. At first, I was terrified that he had learned what had happened and was to berate me for my unmaidenly conduct. But what he had to say was almost as bad; Dr Trent had asked for my hand in marriage, and my father had given his consent."

"Why would your father consent to such a marriage? The man must be more than twice your age?" Lily asked. Of course, Tabitha was less surprised to hear this. While her late husband Jonathan hadn't been as old as Richard Trent, he had been significantly older than Tabitha. As with so many marriages in their social class, this had been seen as a virtue; an older, wiser man to guide the young, naive girl.

Indeed, this was essentially the tale Vivian told; her father knew Richard Trent as an upstanding member of the community and the church and just the kind of man he felt comfortable entrusting with the care of his beloved daughter.

"I could not tell Papa why I refused to entertain Dr Trent's offer for my hand. Instead, I spoke of being unready for marriage. I was already nineteen by this time, and the excuse was weak, but Papa is a loving and indulgent father, and he patted my hand and said, of course, there was no great rush."

A question nagged at Tabitha, "Excuse me for any impertinence in mentioning your finances, but Lily gave me to understand that you have an independent fortune. Surely this gives you far more freedom than most young women your age, or even older, to determine your destiny."

Vivian laughed a humourless, bitter sound, "If only money was all there was to it. Papa may be loving and indulgent, but he is also a man who expects that, as head of the household, his word is the law. I do not doubt that having given his blessing to such a marriage, my father expected that within a short time, his wish would be realised. I believed I would pay a high price for such disobedience, perhaps even losing my family."

Tabitha asked, "Had you met Peter at this point?"

Vivian shook her head, "No, the marriage proposal came just before I met Peter, and my only thought then was to prevent a betrothal. But once I met Peter, I needed to persuade my father that not only could I not marry Dr Trent, but that Peter, a penniless orphan, was worthy of my hand. I hoped that once I was of age, Peter might be sufficiently advanced in his career that my father would not reject the match immediately. And if he had, well, then, to be with the man I loved, I was prepared to accept my expulsion from the family if it came to that."

Tabitha thought about the story Vivian had told. It was evident that the harsh, moralising facade Dr Richard Trent imposed on the world hid a lecherous, repulsive man. The doctor believed Vivian's father would eventually compel her to accept him as a suitor and was merely biding his time. Tabitha said, "You began this awful story by saying Dr Trent had suspected something of the nature of your relationship with Peter and had thrown it in your face. What did you mean by this?"

"I had managed to avoid Dr Trent at church as I always tried to, but perhaps three Sundays after our encounter in the park, so just over three weeks ago, he managed to corner me after Sunday school. There was no incursion upon my person this time, but he came very close and said in an ugly snarl that he would have me, no matter the dalliance I might be trying to hide from my family."

"Did you make any reply?" Lily asked.

"I did. I told him that I would never consent to be his wife and would rather live estranged from all I knew and loved than ever share a marital home with him."

CHAPTER 30

Once Tabitha and Lily had set out for their morning excursion, Wolf and Bear set out for Princes Street. Hamish had told Wolf it was a short walk from Charlotte Square, and Wolf was happy to travel on foot for a change; walking helped him think through problems. He had decided to take Bear with him. The enormous man's presence usually helped encourage people to be more helpful than they might otherwise be inclined to be. From Wolf's brief conversation with James Sinclair at the MacAlister's soiree, he couldn't imagine the man being inclined to answer his questions without some persuasion.

As they walked, he updated Bear on everything they'd discovered. "You were asked to find this Peter Kincaid, and you did. You found that he died of influenza; a sad outcome, but not a criminal one. Why are you still pursuing James Sinclair?" Bear asked.

"There's little doubt that James Sinclair is bribing mine inspectors to overlook the flagrant flouting of safety regulations and his clear abuses of his workers' rights," Wolf explained. "We know that Peter had somehow got his hands on evidence of this and had confronted Sinclair. And the man is having us followed. Just because he's not the villain in the case of Peter Kincaid's disappearance doesn't mean he's not a villain. I'm no longer a thief-taker, merely a gun for hire, moving from case to case. I'm in a position of privilege and influence. I can't ignore what we've found, even if it isn't the case we were asked to investigate." Bear merely nodded in acknowledgement of these words. He knew that his old friend's unexpected elevation to a position of power and wealth did not sit easily with him.

The walk to Princes Street was pleasant. Leaving Charlotte Square, they proceeded down George Street, which was lined with large, stately, light-coloured stone buildings. There were plenty of storefronts and other commercial establishments, and it was a hub of activity that crisp but sunny morning. Hamish had suggested walking through Princes Street Gardens to reach Princes Street. Wolf was interested in taking a stroll through the Gardens, given the supporting role they seemed to play in Peter Kincaid's story. Princes Street Gardens acted as a narrow, verdant divider between Old Town and New Town; a peaceful respite for the affluent inhabitants on one side and a clear reminder of which side they belonged on to the indigent on the other.

Wolf and Bear strolled along the tree-lined path, which afforded a magnificent view of the castle above. As they walked along, they discussed how Wolf planned to approach the conversation with Sinclair. "Are you planning to reveal that you have the papers Peter sent to the reverend for safekeeping?" Bear asked.

Wolf considered the question; how much was he prepared to reveal their hand? He had no doubt Sinclair would deny all wrongdoing. The man had clawed his way out of the mines to the peak of industrial might. A man such as that wasn't easily cowed. Sinclair was cleverly using the butty system in an attempt to shield himself from any liability for the abuses at his collieries. He would believe he could bluff and bully himself out of any attempt to pierce that shield.

Emerging from the Gardens onto Princes Street, they only had to walk a minute or two to reach the building Hamish had described. From the shiny brass plaque announcing Sinclair Industries, it seemed they'd not only found the right building but that James Sinclair owned all of it. A smartly dressed doorman doffed his cap at the obviously well-to-do gentleman and his huge companion. If he wondered why such a man was walking rather than arriving by carriage, he showed nothing of such musings by the look on his face.

On being told that the Earl of Pembroke wished to speak with James Sinclair, the doorman asked them to follow him into a luxuriously appointed ante room. Everything about the room screamed that the man being waited for was very rich and very important; silk, gilt and marble were the dominant materials. To Wolf's taste, the effect, while clearly intended to be opulent, instead had rather a gaudy feel about it; a high-end brothel trying to emulate the drawing room of a duchess.

Sitting behind a large, ornate desk was a slight young man with nervous, darting eyes. He appeared very curious about the two visitors who he was sure were not in the appointment book he kept so meticulously. The doorman went up to the desk and spoke softly to the man, Ronald MacDougal, James Sinclair's personal secretary. Ronald nodded and the doorman left. Finally, coming from around the desk, Ronald bowed his head quickly to Wolf and said, "Your lordship, please take a seat and I'll see if Mr Sinclair can spare time to meet with ye. May I say what this is about?"

"When you tell him the Earl of Pembroke is here to see him, he'll know what it's about," Wolf answered curtly.

Ronald MacDougal again bowed his head and turned to a door to the side, knocking gently twice and then entering. Within a minute, he had returned and ushered Wolf and Bear into James Sinclair's office. Sinclair had not met Bear, though, of course, he had received reports on him from the man following them, and his eyes widened in surprise at the size of his visitor. But otherwise, his face showed nothing but an insincere pleasure at receiving them.

Sinclair stood and extended his arm to shake Wolf's hand, "Lord Pembroke, to what do I owe this honour?"

Wolf looked at the ruddy-faced man, his bulbous nose shining unattractively in the rather harsh electric lighting and realised just how distasteful he found James Sinclair. In the abstract, he admired a man who could make his own way in the world as successfully as Sinclair had. But Wolf now knew the price others had paid so this office could have old masters on the walls.

Wolf shook the outstretched hand and sat down. His intention was to assume the persona of the Earl of Pembroke, which had been serving him so well recently. "Sinclair, I bring you news about Peter Kincaid. We have solved the mystery of his disappearance, and I thought you should be told."

Sinclair's face showed no emotion at this news, neither curiosity nor guilt, "An' where did ye find the ingrate?"

"In the mortuary. Peter Kincaid is dead." Wolf watched James Sinclair very carefully as he shared this news. Whatever he might be feeling, his face was a mask of indifference. Wolf marvelled at the cold-heartedness of the man; he had known Peter Kincaid since he was eight years old. He had considered making Peter his heir. And yet, for all the world, he could have just been told nothing more dramatic than that Peter had been found in Glasgow.

"I see," Sinclair finally said. "But I'm no' sure why ye came a' the way here tae personally gie me this news. I had nae expectations o' ony further relationship wi' Mr Kincaid; as far as I'm concerned, he was dead tae me the moment he threw my largesse in my face and stormed oot o' my hoose."

The harshness of these words was staggering, and Wolf wondered, for a moment, if Sinclair had killed Peter Kincaid and somehow managed to make it seem like he died of influenza. However, Wolf wasn't sure how such a thing would be possible. He had more knowledge of poisons than the average person might, but he'd never heard of anything that could mimic the symptoms of a disease in such a way that it could fool an autopsy. He considered the idea again and then dismissed it. Sinclair's reaction wasn't that of a killer; instead, it was the reaction of a heartless bastard.

Deciding there was no point in calling out a man with no conscience, he pivoted and said, "I came to give you the news because you were very interested in the investigation Lady Pembroke and I are conducting. I thought we might cut out the middleman, and I could report to you directly for a change."

Again, the other man's face showed no surprise; Wolf considered what a good card player he must be. "I was wonderin' whether my man had been found oot. His reports were suddenly sae bland."

"Would you care to tell me why you were having us followed?" Wolf answered, attempting to match the other man's sanguinity.

"I keep a close eye on my business, and I keep an equally close eye on anyone who makes my business their concern," Sinclair said calmly.

"Peter Kincaid made your business his concern, did he not? And from what I've heard, he discovered some very interesting information on your reliance on the butty system and its tragic consequences. And then, of course, the final straw as far as Peter was concerned was when he found papers showing your bribery of the mine inspectors."

Finally, something had caused a reaction from Sinclair; the corner of his mouth started to twitch. Perhaps attempting to give his mouth something else to do and distract from the involuntary motion, Sinclair laughed and replied, "I hae nae idea whit ye're talkin' aboot, Pembroke." This overly familiar use of his name did not escape Wolf's notice, but he said nothing. "But if I should hear that ye're spreadin' sick lies aboot me, I'll hae nae choice but tae bring a suit o' malicious slander."

Wolf felt he'd had enough of the man and wasn't sure why he'd bothered to come. Perhaps there was a small part of him that hoped Peter had somehow been wrong and had misconstrued what he'd found and that perhaps Fergus Charles had just been a disgruntled employee with an axe to grind. But after looking the man in the eye, he did not doubt that James Sinclair was guilty of every crime they suspected and likely many others they had no idea about. There was nothing to be gained by continuing this conversation. Instead, Wolf stood up and said, almost as if it was an afterthought, "I look forward to showing the evidence in court then, Sinclair. Because, of course,

it's not slander if it's true."
    And with that, he and Bear turned and left.

CHAPTER 31

Lily had been reluctant to leave Vivian behind. Between her emotional distress after sharing her horrifying story and her overwhelming grief at losing her betrothed, Vivian seemed in no state to help her sister and her newborn. But she had insisted that it would be unbearable to return to Edinburgh just then and be reminded of Peter wherever she went. Better that she stay and attempt to lose herself in the joys of a newborn baby.

The carriage ride was too brief to allow for much discussion about what they had heard. And a train ride with a quite inebriated Uncle Duncan was neither the time nor the place. Arriving back in Charlotte Square just in time for luncheon, any opportunity for discussion was again postponed.

Tabitha was not unhappy to have this time to reflect on what Vivian had told them. It was no great shock to hear that the self-righteous, frequently sermonising, puritanical Dr Trent was, in truth, a hypocritical, lecherous monster. It would hardly be the first time such a man was thus exposed. Watching a still tipsy Uncle Duncan leer at the dowager as he entered the drawing room, Tabitha thought that at least this man was open and transparent about his vices. And she suspected that much of Uncle Duncan's more outrageous behaviour was more for effect than anything. No, men like Dr Trent were the real evil, cloaking their appetites in the trappings of religion and holier-than-thou morality.

"So, you delivered this so-called news to Lily's supposed friend?" the dowager interrupted Tabitha's thoughts with her caustic question.

After the morning she had experienced, Tabitha had no desire to engage in verbal sparring with the dowager and merely answered, "Indeed, Mama. I hope your morning was also productive." Tabitha realised that in asking such a question, she had known full well that she was likely making poor Jane an easy target. But she had no desire to share their conversation with Vivian and knew that providing a distraction was the best way to deflect the dowager's attention. This didn't make her feel less guilty.

"Productive? No, it was hardly that. Truly, as dreary as Jane's company is, I believe that throng of dullards who make up her sewing circle might be even worse. From what I could tell from the very little attention I paid as they introduced themselves, my daughter is the highest-ranking one of their number. Yet, she allows herself to be browbeaten by this appalling, officious woman, a Mrs Shark, no, I believe it is Mrs Shard. Whatever the harpy's name is, she manages to combine the doltishness of Lady Price with the sharp elbows of the Duchess of Lea, which is quite a feat, I can tell you."

All the while, Jane sat at her mother's side, looking even more miserable than usual. Tabitha felt very guilty now for setting this tirade in motion. Luckily, before the dowager could continue, Dawglish announced that luncheon was served, and they made their way to the dining room.

Tabitha hadn't had a chance for even a brief word with Wolf. On his return from visiting James Sinclair, Wolf had spent the rest of his morning in the library to bolster Tabitha's fabrication of his need to tend to estate business and escape the dowager's clutches. Lord Langley had joined him and had brought Melody and Rat with him.

Langley had diligently kept up with Melody's studies during the few days they had been in Edinburgh. And unbeknownst to Tabitha and Wolf, he had also begun working with Rat. That morning, while Wolf sat in a comfortable armchair and read a book, Lord Langley had worked with the children on their reading. Observing his patience and gentleness, particularly with the little girl, Wolf had again marvelled at this recently revealed side of the man. He wasn't sure he'd ever really like Langley, there was still something somewhat reptilian about the man, but he had a whole new respect for him.

Tabitha sat at luncheon between Wolf and Lord Langley and considered how to get them both alone in the library as soon as possible. Finally, as dessert was served, Uncle Duncan, who had started the meal tipsy and, four large glasses of claret later, was now past the point of good sense and judgment, whispered a rather crude suggestion into the ear of the dowager who was sitting to his right. She stood, threw her napkin on the table, and said in an outraged tone, "I don't know when I've been so insulted. You, sir, are no gentleman! I will not spend another moment sharing a table with such a man. If anyone wants me, I will be in my room."

Just as she was almost out of the dining room, the dowager turned and said, "And Lily, do not think for a moment that your secretive outing this morning excuses you from your studies today. I expect you to join me within the hour, and we will spend our afternoon reciting the royal lineage and discussing the best tactics for avoiding Bertie's wandering hands." Lily rolled her eyes, but luckily her grandmother had already left.

With the dowager and her bat-like hearing safely out of the room and Uncle Duncan and his increasingly bawdy jokes occupying Hamish and Jane, Tabitha whispered to Langley and Wolf, "Meet me in the library, as soon as you can." Then she added, "And be discreet." They both nodded.

Tabitha slipped away from the table as soon as she could. She didn't even want Lily to suspect they were meeting; the girl was too fragile at the moment, and Tabitha wanted to discuss some ideas that she wasn't comfortable saying in front of an innocent young girl.

Tabitha made her way to the library, where she wrote up notecards for all she and Lily had learned that morning. Now that the dowager knew they were using this room as a command centre, Tabitha did consider whether pinning notecards to the corkboard was still a good idea. But at this point, the dowager knew almost everything. And while Tabitha still wasn't sure how much the dowager had realised about Peter's political leanings, there was nothing in Vivian's story that gave any more of that away.

When the door opened, and Langley and Wolf joined her, she had just finished writing the notecards. Gesturing for them to shut the door behind them quickly, she then stood and pinned the notecards to the board. Turning back to the men now seated in matching leather armchairs, Tabitha proceeded to tell them everything she had learned that morning. She also told Langley about their visit to the mortuary and what they learned about Peter's death.

When she finished her story, Lord Langley sat back in his armchair and steepled his fingers together, his eyes narrowed as he considered what he had been told. Finally, he asked, "I'm assuming you believe this Dr Trent somehow had something to do with Mr Kincaid's untimely death?"

Tabitha nodded, glad it was as obvious to him as it was to her. "I don't know how, but I believe it's clear why. Everything points to him as the culprit; he claimed he didn't know Peter Kincaid, yet that was a lie. We now know he had a sick obsession with Vivian Wakely and was determined to possess her. Six weeks ago, he stumbled across Vivian and Peter together and suspected some romantic entanglement was standing in the way of Vivian agreeing to marry him. Three weeks ago, he finally caught Vivian alone and confronted her with this, and the truth of his suspicions became evident."

Wolf wasn't entirely convinced, "I agree the man certainly had motive, but Peter died of influenza."

Tabitha shook her head, frustrated that her normally perfectly in-sync investigative partner was being so blind, "We believe he died of influenza because the medical examiner who performed the autopsy put that in the post-mortem report. But that medical examiner was Dr Trent."

Tabitha directed her arguments to Langley, "Even the superintendent seemed surprised that Dr Trent had performed the post-mortem without an assistant. Remember, Wolf? He commented about Dr Trent having written the report himself, which was unusual."

Now she mentioned it, Wolf did remember. It had been a passing observation at the time and seemed to be about how bad the handwriting on the report was more than anything. Wolf asked, "Let me play your line of thought out then for a moment: your claim is that Trent lured Peter Kincaid to the mortuary, killed him somehow, and then created a fake autopsy report for an anonymous corpse. And finally, because the corpse is anonymous and unclaimed, he can send it to the medical school for use in his own anatomy classes, thereby saving him from having to dispose of the body. Is that the narrative you are claiming?"

"That's exactly it. And I believe there may be a way we can prove it. Or at least prove the key part of this, that Richard Trent did not perform an autopsy on an unnamed corpse that night."

Tabitha told Langley and Wolf her suggestion. Wolf considered it and said, "That is quite a long shot. What are the odds?"

"Do you have a better idea?" she asked. Wolf and Langley both admitted they didn't.

CHAPTER 32

Before leaving the library, Tabitha had a thought. Telling Wolf and Langley to follow her down to the drawing room, she went in search of Lily. She found the young woman being drilled by the dowager.

"No, Lily, how many times must I tell you, Prince William, the Duke of Clarence, was Queen Charlotte's second child. It was Prince Edward, the Duke of Kent, who was her fourth," the dowager was saying with the impatience of someone who had repeated this fact many times in a brief period.

"I just don't understand why it matters, Grandmama," Lily pleaded. "None of these people are alive and haven't been in a long time. Who cares?"

"I care! The royal family cares! Heaven forbid you should find yourself in an audience with Her Majesty and the topic should come up and you say the wrong thing."

"Is the topic likely to come up?" Lily asked with genuine curiosity.

"Queen Charlotte was Her Majesty's grandmother. The Duke of Kent was her father. I have first-hand experience of how much such things matter to Her Majesty. It is of the utmost importance that you get this right. You somehow manage to remember all those inane facts about plants, but the lineage of your sovereign seems to be something you can't keep straight for more than five minutes."

The exasperated dowager turned as the threesome entered the room, "Ah, Tabitha. Perhaps you can impress upon Lily the importance of understanding the family trees of the most important families in the realm, particularly the royal family. Your mother can be faulted for many things, but I believe she always placed an appropriate emphasis on lineage."

Tabitha felt there was an insult in there somewhere, but if it was directed at her mother, she was disinclined to argue. Instead, she said, "Mama, I must beg for your forgiveness and steal Lily away for just a few minutes."

Lily looked thrilled at such a possible reprieve, but the dowager glowered. "We lost this morning, and most of the day yesterday, and now you expect me to give up the afternoon?" Tabitha wanted to point out that the dowager had been unable to work with Lily the day before because she had insisted on accompanying Tabitha and Wolf to Stirling. However, she realised little would be gained by pointing out such inconsistencies in the woman's logic and instead tried to appease her, "It is very important. You would be making an enormous contribution to the case, which will not be forgotten."

The dowager harrumphed, as she was wont to do, but let her granddaughter take a break.

"Where are we going?" Lily whispered as they swept out of the drawing room before the dowager could change her mind.

"We're going to find Bear," Tabitha answered. Langley and Wolf exchanged confused glances. They had no more idea than Lily what was happening. Once their escape from the drawing room was assured, Tabitha turned to the two men and said, "Go and find Bear. Tell him to meet us in the small, unused parlour." She paused, then added, "And tell him to bring his drawing materials." Now Wolf was truly confused. But he knew better than to argue, and he and Lord Langley set off in opposite directions to find Bear while Tabitha led Lily to the parlour.

Safely settled there with little chance of being discovered by a nosey dowager, Lily asked, "What is this all about?"

"I need you to describe Peter in as much detail as you can so that Bear can draw him. I need to show his likeness to someone."

Five minutes later, Bear entered the room, followed by Wolf and, shortly thereafter, Lord Langley. Tabitha explained what she wanted; Lily would describe Peter, and Bear would try to draw him. Lily would then suggest corrections until they arrived at as good a likeness as possible.

Privately, Langley was highly sceptical that this would work, but he kept his own counsel and observed the proceedings with interest.

Lily and Bear sat beside each other, and Lily thought for a few moments. Then, she started to describe Peter to the best of her memory, being sure to include the unusual birthmark below his ear. When she was finished, Bear started to draw. He was using a graphite pencil and had a rubber at hand for any corrections. Bear drew in quick, sure strokes, and, a few minutes later, turned the paper around to show Lily. She quickly commented and corrected; the nose was too long, the face too wide, and the forehead too high.

After twenty minutes, she finally said, "Yes, this is Peter Kincaid."

"Thank you, Bear. And thank you, Lily. Now, you better return to your grandmother before she eviscerates both of us," Tabitha said.

Lily unwillingly returned to the drawing room, and Bear went to find Rat and Dodo. Tabitha held up the drawing and said, "I hope this gets us what we need. We must make haste. I want to be sure to get there early enough to catch him."

The three of them then headed to Hamish's study, where they hoped to find the laird hiding, as usual, from his mother-in-law. They were in luck, and he welcomed them into his study and offered everyone some whisky. Wolf and Tabitha politely declined, but Lord Langley, who greatly appreciated a fine single malt, was happy to oblige.

Langley appreciatively sipped his whisky while Wolf deferred to Tabitha to tell the narrative she had pieced together. It wasn't that he didn't agree with her conclusions, but he felt it was her story to tell. Tabitha patiently explained all they had discovered about Dr Trent and his prurient interest in Vivian Wakely. Hamish raised his eyebrows, surprised at what he was hearing about the supposed morally rigid doctor, but did not comment. Tabitha then told Hamish the timeline of Peter's introduction to Vivian, their clandestine betrothal, and their unfortunate encounter with Dr Trent six weeks before.

"And yet," Tabitha explained, "when I asked Dr Trent about Peter Kincaid on the night of your soiree, he denied any knowledge of his son's friend. While it might be believable that he had forgotten a student of his from a year before, is it credible that he had forgotten a man he met less than two months ago? Particularly a man he met in the company of the woman he hoped to marry."

Hamish was a rational man; Lily had inherited her scientifically inclined brain from her father. He thought about what Tabitha had said and asked, "Is it no' possible that Dr Trent didnae put the name Peter Kincaid together wi' the young man he encountered in the park that day?"

Tabitha had briefly considered this before remembering the letter Peter had sent Lily describing the encounter: "In his letter to Lily, Peter specifically said that Louis had introduced him to Dr Trent. And given what we now know about Richard Trent's intentions towards Vivian Wakely, it seems highly unlikely that the name of the man Trent suspected she had a romantic interest in wouldn't have stuck in his mind."

Hamish agreed that this seemed unlikely. Tabitha continued, "When I first mentioned Peter Kincaid to Dr Trent, I wondered at his sudden unwillingness to continue speaking with me. He had been almost chatty up to that point. But as soon as I asked about Peter, he disclaimed any knowledge and abruptly walked away. At the time, I found it rather odd and a little rude, but I didn't think much else about it. But now, I reflect on that conversation in a whole different light."

Hamish nodded in acknowledgement of her logic, and Tabitha then told him about their visit to the mortuary, the post-mortem report of the unnamed young man and the interesting coincidence that Dr Trent had been the person to perform the autopsy and then send the unknown and unclaimed body to the medical school. At this point, Tabitha held up the drawing Bear had made. "The one weak link we have in this narrative, at least so far, is confirming that Peter visited the mortuary. With Lily's help, Mr Caruthers drew this likeness of Peter. We are hoping to use it to get such confirmation."

"An' then whit?" Hamish asked.

Wolf stepped in, "Hamish, we are not sure if things in Scotland work similarly to how they do in England. In your capacity as a local landowner, are you a Justice of the Peace?"

"Aye. I hae authority in my commission area, but no' in this burgh."

Now it was Lord Langley's turn to step in, "Laird MacAlister, I do have some knowledge of how such things work in England. In specific circumstances, I believe it is possible for someone highly placed in the government to grant a Justice of the Peace authority outside of their normal jurisdiction."

"Aye, it's possible. Various authorities can grant that, includin' the Secretary o' State for Scotland."

At this, Langley's eyes lit up, "I believe I can help with that. Lord MacAlister, can you arrange for a telegram to be sent on my behalf?" Hamish assured him he could. Langley wrote out the telegram he wished to send, folded the paper and then Dawglish was summoned to ensure it was sent immediately.

"How can we be sure the telegram will arrive and be dealt with promptly?" Tabitha asked.

Langley merely smiled and answered, "Trust me, it will be dealt with expeditiously at every stage, and I expect the authority to be granted, by the Home Secretary himself, within the next two hours."

Hamish didn't ask how the earl, who had invited himself to stay just a few days before, could be so sure of such things. However, he did say, "If ye're sure, then I'll hae the warrant made oot."

CHAPTER 33

True to Langley's word, Hamish received official authorisation from the Home Secretary himself no more than two hours later. Again, if he wondered at his guest's ability to achieve such things, he did not mention it. By this time, it was past 4:30 in the afternoon, and Tabitha was concerned that they would miss their chance that day if they didn't hurry.

"Lord Langley, Wolf, I believe we must set out for the mortuary, post haste. Hamish, we will leave the rest in your hands."

All three men agreed, and Langley, Wolf and Tabitha gathered their outerwear and called for the carriage. On the drive, they agreed on the approach they would take, and when they arrived a short while later, following their plans, Wolf alone alighted from the carriage. He was happy to find Archie McKay still working even though it was almost 5pm.

For his part, Archie was delighted to see that the toffs had returned. Mrs McKay had been quite delighted with the story he had told the other day and had given him some extra pie as a reward for the entertainment he provided over dinner. He knew for a fact she was making hot collops and plum pudding for dinner that night, and he was sure that a new tale of the Earl of Pembroke would ensure second helpings.

Tugging again at his non-existent forelock, Archie said, "Gude day, yer lordship. Back again? How can I be o' service?"

"Mr McKay, I'm delighted to find you still at your post," Wolf said sincerely.

"Ye'll find Archie McKay at his post frae 7am till 5pm, Monday through Friday, and half-days on Saturdays. Come rain or shine," the man said proudly.

"That's what I've come to ask you about, Mr McKay." Wolf pulled out the likeness that Bear had drawn of Peter Kincaid. "Is it possible this man was a visitor here, perhaps a little over two weeks ago?"

Archie studied the drawing. As it happened, the mortuary didn't have many visitors. Well, not live ones, at least. Carts came and went with corpses, and some families occasionally came to identify bodies. But people arriving with appointments were a rarity, so any such occasions were memorable.

And this young man had been particularly memorable. Archie McKay was an observer of the human condition, after all. He liked to think that all that observing had given him insights into what made a man tick. He saw every human emotion play out on the streets before him, so he knew what desperation looked like when he saw it; he'd seen it that day.

"Aye, he was here. He said he'd been asked tae come an' speak tae Dr Trent aboot a possible job as a mortuary assistant. In my mind, the man seemed o'er eager tae get the job. As if he was doon tae his last bawbee," he said, referring to the Scottish equivalent of an English halfpenny.

Since Peter Kincaid had recently refused his living scholarship from James Sinclair, Wolf suspected he may have been as desperate as he looked. Wanting confirmation, he asked again, "So, this man was here about two weeks ago to meet with Dr Trent about a job?"

"Aye. Ye're lucky it was that evenin'. As I said, normally I'd be away by five, but Mr Murray was waitin' for a delivery and had asked me tae stay a wee bit longer."

"One more question; Is Dr Trent here now? I'd like to have a word with him."

"Aye. Ye'll find him in his office or the post-mortem room. But ye'd best hurry up. He'll be finishin' up for the day."

Thanking Archie for his help, Wolf indicated that Tabitha and

Langley should follow him, and they made their way into the building. After a few wrong turns, they came to a door marked "Post-Mortem" and knocked on it. After a terse "Enter", they filed into the room.

Dr Richard Trent looked up from something he was writing, a scowl crossing his face when he realised who his visitors were. "To whit dae I owe the pleasure o' such an illustrious visit?" he growled.

Looking past where the pathologist was sitting, Tabitha realised a corpse was laid out with a gaping hole in the chest. Dr Trent noticed her glance in that direction and then quickly avert her eyes, "This is nae place for a woman. Whitiver were ye thinkin', Lord Pembroke?"

Pulling herself together, Tabitha answered defiantly, "I am an independent woman, Dr Trent. No man, including Lord Pembroke, dictates my movements."

"An independent woman is an abomination in the eyes of the lord, Lady Pembroke. Yer duty is tae be subordinate tae the menfolk in yer life. Lord Pembroke, from whit I've heard o' yer domestic setup, the guid lord has put a strong temptation in front o' ye. I can only hope ye're no' nurturin' a viper in yer bosom," Dr Trent pronounced with all the disdain and judgement such a man could muster.

Noticing Langley at the back of the group, Dr Trent paused his moralising and asked, "And who is this ye bring wi' ye?"

There was an awkward pause, and it seemed to Lord Langley that neither Tabitha nor Wolf was sure how best to introduce him and how much of his official role to allude to. Stepping forward but not extending his hand in greeting, Langley said in a particularly arrogant tone dripping with condescension that Wolf made a note to try to emulate, when necessary, "I am Maxwell Sandworth, Earl of Langley."

"And whit would yet another earl want wi' a simple doctor like me?" Trent asked cocking his eyebrow. The man's demeanour was calm, and he seemed curious but unconcerned by their appearance in his post-mortem room. If he was guilty of murder, he was impressively imperturbable.

Wolf stepped in, "Dr Trent, just over two weeks ago, you performed an autopsy on a young man who you reported had died of influenza. The report stated that the unidentified body had been delivered from an unnamed hospital. In writing the report, you did not correct the labelling of the corpse as unidentified. Do you remember conducting that post-mortem?"

Dr Trent licked his lips, the first sign he had given of any nerves, "I perform many autopsies, and cannae possibly be expected tae mind them aw."

Tabitha asked rather sarcastically, "Do you perform that many on young men in their prime that one such wouldn't stand out?"

"Mind yer tongue, lassie," the doctor snapped dismissively. "I dinnae ken how things are done in yon Satanic-worshippin' place o' London. But here, women ken their place."

"Do they indeed? Did Vivian Wakely know her place? And was that place in your bed?" Tabitha countered.

Richard Trent stood and spat, "Get awa' frae me, Satan. Whit sinful words are these?"

"Sinful? Is that what my words are? What about assaulting an innocent young girl, and in a church no less? Isn't that considered sinful, Dr Trent?"

"I hae nae idea whit ye're talkin' aboot. I hae nae knowledge o' any assault," the man protested, but with noticeably less authority and confidence.

"Vivian Wakely. The young woman you lusted after whose affections you suspected lay elsewhere," Tabitha explained dryly.

"Another hussy, much like yersel', from whit I can see. If she has deceitfully engaged hersel' in a sinful relationship, I ken naethin' aboot it."

Realising nothing was to be gained by continuing this line of conversation, Tabitha said, "Mr MacKay has just confirmed that Peter Kincaid visited you here approximately two weeks ago at your request. Why did you ask a man you claim not to know to visit you? A man on whose body you subsequently performed an autopsy, writing a post-mortem report that said the corpse had come unnamed from an unspecified hospital."

Before Dr Trent could answer, Tabitha looked around the room at the cabinets and drawers full of instruments and chemicals. "I wonder what toxic materials a post-mortem room might contain. Or perhaps you brought something with you, something that wouldn't be detectable. Cyanide perhaps? I'm assuming you have syringes to hand," she mused.

"I dinnae ken whit ye're presumin', but I've had enough o' this nonsense. I dinnae need tae answer yer questions. The only authority I need tae answer tae is the almighty, and I will dae sae on my day o' judgement."

As Dr Trent spoke these words, Tabitha heard the door open behind them. All heads turned as Hamish entered the room, flanked by two police constables in their dark blue uniforms, highly polished brass buttons gleaming, and black truncheons held at their sides.

"There may be anither authority ye need tae answer tae afore that, Richard," Hamish said with a dramatic flourish enjoying the opportunity to use his authority for something a little more exciting than a breach of the peace or a dispute over sheep.

CHAPTER 34

"I cannot believe you left me out of all the excitement," the dowager complained, not for the first time that evening. She held up a hand to forestall any anticipated excuses, "Please don't claim to have had no idea of the melodrama that was to unfold. Apparently, Hamish was so excited about his role that, on your return, he bothered to seek Jane out to marvel at how he had swooped in at the last moment, holding his warrant aloft like a blazing sword. Jane! Yes, I had to hear this story from Jane, of all people."

Hamish hung his head guiltily at his part, and Tabitha, Wolf, and Langley attempted to look suitably contrite. The dowager was not fooled, "Don't bother to make that absurd face, Maxwell. It didn't work on me when you were in short pants, and I caught you stealing sweetmeats, and it won't work now. If you remember that particular transgression, I believe I pulled those short pants down and delivered a well-deserved spanking. I'm sorely tempted to repeat that punitive measure."

If the Earl of Langley was unconcerned that the diminutive Dowager Countess of Pembroke would follow through on her threat, he still had the good sense to grovel appropriately. "Lady Pembroke, I can assure you that your absence from our interrogatory activities was a true oversight. We knew you were otherwise engaged this afternoon. A convergence of events, including a response from the Home Secretary that came in a timelier manner than expected, led us to confront the villain."

Tabitha almost gasped at this bald lie; Langley had fully expected a swift reply to his telegram. However, his words seemed somewhat of a balm soothing the dowager's indignation. She sniffed and said, "Well, the least you can do is fill me in on what I missed." Even though they were all seated at dinner, the dowager turned to her tyrannised daughter and said, "Jane, you may wish to leave the room. I suspect such a sordid tale may bring on another fit of the vapours."

Jane, unwilling to leave her own dining table in the middle of a meal, seemed unsure how to answer. She was saved by her husband, who said with quiet authority, "Lady Pembroke, I dinnae believe there are any aspects o' this story that Jane isn't robust enough in mind and body tae hear." From across the table, Jane gave her husband a grateful smile.

Whether or not the dowager was convinced of Jane's fortitude, Tabitha and Wolf told the whole story. When they arrived at the part where Hamish had marched in with two police constables and arrested Dr Trent, the dowager exclaimed, "Well, if that isn't straight out of a penny dreadful, I don't know what is! All that was missing was this Miss Wakely tied up on the tracks by the villainous doctor as a train approached. 'If I can't have her, no one else will,' he declares," the dowager improvised, brandishing her fork.

Lily had been very quiet during dinner. Now she asked her father, "What will happen to Dr Trent? Is there any chance he will not be found guilty?"

Hamish said, "I believe that once a' the Edinburgh hospitals hae signalled they never sent a body matchin' Peter Kincaid's description tae the mortuary, Dr Trent will hae a hard time explainin' how he ended up performin' a post-mortem on a man who had been alive when he entered the mortuary."

Langley continued, "No conviction is ever guaranteed, but the circumstantial evidence against Dr Trent is compelling. The police will be visiting the medical school tomorrow to retrieve Peter's body. I believe his friend, Louis Trent, will be asked to identify it. Quite ironic given the circumstances."

"Why did Dr Trent send the body to the medical school? Couldn't he have disposed of it in a more effective manner?" the dowager asked.

Langley laughed humourlessly, "Ever the frugal Scot, he saw no reason to waste a perfectly good corpse. It's hard enough for medical schools to source bodies." He caught himself and looked at his hosts, "Apologies, I meant no offence."

"Nae offence taken. It's a fair comment," Hamish chuckled.

"And what about James Sinclair?" Tabitha asked. "While he may not be guilty of Peter's murder, he's hardly innocent in the deaths of so many men at his mines."

Wolf smiled, "Oh, you don't have to worry about Sinclair. I believe he will be getting his comeuppance. I sent the papers we found, plus a detailed report on our findings, to my journalist associate Andrews in London. I believe his newspaper will have a front-page scoop within a couple of days detailing the outrageous conditions in Sinclair's mines, the horrific accident that recently happened because of those conditions, and his overly close relationship with some of the mine inspectors. I'm sure Mr Sinclair will have some answering to do."

Hamish chuckled, "I'm proud of ye, lad. It's been a long time comin'."

Noticing Uncle Duncan had not joined them for dinner, Tabitha asked where he was.

Lily answered, "While you were all busy this afternoon, Mama decided it was perhaps time for Uncle Duncan to spread his bonhomie around to some of his friends in Edinburgh. At least for as long as Grandmama is with us."

The dowager's look of genuine surprise was priceless, "Really, Jane? You did that? For me?" Her daughter shyly nodded. "Well, I never. Who would have thought you'd have the gumption to face down a boor like that. Perhaps there is some hope for you after all. Perhaps you can try standing up to Mrs Shank, or whatever her name is, next."

"I believe that it is time for us to also take our leave of you, Cousin Jane," Wolf said. "We plan to catch the early train tomorrow. Will you be joining us, Langley?"

Langley was deciding whether he was ready to face his

mother when Dawglish entered the dining room. He approached Wolf and handed him a telegram.

Wolf read the telegram. Then reread it. Tabitha tried to read his expression but could not tell if the telegram was good or bad news. Though, how often was good news sent by telegram? Finally, Wolf looked up and said, "Actually, I have a change of plans. I find I must make a detour before returning to London."

"What kind of detour?" Tabitha asked, sensing that Wolf was planning to make this detour alone.

"An old friend is in need of my help. It seems she tracked me down to Chesterton House and begged Talbot to contact me."

"She?" Tabitha couldn't help asking. Who was this old female friend that she could command Wolf's help so easily?

"Bear and Langley will see you all home from London and I will continue to Brighton," Wolf explained.

"Brighton? What on earth is in Brighton besides pebbles and crass summer entertainment for the masses?" the dowager asked.

"My friend is living in Brighton, apparently," Wolf explained, clearly uncomfortable about revealing too much.

"And she needs your help? Is this another investigation?" the dowager asked, gleefully clapping her hands. "How exciting. I'm assuming it goes without saying that you will not be 'accidentally' leaving me out of the best parts of this one!"

Wolf looked at her, realising what the woman was implying, "Lady Pembroke, there is no need for any of you to join me. I assure you that, whatever my friend's need is, I can handle it alone. I know you still have important work to do to prepare Lily," he added, hoping this would sway the woman.

He should have known better, "Poppycock! Lily will come with us, and we will use Brighton to practice her introduction into society. This works perfectly. It's hardly as if anyone who matters will be in residence there, and yet it is near enough to London that one would hope they have a little more sense of things than these Scots seem to. We may even be able to find a serviceable modiste there." The dowager paused, and then said pointedly, "Anyway, based on things I've learned recently, I believe the sooner we get Lily away from certain unsuitable influences in Scotland, the better!"

Lord Langley, seeing a golden opportunity to avoid his mother for a little longer and willing to stab Wolf in the back to seize that opportunity, said, "Yes, Pembroke, I believe we should all come and assist you."

"Do you? Do you indeed, Langley?" Wolf asked bitterly.

EPILOGUE

Despite his stated desire to leave the morning after receiving the telegram from his mysterious female friend, the unwanted addition of the enormous entourage of the dowager, Tabitha, Lily, Langley, Bear, Rat, Melody, all their servants and the dog, meant that Wolf had to postpone his departure by at least a day.

While he hadn't been concerned about where he might stay alone in Brighton, the extra day was needed to secure appropriate accommodation for the large and illustrious travel party that was now to accompany him. The dowager, who seemed to know more about Brighton than might have been imagined from her derisive comments about the town, had said, "I believe Lady Willis visited last year to take the sea air to cure one of the many imaginary complaints the woman believes herself at risk of dying from. If memory serves me correctly, and it usually does, she stayed at The Grand Brighton. While the woman has terrible taste in husbands, she does have quite unimpeachable taste in other things. If The Grand Brighton was good enough for her, I'm sure it will at least suffice for me."

A telegram was immediately sent to the hotel. Luckily, given that it was now the low season, they were happy to reply immediately with confirmation of the required number of grand suites and other rooms. The dowager's modiste had not managed to send the requested gowns in time, and so at least two hours were spent with the dowager and Tabitha sorting through Lily's wardrobe to see if any of the clothes the young woman owned were deemed appropriate "to be seen wearing when travelling with a dowager countess." Finally, with some gentle persuasion from Tabitha and some pointed reminders that if they couldn't travel the next day, Wolf might be inclined to leave the dowager and Lily behind, a few sufficiently decent pieces were chosen.

Tabitha had wondered if Jane would be inclined to accompany her daughter. But the much put-upon woman seemed thrilled to be getting rid of her mother sooner than expected, and it was all Jane could do to tamp down her enthusiasm for their departure. There were some vague comments about perhaps coming down to London in time for the season. Still, Tabitha suspected Jane would rather have her eyes gouged out than deal with the dowager's expectations for how her daughter should behave in London society.

Finally, only twenty-four hours later than Wolf had wanted, the large party of twelve, including servants and children, was ready to be ferried to the train station.

Waiting in the vestibule for the carriage to be brought around, the dowager took Melody's hand. "Now, you will sit with Granny on the train and can show me how improved your reading is."

"And then, will you tell me stories, like Uncle Maxi did?" the excited little girl asked.

"Indeed, if you are a good girl. I will tell you the story of Cinderella and how she was saved from a life of social ineptitude and a bizarre obsession with flowers by a wonderful fairy grandmother who managed, against great odds, to transform her into a wife worthy of a prince." As the dowager said this, she glanced over at Lily, who luckily seemed not to have heard how a beloved fairy tale was being co-opted as a cautionary tale about her.

Looking at the large group he had somehow been persuaded to take with him, Wolf could only inwardly sigh. He'd been surprised to receive the telegram from Arlene. He couldn't imagine what would make the woman so determinedly seek him out after so many years, but he knew what he owed her. There had never been any doubt that he would do whatever he could to help her. However, he couldn't imagine how he would introduce Tabitha to the first woman he had ever loved.

* * *

Find out what Tabitha's wedding day to Jonathan was like before things started going horribly wrong. For this and other short stories, as well as insider tidbits and previews, signup for my newsletter or at sarahfnoel.com.

Continue reading for a sneak peak at the next book, **An Inexplicable Woman**

On the journey to Scotland, Wolf had marvelled at their excess of luggage. But now, as he looked around at the even greater throng of titled personages, servants, children and pets and all the attendant bags and boxes they were leaving Scotland with, he wondered how he had let himself be bullied into allowing this travelling circus to accompany him to Brighton.

Of course, he couldn't imagine what he might have done differently. Despite what he might wish otherwise, it was hard to imagine that Tabitha would have agreed to be left behind. So already, that was two people and two servants. Then, of course, the dowager, sensing an investigation, had insisted on joining and bringing her granddaughter, Lady Lily, along. Given that the Dowager Countess of Pembroke had travelled to Scotland with her maid and her butler, Manning, and that Lady Lily had her maid, that was another five people (though in an act of surprising thoughtfulness, the dowager had allowed Manning to go off and finally have a real holiday while they were in Brighton).

In addition, there was Bear, of course. Under normal circumstances, Wolf would have welcomed his old friend's company. But Wolf's original intention had been to travel alone to Brighton and that his friend, former thief-taking partner, then valet and now personal secretary, Bear, with Lord Langley, would escort the dowager, her granddaughter, Lily, and Tabitha back to London. But once the dowager and Tabitha had decided to accompany him, their burgeoning group had been joined by Maxwell Sandworth, Lord Langley and his valet. Because Langley wasn't going back to London, this also meant that rounding out their group was Melody, Tabitha's four-year-old ward, her brother Matt, known as Rat, and her mischievous puppy, Dodo. Oh, and Melody's nurserymaid, Mary.

Wolf didn't understand why Langley needed to accompany them to Brighton. Maybe that wasn't wholly accurate; he knew why. Langley wished to avoid his mother. Wolf shook his head as he considered that Langley was a grown man, a Peer of the Realm, and, to top it off, he worked for British Intelligence. Yet he was scared of his own parent! Langley had been left in charge of Melody when Wolf and Tabitha had been summoned to Edinburgh by the dowager but had followed them up to Scotland when his mother had turned up to redecorate his London house. Rat, who had been working as a servant at Pembroke House, had also been brought along because it seemed the boy would now live with Langley and be educated and trained to help him in his intelligence work.

As they descended from the train in Brighton, Wolf did a quick count of heads: minus Manning, that was eleven adults, two children and a dog. He wanted to ensure they all arrived together at The Grand Brighton, the palatial hotel they were almost taking over. It was lucky it was off-season, and all the hotel's suites had been available at such short notice. As it was, while the dowager was getting her own suite, Tabitha and Lily were sharing, as were Wolf and Bear. Surprisingly, Langley had offered to share with the children.

Wolf looked around at the large group and the huge number of bags and hat boxes and wondered how his life had changed. While his thief-taker life had sometimes been hard, there had been a simplicity to it that he sometimes missed. He and Bear had owned not much more than the clothes on their back and often didn't know where their next meal was coming from. But they'd been free to come and go as they pleased. They owed nothing to anyone, and no one had any expectations of them. Now, he was a landlord and business owner with many employees and tenants who relied on him. In addition, there were all the people living and working at Pembroke House, not the least of whom was Tabitha.

AFTERWORD

Thank you for reading An Independent Woman. I hope you enjoyed it. If you'd like to see what's coming next for Tabitha & Wolf, here are some ways to stay in touch:

SarahFNoel.com
Facebook
Twitter @sarahfNoelAuthor
Instagram sfnoel
YouTube
TikTok @sarah.f.noel

ACKNOWLEDGEMENT

I want to thank my wonderful editor, Kieran Devaney and the eagle-eyed Patricia Goulden for doing a final check of the manuscript.

ABOUT THE AUTHOR

Sarah F. Noel

Originally from London, Sarah F. Noel now spends most of her time in Grenada in the Caribbean. Sarah loves reading historical mysteries with strong female characters; the Tabitha & Wolf Mystery Series is exactly the kind of book she would love to curl up with on a lazy Sunday.

BOOKS BY THIS AUTHOR

A Proud Woman

Tabitha was used to being a social pariah. Could her standing in society get any worse?

Tabitha, Lady Chesterton, the Countess of Pembroke, is newly widowed at only 22 years of age. With no son to inherit the title, it falls to a dashing, distant cousin of her husband's, Jeremy Chesterton, known as Wolf. It quickly becomes apparent that Wolf had consorted with some of London's most dangerous citizens before inheriting the title. Can he leave this world behind, or will shadowy figures from his past follow him into his new aristocratic life in Mayfair? And can Tabitha avoid being caught up in Wolf's dubious activities?

It seems it's well and truly time for Tabitha to leave her gilded cage behind for good!

A Singular Woman

Wolf had hoped he could put his thief-taking life behind him when he unexpectedly inherited an earldom.

Wolf, the new Earl of Pembroke, against his better judgment, finds himself sucked back into another investigation. He knows better than to think he can keep Tabitha out of it. Tabitha was the wife of Wolf's deceased cousin, the previous earl, but now she's running his household and finding her way into his life and, to his surprise, his heart. He respects her intelligence and insights but can't help trying to protect her.

As the investigation suddenly becomes far more complicated and dangerous, how can Wolf save an innocent man and keep Tabitha safe?

An Inexplicable Woman

Who is this mysterious woman from Wolf's past who can so easily summon him to her side?

When Lady Arlene Archibald tracks Wolf down and begs him for help, he plans to travel to Brighton alone to see her. What was he thinking? Instead, he finds himself with an unruly entourage of lords, ladies, servants, children, and even a dog. Can and will he help Arlene prove her friend's innocence? How will he manage Tabitha coming face-to-face with his first love? And how is he to dissuade the Dowager Countess of Pembroke from insinuating herself into the investigation?

Beneath its veneer of holiday, seaside fun, Brighton may be more sinister than it seems.

An Audacious Woman

The Dowager Countess of Pembroke is missing!

While Wolf is contemplating whether or not he wishes to continue taking on investigations, it seems that the dowager has taken the matter into her own hands and is investigating a case independently. But why has she gone missing from her home for two nights and what mischief has she got herself into? Tracking down the elderly woman takes Tabitha and Wolf into some of the darkest, most dangerous corners of the city.

What on earth is the exasperating dowager caught up in that she seems to have become entangled with London's prostitutes?

An Indomitable Woman

The Investigative Countess, Rapier Sharp Logic paired with Great Insight and Boldness. A Private Inquiry Agent.

When the dowager countess receives her first assignment as a private inquiry agent from Miriam Tuchinsky, an East End gangster, she immediately throws herself into the case with gusto. Meanwhile, Lord Langley hires Tabitha and Wolf for an assignment that takes them deep into London's Jewish neighbourhood. Is there a connection between the two investigations? More importantly, can the two investigative teams work together?

Wolf has made his peace with continuing to take on investigations and with having Tabitha partner with him, but how will he manage the dowager countess' continued meddling in such a dangerous case?

Printed in Great Britain
by Amazon